Readers Love Amanda Meuwissen

A Model Escort

"The aspect of 'Beauty and the Geek' is subtle but effective here.... This would be an attractive story for readers looking for more STEAM/STEM in their romances."

—*Library Journal*

Their Dark Reflections

"I thoroughly devoured this book. Amanda Meuwissen has a gift for creating multi-dimensional characters, full of moral ambiguity, and making you fall in love with them. This book is no exception."

—Paranormal Romance Guild

"The concept of the story was simple, the execution – delightful – one that kept me turning the page."

—Love Bytes

After Vertigo

"With its endearing main characters and a story that held my attention, *After Vertigo* was a fun read and perfect to unwind with at the end of long day."

—Joyfully Jay

Coming Up for Air

"*Coming Up For Air* by Amanda Meuwissen is the first book that I've read by this author, but it won't be the last…"

—OptimuMM

By AMANDA MEUWISSEN

Coming Up for Air
Their Dark Reflections

DREAMSPUN DESIRES
A Model Escort
Interpretive Hearts

MOONLIGHT PROPHECIES
By the Red Moonlight
Blue Moon Rising
Wane on Harvest Moon

TALES FROM THE GEMSTONE KINGDOM
The Prince and the Ice King
Stitches
The Bard and the Fairy Prince

Published by DSP Publications
After Vertigo

Published by DREAMSPINNER PRESS
www.dreamspinnerpress.com

WANE ON
Harvest Moon

AMANDA MEUWISSEN

DREAMSPINNER
PRESS

Published by
DREAMSPINNER PRESS

5032 Capital Circle SW, Suite 2, PMB# 279, Tallahassee, FL 32305-7886 USA
www.dreamspinnerpress.com

Wane on Harvest Moon
© 2022 Amanda Meuwissen

Cover Art
© 2022 Kris Norris
https://krisnorris.com
Cover content is for illustrative purposes only and any person depicted on the cover is a model.

Trade Paperback ISBN: ISBN: 978-1-64108-495-6
Digital ISBN: 978-1-64108-494-9
Trade Paperback published December 2022
v. 1.0

Printed in the United States of America
∞
This paper meets the requirements of
ANSI/NISO Z39.48-1992 (Permanence of Paper).

Chapter 1

"WOW, THE architecture here is badass!"

Preston followed Luke and Jesse out of the parking garage to better take in the view of downtown Glenwood. They'd driven from Centrus City since there wasn't a direct train route like from Centrus to Brookdale, and three plane tickets wouldn't have been worth the short distance.

Glenwood was impressive, with more skyscrapers than either of the other cities and an Old World feel like it might have been a century in the past if not for several more modern buildings. Old stonework with carved designs and even lions or gargoyles peering down at them from several stories up was just as common as reflective glass, and everything had a gray or black look to it that said as soon as the sun set, they might as well be in Transylvania.

"How... gothic," Preston said, brushing aside the strands of hair that had fallen loose from his disturbed bun, since he'd been the one driving all afternoon.

Jesse didn't respond. She had her arms crossed in front of her, with shoulders hunched in typical annoyed teenage fashion.

"Come on, you two." Luke threw an arm across her shoulders. "No being sourpusses while we're on vacation!" For a werecat, he had the temperament of an overactive puppy, which on a good day, Preston adored, but on a bad, sort of made him wish he could lock Luke in a kennel.

Jesse was more the temperamental type, but instead of an alley cat, she was a tiger, and their very recently adopted daughter.

Preston, or rather, Preston James Rathaway III, wondered what his parents would think of finally having a grandchild only for it to be their gay son having adopted from the cat tribe. They were the epitome of traditionalists, preferring to keep to rat shifter circles. Preston didn't talk to them anymore, hadn't in years, but maybe he'd send a Christmas card, just to imagine the look on his mother's face when she saw him happier than ever with his found family.

Well, "happy" was subjective lately. Ever since Jesse moved into the den, Preston and Luke hadn't agreed on much of anything, other than this trip, which wasn't starting off all that great, given Jesse looked like she wanted to crawl back into the car and hide.

"This isn't exactly a vacation," Preston reminded them, adjusting his glasses more out of habit than crookedness. "We have official circle business to attend to."

As Centrus City's Magister in charge of all things magic related, Preston often took on complicated mysteries of unknown origin, and Luke, the city's Councilor, who watched over community relations, knew best how to get even the most closed-off pack members to open up. They had been tasked by their Alpha, Bashir "Bash" Bain, to discover where a suspicious set of creation tablets had come from, which depicted the history of shifter-kind. All they knew currently was that the tablets had been sent to Brookdale from a museum in Glenwood, though with no idea who originally donated them.

Solving a mystery together had been how Preston and Luke first got to know each other after taking on their roles in Centrus City's circle almost a decade ago.

Luke cast Preston a sharp look, and his blue eyes flashed to shifter Stage One. The intensity enhanced his youthful attractiveness, with ginger hair and the hint of strawberry blond highlights, an echo of his tabby-striped cat form. He was shorter in stature, barely five foot eight, and therefore, one of the smallest of their pack's inner circle, other than Preston, who was five foot six. But while Preston had an average build, Luke had a lankier litheness to him that betrayed his feline heritage.

Which included an occasional burst of temper.

Luke jutted his chin toward Jesse, and Preston had to admit he was the one at fault this time, since Jesse needed support.

"However," Preston amended, stepping up to Jesse's other side, "we will also make time to see the sights and… have fun."

Jesse snorted but allowed a small smile as she leaned against Luke. Her dark hair with its streak of blue contrasted Luke's ginger as she easily succumbed to his casual physicality.

To any passersby, they probably looked more like siblings than child and parent, but Luke and Preston were technically old enough to have a thirteen-year-old daughter—if they'd had her when they were young teens themselves.

"Buck up, pixie girl," Luke tried once more to coax her from her funk. "I thought you wanted to visit."

"I did. I just haven't been back here since...."

Since her parents died.

A car accident over a year ago had claimed both their lives while she was at school, and since she had no other living relatives, she'd ended up at Glenwood's Shelter—the place in each city where shifters without any other place to go or who couldn't control their shifts were allowed to live under pack protection. As Preston understood it, Jesse had asked to be transferred to Centrus City after the first month.

"I really wanted to get away back then," she continued, "but I was missing home and thought... I don't know." She rested her head more snugly against Luke's shoulder. "You were always from Centrus, right?"

"Born and bred."

"What happened to your parents?"

Preston watched a thin smile overtake Luke's expression. Neither of them talked about their families, and for good reason—they weren't nice stories.

"I don't really remember them," Luke said. "I was a lot younger than you when I ended up at the Shelter. I'm sure having memories of your parents makes things tough, but it's also good to have them, right?"

Jesse hesitated but eventually said, "Yeah, I guess. What about you?" She glanced at Preston. "You never lived in the Shelter."

"No. My family is alive, but trust me, having no memories of them would be better. Come on." Preston indicated the hotel behind them, where they would be staying while they were in town. "If we want to get to any vacationing, we need to handle our assignment first."

He headed in that direction, but slowly to allow Jesse and Luke to catch up. Preston wasn't as physically affectionate as Luke, but although Luke had always been understanding of that where it concerned him, he kept passing disapproving glances at Preston for holding back with Jesse—like now.

Swallowing a sigh, Preston reached out to gently squeeze Jesse's shoulder.

She smiled and briefly leaned into his side like she had Luke's.

Preston hated when Luke was right, especially when he looked so smug afterward.

"Why didn't you bring Basil and Dr. Dawson?" Jesse asked.

Those were Preston's most treasured rat companions, who were family as much as pets. Rodents he had a connection with tended to live longer, but even then, they rarely lasted more than five to ten years max. Before Basil and Dawson, he'd had a different set of rat friends.

"Hotels tend to frown on that," he said, and Jesse snorted.

The hotel in question was as gothic as the other buildings on this block, refurbished but not too outlandish, providing both sensibility and a show of wealth from Glenwood's circle, since they would be footing the bill. Inside the high-ceilinged lobby, waiting for them, was Glenwood's Alpha, Kate Romero, and her Second—

"Jude!" Luke exclaimed, neglecting any sense of decorum as he bounded toward their old friend and embraced him by practically leaping into his arms.

Jude Marley was a fox shifter, which technically put him in the wolf tribe with Kate, though it was rare for a wolf-run city to let foxes be so high ranking—aside from Bash's circle in Centrus, which was a mix of almost every tribe.

Jude easily encompassed Luke in a hug, being nearly a head taller than him, with long ginger hair, a shade lighter than Luke's, amber eyes, and a trim beard.

"Hey there, Kitten!" Jude exclaimed just as jubilantly.

To Kate's credit, she didn't look at all put out by the casual display. She too was a young Alpha, since all Alphas in the three major cities had been replaced within the last decade or so—Glenwood's, Kate's father, who passed away, Brookdale's, who retired and left things to Jeffrey "Jay" Russell, and Centrus City's, Bash's father, who Bash personally killed to usurp.

Kate had the sort of biker-chick look that reminded Preston of fellow circle members back home, Deanna and Siobhan. She had a darker complexion, with a dark shorter hairstyle, not quite shaved on the sides like common fashion, but still longer on top like a 90s teen boy heartthrob. While taller and trim like an androgenous model, there was no doubt by the way she held herself that she could clobber anyone who foolishly tried to pick a fight.

"Wow," Jesse muttered as they approached at a slower pace. "I forgot the hotness factor."

"For which one?" Preston asked.

"Both. Definitely both."

That brought a smile to Preston's face that he fought to not let crumble into a sneer. Kids sure had it different these days, more allowed to explore what and who, if anyone, they were attracted to. Not to say it was *easy*, but he did envy them sometimes.

"Jude." Preston nodded and shook the fox's hand once his mate was no longer attached to him. "Madame Alpha."

"Kate's fine," she said, shaking Preston's hand next. "It's good to meet you, Mr. Rathaway. And Mr....." She frowned, not knowing Luke's surname, which was common.

"Legally it's Smith, since I don't know what it actually was." Luke shrugged. Smith or Jones were common choices for orphans at the Shelter when forging paperwork. "But if you're Kate, then we're just Luke and Preston."

"You obviously already know my Second," she said.

"For almost, what, ten years now?" Luke finally remembered his manners and shook Kate's hand too. "Man, are we getting old!"

"I'd argue," Jude said, assessing Jesse between them, "but I never expected you two to adopt. Nice to see you again, Jesse. I'm glad Centrus led you to a good home—though I don't know if I can truly vouch for these two." He winked.

The way she averted her eyes without the usual snarky comment said plenty about how attractive she found him. "They're not so bad."

"How are you, Miss Kane?" Kate asked. "Or is it something new now?"

"Please," Jesse scoffed, "and let them force a hyphen on me? *So* lame."

Preston would have teased they'd do it anyway for that comment alone if he didn't remember having the same holier-than-thou attitude about being "cool" at her age.

"Hey, man, how's your sister?" Luke asked with a smack to Jude's arm.

A squeal was heard before heeled feet bounded toward them with audible warning clicks.

"Ask yourself," Jude said and knowingly stepped aside to grant entry for Jordana Marley, who leapt into Luke's arms even more raucously than Luke had leapt into Jude's.

"Kitten!" she cried. "Oh my God, you look amazing!"

The jaw-drop from Jesse proved she hadn't yet met Jude's sister, who had identical coloring to her brother, including waist-long ginger hair. If Jude was basic casual, and Kate a biker chick, then Jordana was the odd one out, as if she'd stepped from the screen of any *Real Housewives* episode, though without the excess makeup or blatant fakeness.

Not that Preston had ever watched any of that—willingly.

"Hey, foxy woman, I was hoping we'd see you!" Luke greeted.

Unlike Jude, who'd respected Preston's self-imposed bubble, Jordana glomped onto him next. "And Fievel! Your hair is getting so long! You should totally wear it down—"

Preston swatted her from pulling loose the tie from inside his tangled bun. "Oh no. You can fuss when I don't have hours' worth of car ride on me."

She pouted at the denial but didn't try again. "And this must be Jesse. Look at you!" She rebounded, pulling Jesse in for a slightly less resistant hug than Preston and was even allowed a near immediate twirl of her fingers through Jesse's blue streak. "Rocking the badass punk look like my Kate, huh? You are too precious."

Jesse's understandable shock from meeting the whirlwind that was Jordana was likely to blame for her once again not throwing up defenses—or because Jordana was a literal bombshell. "Are you part of the Glenwood circle too?" Jesse asked.

Jordana flew to the other side of their tight gathering and affixed herself to Kate. "Only as mate and whisperer in ears on occasion. Glenwood pack dynamic sort of frowns on mated pairs both being in the circle. Unlike Centrus City's blatant nepotism," she added in mock-whisper.

"Hey!" Luke defended. "Bash chose us for our roles before we mated."

"And that lasted all of a few days, if I remember."

"That was a long time ago," Preston said.

"Yeah, you two weren't even legit back then." Luke nudged Jude, indicating the… *profession* the two had had when they first met them.

"Like any of us are wholly legit now." Jude chuckled back.

Being *professional thieves* was a bit different from mob-like business dealings, but not by much.

Jesse's curious glances between them would likely demand explanations later, but for now, Preston was glad to have Kate as another voice of reason.

"Let's continue this away from prying ears," she said, placing a hand on Jordana's that was curled around her arm. "We'll treat you to a late dinner and fill you in. Your things?"

"Still in the car," Preston said. "We figured we'd grab everything after we checked in."

"Then let's get you settled. We have a lot to tell you."

THE HOTEL restaurant would have felt far too fancy for them if Kate and Jude weren't also more casually dressed. Besides, Jordana, with her model-perfect accessorized ensemble and infectiously charismatic personality, made the rest of their table more polished by association.

Luke liked seeing the twins again, a reminder of when he first met Preston, first fell in love with him, first knew that this acerbic and fiercely intelligent rat was destined to be his mate. They'd kept in touch with Jude and Jordana, even visited a few times and vice versa, but it was difficult to remain close with people who lived in a different city.

Sometimes even in the same city....

Luke stretched his smile to counteract that bitter thought. He hated how off the chemistry between him and Preston had felt lately. They'd had fights before—everyone had fights—but the tension had been almost constant the past few weeks. Jesse was the only thing that had changed in that time, which Luke hated thinking. She wasn't the problem, but then what was wrong with them?

"Luke?"

He blinked stupidly at Kate. She wasn't a traditionalist asshole who was going to give him a hard time for drifting, but he didn't want to seem too much like a space case. "Sorry, just my hunger brain distracting me. I'm listening."

He was seated between Jesse and Preston, with Jude on Preston's other side, then Kate, then Jordana, and back to Jesse, who seemed entirely enamored with the older fox woman. She was allowed a crush, which seemed to expand to more than just Jordy.

"I was saying we're sorry to have to report another dead end for you," Kate explained.

What they'd already known about the creation tablets was that the museum here had them donated with the explicit instructions to send them to Brookdale, and then to eventually have them sent back. They never would come back, however, because Bari Bain, Bash's brother, destroyed them after an eerie encounter with an unknown female vampire, who was apparently bent on taking over shifter society.

It was seriously freaky and messed up, and all the fear Luke used to feel toward vampires before meeting and befriending Ethan Lambert—who was the coolest and a totally on-the-level fanger—was rearing its ugly head again.

It seemed even after being told all this, the Glenwood Museum director, who himself was a shifter, still wasn't budging on giving up the anonymous donor's name, only now they knew why.

He didn't know it.

"He claims the name disappeared," Kate continued, "and almost all the paperwork with it. He kept shutting down Mr. Bain's efforts, and mine, because apparently, this is someone who's donated before, and he didn't want an investigation scaring them from donating in the future."

"Fortunately or unfortunately," Jude spoke up, "there was one thing the director still had—the original request notes from the donation report, just without any signature or name." He passed the slip of paper across the table between Luke and Preston.

"Okay…." Preston prompted, and Luke likewise had no idea what they were supposed to notice.

Then Jude passed over another piece of paper, almost identical, but clearly worn from age.

"Do those handwritings look like a match to you?" Jude asked.

They were indeed the same, but while the newer slip described the creation tablets, the older one described….

Shit.

"That's not from…." Luke couldn't say it but met first Preston's eyes and then Jude's.

"It is."

Another blast from the past, because even an artifact they'd encountered ten years ago was involved in all this.

"Why did you keep that?" Preston asked.

"It was the only thing I had to remember it all by." Jude shrugged. "And I never wanted to forget what almost happened… or what we might have lost." He glanced furtively at his sister.

Jordana glanced over too, meeting her brother's gaze and then landing on the older piece of paper, but since they'd been talking quietly, she valiantly returned her attention to Jesse, who she'd been keeping occupied and away from dangerous shop talk.

That paper would indeed be the only thing left, since the artifact itself was gone.

Luke could still picture it, like a handheld totem pole, depicting each of the five shifter tribes, starting from the bottom: wolf, cat, rat, lizard, and finally raptor, which was the bird tribe. He remembered kind of liking it, thinking it a cool representation of their heritage.

If it hadn't come with a curse and a prophecy that would have destroyed all shifter kind back then if it had come true.

There had been a lot of those prophecies lately, between Bash, Ethan, and now Bari all being Seers with the ability to predict the future.

"Whoever this regular donor is," Kate said, "it has to be someone local who is part of our world and knows their anthropology. I can give you a list of people with enough resources and knowledge to have access to such things, but I can't imagine any of them being involved in this. Then again, I realize pack betrayal isn't exactly unheard of right now."

As fellow Alphas, Jay and Bash had shared with Kate their knowledge of events over the past several weeks. Kate knew vampires were in both cities—good, trustworthy ones, not only the menacing woman whose identity they needed—as well as how several members of Brookdale's inner circle had rebelled against their Alpha, Jay, per the mystery vampire's direction.

Times were shit, but at least they had somewhere to start with unraveling the next part of the mystery. Just in time too, because the waiter arrived with their food.

For now, they'd eat, finish settling in, and relax before tackling more tomorrow. Luke was just glad Jesse had been distracted enough by Jordana to not pay much attention to their conversation.

"So, what's with these creation tablets and old totem?"

Or so Luke thought, before that question was the first thing to leave Jesse's lips when they got to their room.

"Nothing you need concern yourself with," Preston said.

Luke flinched at the authoritative tone. He hated when Preston used it, especially since he didn't think Preston realized how much that made his voice sound like....

Another figure of authority.

They had a suite, with a separate room for Luke and Preston through a door they could close, and a pullout sofa in the main space for Jesse. Rather than start getting ready for bed, however, Jesse flopped down onto the sofa and turned on the TV.

"What are you doing?" Preston asked with hands on his hips.

"Um, unwinding?"

"It's late. You should get to bed."

"I'm not seven."

Luke snorted. "Yeah, Pres, come on, she can stay up a little. It's vacation!"

The glare Preston shot at him made Luke's smile instantly drop.

"Half an hour," Preston told Jesse.

"What was with those nicknames anyway?" She basically ignored him. "Kitten is obvious, but Fievel? What's that even mean?"

"Oh, we are so adding *An American Tail* to our classic movie night." Luke dropped down beside her. "Fievel is the main character, a mouse, and there's this cat—"

"Luke," Preston used his authoritative tone again before Luke could get settled, "can I talk to you, please?"

Great.

Much as Luke wanted to protest, they'd made a point to not argue too much in front of Jesse, and he knew refusing would not go over well.

"One sec, Jess," he said and followed Preston into the bedroom—slowly.

Apparently his feet-dragging pace was too slow, because before he could reach the threshold, a glowing coil of magical spirit chains wrapped around his middle and tugged him the rest of the way inside.

"Dude, I'm here." Luke brushed his hands through the chains until the translucent bindings vanished. It was especially unfair having them used against him that way when during better times they could be used for… recreational purposes. "What's up?"

"I would appreciate it if you didn't undermine literally everything I try telling her."

"It's not *literally* everything." Luke fought to not roll his eyes. "But maybe every little thing isn't that big of a deal."

"Of course you'd think that," Preston huffed.

"Meaning?"

"Nothing." He tried to exit, but Luke grabbed his arm.

"No, what?"

With a wrench free from Luke's hold, Preston fired back what had obviously been on his tongue. "You didn't exactly have much authority growing up, did you? The best you got was being swept up by Bash's bastard father to be a child runner."

"So? It sucked. That means I don't get an opinion?"

"You don't understand—"

"What? How to raise a kid, 'cause I turned out so terribly?"

Finally, some of the walls Preston had thrown up crumbled, but it didn't change what he'd said. "That's not what I meant."

"It is what you think. You'd rather turn into your own father—"

"Excuse me?"

"You're trying to control every second of her life!" Luke snapped, much as he was trying to keep his voice down. "Because obviously a bunch of rules and rigidity was so the right call with how your parents raised you."

Preston rocked backward, and the moment Luke saw the hurt that marred his expression, he regretted saying anything.

"Shit, I... I didn't mean to say it like that." They were going in circles, both saying things they didn't mean. "It's just been a lot lately, ya know? Jess, these crazy prophecies, and now finding out whoever originally owned that totem a decade ago might be the same person who donated the tablets? That's why I wanted this vacation. Not only for Jess, for us." He reached for Preston's hands, grateful that his softer tone kept his mate from pulling away. "I barely even remember the last time we didn't just fall asleep when we got into bed."

Preston sagged closer, and Luke gently dropped his forehead down for theirs to meet. Slowly, he brought one hand to Preston's cheek and tilted his chin up to steal a kiss. He couldn't even remember the last time they'd done that, other than a peck hello or goodbye in passing. Sure, becoming parents didn't leave as much free time, but Jesse didn't need constant care like a newborn. The real reason they hadn't been together much was because of all the fighting, and it made Luke's insides ache.

He ached in far sweeter ways kissing Preston now. Preston's bit of scruff at the end of the day was a pleasant scratch, contrasting his soft lips as Luke coaxed them to open and slid his tongue between them. Preston's East-Asian background might have made him as unlikely to get five o'clock shadow as Luke with his fair Irish looks, but he always got that scruff, and Luke loved it. He even sometimes wished Preston would let it stay instead of shaving every morning.

Their kiss was slow, like a drawn-out apology and making up for lost time, not by rushing, but by letting things linger. Luke kept his hold on Preston's cheek and curled his other arm around Preston's waist. Preston had a sweater on, soft and corded, and Luke stroked up the knitting with an eager hand along Preston's back. He was careful not to let his claws out, despite the natural inclination to shift when things got heated, but that was what he wanted, to mark Preston's skin like a renewed claim.

Deepening the kiss further, Luke pushed his hand up beneath the sweater to do just that and rolled his hips forward to prove his enthusiasm.

Jesse laughed at something on the TV.

"We can't." Preston dislodged Luke's hand and the lock of their lips. "She's right there."

"We'll close the door," Luke whispered, trying to pull Preston back to him. "She'll get it."

The sneer Preston responded with was not conducive to foreplay. "Seriously? Just because you grew up without rules or modesty doesn't mean I want our daughter brought up that way."

"Again with this? You really think I'm just some low-brow alley cat who doesn't know any better? It's like ten years ago all over again."

"You're certainly acting like you did back then."

"So are you!" Luke snarled. "Like an uptight asshole who never thought I was good enough."

The second Luke turned to leave, he regretted saying that too, like every barb they'd exchanged lately, but he couldn't look at Preston right now, and the only way he could imagine keeping the sting of tears from his eyes was by joining Jesse on the sofa for some late-night *Conan*.

If her shifter ears had caught any of their argument, she gave no indication, but after a few minutes passed without Preston joining them, his voice came instead.

"I'm getting ice," Preston said, and Luke didn't stop him from leaving.

THAT DAMN… *cat*. He was so frustrating.

Especially after Preston cooled down enough to admit Luke was right.

Not about everything—some discipline was needed, and Preston had never believed Luke wasn't good enough for him—but turning into his parents wasn't what he wanted either. He really hated hearing Luke say that. Luke didn't know what it was like growing up in a house where your entire life was laid out for you, planned to the letter, and the slightest deviation made you an instant disappointment.

Just like Preston didn't know what it was like growing up with no family at all.

Dammit. Preston didn't even know what floor he was on anymore, or what hallway he was walking down, but he paused between a set of doors to lean his head against the wall and took a deep breath. Jesse wasn't the problem; he knew that. She'd merely been the catalyst, because even after ten years, their pasts plagued them.

Maybe they weren't ready to handle adopting a child when they clearly hadn't gotten over their own issues.

Missing the constant companionship of Basil and Dr. Dawson, Preston closed his eyes and reached out with his Rat King abilities to locate any nearby rodents. This was definitely a nice hotel, because all he found was one lonely mouse.

Come, Preston called, and he could sense the mouse hurrying through walls and seeking the fastest route to reach him. After a few minutes, the small gray creature was climbing up Preston's leg to find perch on his shoulder.

A very simple runic spell cleaned and rejuvenated the poor thing, though as a shifter, Preston didn't fear any diseases the mouse might carry. It was as healthy as the most pristine of pet mice in moments, and it showed its appreciation with a nuzzle at Preston's neck.

Sometimes Preston still thought the way he used to as a child—that rodents were easier than people.

He couldn't be certain how much time had passed since he left the room, not wearing a watch or having taken his phone. After securing the mouse in his pocket in case he ran into other guests, Preston found the elevator instead of using the stairs and realized he'd paced down and around five floors.

The TV was still on when he slipped inside the room, but he couldn't see Jesse or Luke. He didn't have ice—he hadn't taken the bucket—but he knew that didn't matter. Moving quietly to the sofa, he found a half-grown tiger curled up asleep in the corner with an orange-striped cat snuggled atop her.

Preston smiled. This wasn't the first time he'd caught them this way, either in a nap or late at night like this. It made him think of the first time he ever saw Luke's Stage Four form, which he'd fought at the time to not find adorable and failed. Seeing it now, through such a simple act of trying to be a good dad, just there and understanding and present for the girl they'd brought into their family, was the warmest reminder Preston could imagine of how much he loved Luke.

He wished he could get over himself enough to show him that and stop saying things he didn't mean. It hadn't been any easier a decade ago, and just like during that time, Preston was dangerously close to screwing this up.

Not wanting to disturb the pair, he padded into the bedroom to sleep alone.

LUKE WOKE with a start, having stretched, rolled, and nearly tumbled right off Jesse onto the floor. Being in cat form, however, had the perk of better reflexes, and he righted himself just in time to land on his feet.

After a larger stretch of his back and hind legs, Luke hopped onto the coffee table to check on Jesse. She was still fast asleep.

She was only medium-sized in tiger form, since she was still young, and he mused at how much larger she would be one day. They hadn't practiced much with getting her to Stage Two or Three. Before puberty, kids tended to shift straight to animal form just from trying to sharpen their eyesight, and the nuances of holding the different stages came slowly. He knew she'd be a quick study once they put more focus on it.

Glancing down at his phone beside his paws, Luke saw how late it was and realized with a quick glance around the room that he had no idea what had become of Preston. He jumped down from the coffee table to search, shifting human once he was behind the sofa, naked but not too concerned with finding clothes.

Hearing gentle snores coming from the partially closed bedroom door, he peeked inside to find Preston asleep, with an unknown mouse friend snuggled on the pillow beside his head. He always looked so disarming with his hair fanned out and no glasses on. His hair *was* long, like Jordana had said, having only been a little shaggy when they first met, since growing it out was one of Preston's many rebellions against his parents.

At least he'd had parents to rebel against, but even thinking that caused a twinge of guilt in Luke's gut. He'd never wish on anyone controlling, disapproving parents who'd want their son out of the house just for being gay and becoming mates with someone of a different tribe, just like he knew Preston would never wish on anyone growing up an orphan. They'd both had it tough, and Luke thought they'd come to understand and respect that about each other, only now, they kept getting tangled, all because they were overcompensating to give Jesse something better than they had.

Luke couldn't believe he was letting his stubbornness ruin this.

Just like he almost had when he and Preston first met.

Chapter 2

TEN YEARS AGO

"YOU WANT me to *what?*"

"I want you to be the new pack Councilor."

Luke stared at Bash like the werewolf had grown another head. Considering Bash was a twenty-three-year-old Alpha who had just murdered his own father to get the job, Luke shouldn't have been surprised by much, and he had heard Bash was recruiting younger shifters for his circle, but him? Luke?

"Dude, you know I, like, just turned eighteen, right?"

"Which means you are old enough to be a viable candidate." Bash was seated beside him in the room Luke shared with several other teens at the Shelter. Even though Luke liked Bash, being around the young wolf—now *Alpha*—was sort of like convening with royalty. Bash was educated, poised, dangerous, yet with an air about him that made Luke really want to listen, something he had never felt toward Bash's father, Baraka Bain.

Bash was tall, handsome, with brown skin and wavy chestnut hair that was long enough to be tied up. Even without the glow of his shifter nature, his eyes were golden, commanding the attention of anyone around him. He was not the sort of person you wanted to cross but also seemed noble in a way his father never had, so that Luke never feared Bash the way he had Baraka, because he knew Bash had the pack's best interests in mind, no matter what actions he took or which tribe someone came from.

Luke was seriously doubting Bash's leadership skills at the moment, though.

"I thought your brother was going to be Councilor."

"Bari is not planning on sticking around. He's never cared for all this, and that's his prerogative."

Luke frowned, trying to place the word. His schooling hadn't exactly been formal, since he'd grown up at the Shelter since he was six, and Baraka, asshole Alpha that he'd been, had cared more about using the Shelter *for* resources than giving any to the people who needed them.

"His *choice*," Bash clarified, and not with any condescending like someone else might have used. That was another reason Luke liked Bash and had maybe done a little cheer and dance when he heard about the takeover, but he'd never expected to be part of that takeover.

"Why me? I'm just an alley cat, a nobody."

"Everyone here trusts and adores you," Bash countered, "and you know everything about all of them. I wouldn't call that nobody. It's what I need in my circle. And, I'll have you know, that everyone else I've chosen is from a different tribe. Not a single wolf other than me."

If Luke's mouth could have dropped open farther, his jaw might have unhooked like a lizard. "That's insane."

"I prefer to think of it as the future." Bash grinned. "But I didn't choose random shifters just to make a statement. Each of my circle members was chosen because they are the best option. There is even another cat, Deanna, the panther, as my Second."

"Sure, I know Deanna. She's a good choice for Second."

"And you are a good choice for Councilor. If we had any raptors in town who fit the bill, I would have gone with them just to prove all tribes can work together. But, seeing as how there isn't and a simple *alley cat*," Bash said with a playful lilt, "is the best option, I want you. I even asked a human to be part of our circle."

Apparently Luke's mouth could drop open wider. "You're nuts. Like, totally bonkers. And… I kinda love it? But I don't know, man. That's a lot of responsibility. All the shifters in the city would rely on me, especially the ones at the Shelter."

"Way I hear it, that's how it already is. You even helped keep my father away from some of the younger children so what happened to you wouldn't happen to them. You were willing to risk his wrath by keeping those kids under his radar. Not many people were willing to stand up to him."

"I probably would have pissed my pants if he ever caught me." Luke rubbed the back of his neck.

Baraka had been seriously frightening and used brute force to run the city more than love or loyalty. It's why few shifters inside Centrus had balked at Bash's claim as Alpha after the coup.

"Nothing like what he put people through is ever going to happen again," Bash vowed. "No more child runners, and any involvement in pack inner workings is voluntary. We're going to make the Shelter what it was meant to be, a place of refuge, not assets to exploit. And we're going to take things one step further and become a new kind of pack, showing all nearby cities that they are wrong for only letting one kind of tribe lead."

Wow, Bash was the kind of guy who could have talked someone into walking through hell for him—which was sort of what he was asking of Luke. "Unless they wipe us out first," Luke mumbled.

"They'll hold off to see what we do," Bash said, showing an impressive amount of confidence considering the scope of all this. "See if we implode on ourselves before they risk making a move. We just need to prove them wrong, prove we're strong players among our sister cities and not to be underestimated. You're my last chess piece, Luke. You're my rook."

"I, um… don't really know chess."

"It means…." Bash smiled. "If I'm king and Deanna queen, then the next most important person in this circle is you."

"Ha!" Luke rocked forward, glad he was sitting down or his knees might have buckled. "No pressure or anything. But… ah, fuck it. I'm in! You are off your rocker, but I think that might be what this city needs."

Bash clamped a hand on Luke's shoulder with a supportive squeeze. "This also means you get to move into the den."

"Oh shit." Luke might need to lie down with how much his world was being flipped. "Uh… do I gotta? I really appreciate it, seriously, but… maybe not right away? I've never lived anywhere but at the Shelter. Plus, you might want me here since it's the beginning, ya know, make sure no one plans to off you while your reign's still young."

Bash patted Luke's shoulder once more. "If you prefer. It would be best to eventually have the entire circle under one roof, but take your time."

"Thanks. So… what now?"

"Now…." Bash rose from the cot they had been sitting on. "You meet the rest of the team. Come on. Even if you're not ready to move in, we're having our first circle meeting at the den in half an hour."

Luke felt a flash of his stripes come in as a jolt of anxiety almost made him shift. He needed to keep it together, but this was way too… *Cinderella*. Like, he was definitely an imposter in rags being taken to the ball, where everyone else knew what they were doing and he would absolutely give himself away that he did not.

Even the fancy car waiting outside was like the pumpkin carriage. *Shit.*

Luke had seen Baraka driving by in that thing, but no runners or non-wolf tribe members had ever been allowed near it. That was fine, honestly. Baraka hadn't been, like, a creepy pedophile sleaze or anything, but you still sort of felt like you needed a shower after meeting him.

Usually, he'd delegated talking to the "lesser races" to his circle members, all of whom had been kicked out of the den, Luke heard, so Bash could form his own, and some of them weren't too happy about it. But unless they wanted a tribal war on their hands, there was a grace period after someone usurped an Alpha, though the only reason they'd likely respected that was because the killing had been done by Baraka's rightful successor anyway.

Now Luke was being gestured inside Baraka's car by the *new* Alpha, who was literally holding the door for him. He almost pinched himself to be sure he wasn't dreaming.

"Welcome to the party, kid." A familiar voice greeted him as he slid into the back. Deanna's presence in the driver's seat eased Luke, another person from the cat tribe, someone he knew and who wasn't exactly highbrow.

"Hey, Deanna. Congrats, I guess? This is super weird."

Bash got into the back with Luke, which made it weirder, like they were being chauffeured by some fancy driver instead of a former pack enforcer.

Deanna had been a Shelter kid once too, an Asian panther with black hair she had coiled into a french braid and nearly violet eyes. She was pretty, but in the "don't hit on her unless you're ready to get your teeth knocked out if she's not feeling it" sort of way.

"Relax, kid," Deanna said as she drove them from the Shelter. "The old regime was well overdue for a change. We're gonna show those traditionalist pricks in the other cities what a real pack looks like even if it takes us decades to convince 'em. Right, boss?"

"That's the plan," Bash said.

"So, uh...." Luke fidgeted with a flex of his hands on his thighs, afraid to touch the leather upholstery too much. "Being at the Shelter my whole life, being a runner, I've had my hands in a lot of the Alpha's... I mean, *Baraka's* business. You know, the less-than-legal stuff. Heard a lot too. Rumor was he suspected Bari might try to off him someday, and that's why he sent him to another city."

"That's true." Bash nodded.

"You and Bari were in on it together, then, just bided your time?"

"I'll explain at the den. Most of the others don't know the whole story yet either, only Deanna. But I don't plan on keeping secrets from my circle. You will know everything—always."

"Cool." Luke shrunk from the intensity of Bash's gaze. "Kinda freaking me out more, but... cool. Can I still pick a room even if I'm not ready to move in yet?"

Bash laughed. "Absolutely."

THE DEN, which had been the home of Centrus City's inner circle for generations, was a gated and renovated warehouse that almost looked abandoned from the outside, other than a few cars parked out front, but inside was a cozy living space with communal areas like any large home and private apartment-like rooms for each circle member, as well as a few rooms for member families and potential guests from other cities.

Luke had never been inside before, and going from the familiar facade of a warehouse, not unlike the Shelter, to a high-end interior that showed off the wealth Baraka—and the Alphas before him—had made for himself was a cold splash of reality. Luke could never imagine living here.

"Don't get too attached to the antiques," Bash said, leading him farther inside. "I only plan to keep what we need and a few items of personal significance. The rest will be sold and the money put to better use."

The place was a bit cluttered with antiques, to be honest, like an art dealer's place, but at least the furniture in the living room looked well-worn and comfortable. That's where Bash brought Luke, with four others awaiting them.

"I'll grab us some beers," Deanna said and made a beeline out another door.

Luke recognized most of the room's inhabitants. In an armchair was Bash's twin brother, Bari. They looked identical, but Bari wore brighter, more fashion-forward attire, and the way they carried themselves was like night and day. Where Bash was reserved and calculating, Bari was flamboyant and exuded chaotic energy.

He was chatting with a human woman in another armchair, Nell. Luke had heard she was a witch, who therefore made sense as an addition, but having humans in a pack's inner circle had never been done before. Witches weren't always part of shifter society but usually knew about it, since magic in a city was overseen by a pack's Magister. Maybe that was her role.

She had light brown hair down to her waist, pale blue eyes, and wore a colorful dress and jewelry on every available body part.

On the floor, leaning against one side of the sofa, was Siobhan, a lizard shifter, who had the same kickass air about her as Deanna, since she had also been an enforcer. Enforcers were the muscle under a pack's Warden, who kept the peace like a sheriff. If there was trouble, usually of the physical kind, people like Siobhan were the ones sent to deal with it. If Deanna was Second, then she must be Warden.

Everything about Siobhan was pale gold, from her honey-colored eyes to her platinum hair shaped into a faux-hawk. She had a few visible tattoos on her forearms and was smaller and trimmer of stature than Deanna, who was tall and curvy. Siobhan was listening to whatever Bari and Nell were talking about, since conversation with the fourth and final member would have been difficult with him scooted to the opposite end of the sofa staring at his cellphone like a lifeline he didn't want snipped.

Luke didn't recognize him, but wow, was he pretty.

And *young*. They were all young, only early twenties, with Luke just eighteen.

How the hell were they going to run a city?

"Hey, our fearless leader and mascot at last." Siobhan grinned at them, her eyes going momentarily slitted.

"Hi." Luke waved. "Mascot?"

"Sorry. Only coz you're such a baby-face, kid." She laughed. "But I know how well you handle the streets and what goes on in them."

Kid. Luke had a feeling that was going to be a common nickname.

Maybe he shouldn't have worn his "In My Defense I Was Left Unsupervised" shirt.

"Luke," Bash said, guiding him forward, "you know Siobhan. Nell too, I hear. And—"

"Bari." Bari thrust his hand up at Luke from his perch in the armchair, a little daintily, almost more like he wanted Luke to kiss it rather than shake.

Luke felt totally out of his league. All these people were older than him, most had had higher-ranking titles than him before now, since he was just a runner for basic smuggling and money laundering and the like, and they were all really, really attractive.

Like, Bash was hot, but Bari, with his dazzling smile, made Luke forget to shake hands like a normal person, and he sort of just shook the tips of Bari's fingers.

Bari chuckled, but there was a ring of falseness to it, like maybe he didn't really want to be here. His father had just died, and he usually lived in a different city, so it made sense, but he was putting on an impressive mask to hide it.

"Is it still cool to say sorry about your dad, or… no, that's weird, right?" Luke immediately regretted saying anything with how Bari's mask flickered. "Congrats?"

"It's okay," Bari recovered. "You can be sorry about him. We always were. But you—darling, *you* are seriously pulling off that vintage grunge look. What a cutie." He winked.

Luke's face flushed. He had his moments, but he'd always thought his smile was sort of crooked and goofy, and his outfit probably only looked grunge because it was *grungy*.

"I was happy Bash mentioned you, Luke," Nell said, smiling serenely up at him. She was the type that uninitiated humans might take for a hippie flower child with a love of crystals and tarot readings when, in actuality, she was the real deal. She did have a new-age magic shop, but in the back was a place where shifters could get special medical attention through runic spells without having to risk discovery by normal humans. From what Luke had heard, Nell's mother ran it before her.

"Siobhan's Warden, right? Are you the new Magister?" Luke asked.

"Shaman," Nell corrected, which also made sense, since a Shaman oversaw pack health as well as used magic to keep their culture hidden.

"*This* is our Magister," Bash said, indicating the final member, who had torn himself from his phone long enough to get up and cross to them behind the sofa. "Preston Rathaway."

"Hi! I'm…." Luke trailed off, partially because the name Rathaway was as big as one could be in this town without being part of the former pack leadership. They owned multiple chunks of the city that hadn't been owned by Baraka—or at least secretly run by him—and were literal millionaires.

The other reason Luke stopped short was because Preston was even prettier up close, with delicate Asian features, fierce dark eyes behind his glasses, and shiny black hair he'd swept back like 90s Keanu Reeves. He also brought with him an intoxicating scent.

What *was* that? Luke had never known a rat could smell so….

Delicious.

THIS WILLOWY, cherubic-faced cat shifter smelled *incredible*, which, considering he had just come from the slum of Centrus City's Shelter, should not be possible. Preston couldn't even describe what the smell was, but the moment it struck him, his mouth salivated, and he decided….

He was not going to like this kid at all.

And seriously, with that T-shirt?

"You're… what?" Preston prompted the unfinished sentence. "Barely old enough to drive?"

The friendly smile on the cat's face dropped. Good. Preston did not have time to make nice. They had a city to overhaul, and the others Bash had chosen for their ragtag circle were practically laughable. A human witch, two former enforcers, and this guy? Preston needed them to succeed—to excel—if he was going to admit to his parents what he'd gotten himself into. They didn't even know he'd left college, and he planned to keep it that way until he was ready.

"Preston is also a Rat King, if you're familiar with the term," Bash said.

"Sure!" Luke's smile wasn't deterred for long and had this endearing crookedness to it. His ginger hair could have been better combed, and his outfit was likely Goodwill or Shelter hand-me-downs, but he was impishly and annoyingly… cute. "That means you got normal witch magic and you can control animals, right?"

"Rodents, but yes," Preston droned.

"No wonder you're Magister! That's awesome!"

He was *really* cute, something ingrained in Preston since birth that he was not allowed to think of a cat, let alone another male.

He'd kept his head down for three years of university schooling, because even finally being outside his parents' home, the idea that he couldn't, *shouldn't* indulge in another man's touch like he wanted stuck with him.

Then Bash, who Preston had known when he was a freshman and Bash a senior, had sought him out. Bash hadn't asked Preston to quit school, but Preston had jumped at the chance. He could finish his degree online if it meant being Magister. His parents couldn't rule over him if he outranked them. They'd have to be made to understand that he could carry on the family name in other ways.

They'd *have* to.

But until that happened, a cute catboy was too much too soon.

Preston tried to focus on the annoying part, like how he'd still managed to end up the shortest member of the circle, since Luke completed that travesty by being the same height as Siobhan and Nell, and Deanna was practically five foot ten. An over-six-foot-tall Alpha was no help either.

"We ready?" Deanna returned with a six-pack and immediately popped one open as she set them on the coffee table. She took the sofa seat behind Siobhan's spot on the floor, lightly nudging Siobhan's shoulder with her knee in casual greeting.

Siobhan grabbed a beer next and tossed a couple to Bari and Nell, before draping an arm back across Deanna's thighs in equally relaxed closeness. Preston snubbed the idea of a beer—it was *early afternoon*—and returned to his corner of the sofa, leaving the middle open for Luke, who followed like a lost kitten and then twiddled his thumbs when Deanna asked if he wanted one.

"I'm eighteen."

"So?"

"Deanna," Bash chastised. He didn't take a beer either but remained standing between the sofa and his brother's chair.

Luke was too close. Preston had never known the easy physicality the others were displaying and squeezed himself against the armrest to better escape Luke's smell. It made his insides quiver.

It was probably mold from the Shelter or something.

"Now that everyone has been acquainted," Bash began, "I had hoped we could discuss some long-term plans for changes in the city. Unfortunately, that will have to wait. We have a problem."

"Already?" Siobhan snorted.

"Yes," Bash said plainly. He took a breath before adding, "I've had two prophecies since my father's death."

Preston's head snapped up from watching Luke in his periphery to stare at Bash. It was clear everyone except Bari and Deanna were equally stunned.

"You're a Seer?" Nell inched to the edge of her seat.

"My father never wanted it to be public knowledge. *I* don't want it to be either." Bash cast his gaze around the room to tempt any naysayers, but no one spoke against him. "The first recent prophecy was right after the deed was done. I… go into a trance, and normally, it's rare for me to remember the riddles I spout, but this one I do."

"What was it?" Luke asked with a hush of excitement.

"Less important than the second one. The first references All Hallow's Eve and a red moon, which isn't slated for this year. It may be some time before we deal with that. But the second prophecy I had right before *this* went live."

Bash pulled out his phone and clicked Play on a YouTube video showing something Preston had never thought would be viewable by the public.

A wolf shifter was already at Stage Two, showing fangs, glowing eyes, and sprouts of fur, and continued shifting into her Stage Three form like a movie werewolf, massive and menacing, particularly because she was screaming and tearing at herself like she had no idea how or why she was changing.

On a public street.

She further transformed to Stage Four, becoming a common wolf, with her torn clothing left in tatters on the ground. Afterward, she darted into an alley to escape the crowd beginning to form, with several other phones in hand recording and taking photos. Then the video stopped to a tense silence.

Preston had to give Luke some credit because he summed up the situation perfectly.

"*Fuck.*"

Chapter 3

LUKE FELT a flicker of regret, fear, panic—what was he thinking agreeing to be Councilor when *this* was his initiation, public proof of their species posted online that could topple the entirety of shifter society.

Fuck was indeed the appropriate response.

"It isn't that bad, is it?" Siobhan lifted onto her knees. "I mean, how many people will believe it's real? Even the ones who were there didn't look that rattled. They probably think it was a publicity stunt. We just need damage control."

"I wish it were that simple," Bash said. "But this wasn't the only instance."

He showed two more videos posted to YouTube, one of a male hawk shifter and another of a female lizard. All three videos had thousands of hits.

"Okay…." Luke laced his fingers together, hoping the tight pressure would ease his anxiety. "Not sure I really want to know this, but… what was your second prophecy?"

Deanna must have already heard it, because she sipped stoically from her beer, but although Bari obviously knew his brother was a Seer, he seemed as earnestly interested as everyone else.

Bash recited the words like an ominous nursery rhyme.

> *"It begins with an exodus of siblings and charm,*
> *Neither knowing the extent of their greed's lasting harm.*
> *All beasts will howl on and rage, none immune*
> *If the source is not stopped by wane on Harvest Moon.*

"This is happening fast," he said after letting the verses settle. "It's only a week until the Harvest Moon, and these three incidents happened within days of each other."

"Since the takeover?" Preston asked.

"I don't know if it's connected yet," Bash said, "but we can't rule it out as a catalyst. We need to know who and what has changed or entered this city since the first incident. That the prophecy mentions siblings is honestly more the reason I asked Bari to come home than for our father's funeral." He cast his brother an apologetic look.

"I don't know about exodus." Bari shifted nervously. "I wasn't planning on staying."

"But you know better than anyone my prophecies aren't always literal. And we are experiencing an exodus from Father."

"I suppose I can't deny the charm factor." Bari shook out his hair, not quite as long as Bash's but hanging just shy of his shoulders. Then his smile twitched. "I promise, brother, I've done nothing quite so greedy that would explain shifters in this city losing control. How? From what?"

"You needn't explain yourself to me, Bari," Bash assuaged. "It could simply mean our desire for Father to be gone and to make a better pack from his mistakes is going to have unintended consequences—from others seeking to destroy us."

"Um...." Luke spoke up again, waiting for both brothers to look at him. "You said you'd explain, but... the reason Baraka thought Bari might kill him someday was because you had a prophecy about it, right?"

"Correct," Bash said. "But like this prophecy, the details were vague. Our father assumed the son who would overthrow him would be Bari, because Bari was more outspoken against him. After he sent Bari away, he should have paid more attention to the son left behind."

The darkness and deep-seated hatred in Bash toward his father made Luke shiver. He got it, at least as much as anyone could who wasn't Bash or Bari themselves, because Baraka had been a monster, and to none more than his own children.

"What matters now," Bash went on, "is that we solve this before things get worse."

"I'm going to assume by how you keep looking at *me*," Preston said, "that you want me to take point?"

"You are Magister," Bash conceded. "While there may be a biological component, there is magic at work here, of that I have no doubt. Additionally, I would like Luke to accompany you."

"*Me?*" Luke squawked, voice breaking as the inevitable proof that he did not belong here.

"Why Garfield?" Preston sneered.

"Hey! That's… actually, I kinda take that as a compliment."

Preston huffed. How could someone that pretty be so surly?

Although there was definitely something hidden beneath the grumpy bits.

Luke had to watch how much he naturally wanted to lean toward Preston. He tried to decipher what that smell was, but all that came to mind was what he imagined home-cooked pie was like just out of the oven, with crust and fruit and cinnamon, though his only experience with that was on TV and his imagination.

"Luke's main presence is to help reduce hysteria," Bash said. "These videos are going to keep circulating, and eventually everyone in our community will know."

"And other communities," Deanna jumped in. As Second, her main job was to protect Bash and to be ready to lead in his absence or incapacitation. She was also his main advisor and was clearly worried about what other cities might do with this revelation.

"Very soon all eyes that weren't on us already will be," Bash agreed, "which is why we need to prove we can handle this on our own, succinctly and with discretion. Luke, I imagine you recognized most of the people from those videos?"

"Uh… sure. The wolf was Sydney Hyland. She's a social worker, stops in at the Shelter when she can but mostly works with humans. The raptor was George Lien, another runner. I don't know the lizard's name, but I recognize her from Shaw Street, worked the corner or got, um… picked up when Baraka had guests, ya know?" There was *some* sleaze factor to Baraka Bain, not that anyone looked surprised.

Bash's expression was different, focused more on Luke, as if impressed by his ability to know everyone so well, but… why wouldn't he? As a runner, all Luke did was know everyone. It wasn't as if he had a normal job or went to school.

Bash clearly saw Luke's knowledge as a strength and was trying to impress that upon him with a look—and maybe with some of that look shooting over Luke's shoulder at Preston.

"*That* is why Luke," Bash said.

Ignoring the rising heat from feeling Preston's stare on the back of his neck, Luke asked, "Where are they now? Are they okay?"

"The two you know are home. Both say they haven't had any issues since, but they're understandably spooked and don't want to go out. Frankly, I don't want them out either, not until we know what's causing this.

"As for the unknown, she's MIA, and we need to find her. Use each other as resources. Siobhan, keep recruiting agents. And they are *agents*, not enforcers. Let's focus on the ever elusive 'protect and serve' portion of the job description. I want as many eyes on the streets as possible for the next time this happens. Any of you find magical residue you can't identify, Nell is knowledgeable in her own specialties." Bash met eyes with each of them in turn. "Run into trouble that requires a little muscle or need to put fear into anyone, call me directly, and Deanna and I will be there."

"And Tweedle Dum?" Preston swept a hand at Bari, which nearly made Luke choke on a laugh.

"*I'm* the older twin," Bari defended—then winked again. "And believe me, darling, I am definitely the 'D'."

Luke did laugh then, accompanied by Deanna, Siobhan, and Nell, while Bash looked maybe mildly annoyed, and Preston... sort of clammed up and turned away. Maybe he wasn't all that comfortable around queer people, which honestly was probably everyone else in the room on some level, but Luke had always heard of the Rathaways being uber-traditionalist.

Of course, a true traditionalist wouldn't be here.

"Bari will be around a while longer," Bash said, "at least until we know more and I can be assured of his safety in another city. Otherwise, you all have your orders or know what to be on standby for. Move in, make yourselves available to the pack as needed, and show this city the strength of what we are doing here without being a symbol of fear the way my father ran things. Solving this mystery will be a huge step in the right direction.

"You're dismissed, but feel free to explore the den at your leisure. This is our home now—together."

The others finished their beers in a closer huddle, discussing the situation and plans for the house. Luke and Preston were expected to get straight to work, but Luke met eyes with Bash first, silently luring him in their direction. He and Preston stood and met Bash behind the sofa.

"I don't think he's okay," Luke whispered of Bari. Bari's smile, demeanor, and joking words were all part of the same mask, covering how much pain he was in just by being here.

"I know," Bash said without glancing back.

"Seems fine to me." Preston shrugged.

He was smaller than Luke, which was rare with men, but he was still older and had this almost ageless presence about him that said he suffered no fools.

He wasn't very observant, though.

"You gotta look behind the eyes," Luke said. "Some smiles are faker than if an actor was wearing them, ya know?"

Preston seemed surprised, even clammed up again. Standing so close to him, with that smell emanating and his dark eyes glittering hypnotically, Luke felt a warm pulse between them, like being drawn into the thudding bassline of his favorite song. He'd never felt something so potent and unexplainable before. He'd fooled around with others at the Shelter plenty growing up—there wasn't much else to do if you weren't on a job—but he'd never… yearned.

That was definitely the word for this.

An unlikely but beautiful idea blossomed in Luke's chest, and he wondered—

Preston cleared his throat, and Luke shook himself from staring. He was going to be working closely with this guy. He couldn't have Preston thinking he was a creeper.

"Just to be clear—" Preston turned to Bash. "—the reason your father thought Bari might kill him someday was because he misinterpreted your prophecy."

"Yes."

"Meaning they can be wrong?" Luke balked. "Or… are easy to get wrong?"

"Easy enough, and it's smart of you both to think that way. We need to be vigilant. Use your skills and your intuition to find out something, anything, before this happens again. I'm counting on both of you," Bash finished with severity. "Seven days."

Luke would have laughed at the unintentional *The Ring* reference if any of this was funny. He'd been wrong. The situation alone wasn't what warranted a *fuck* moment.

Being responsible for fixing it was.

DAY 1

NOW PRESTON had to work with this cat? Not playing well with others was a major part of his personality, and he was fine with that. Although he did have to recognize the benefits of having a personable and perceptive companion who knew everyone, since then Luke could handle the interacting part of their assignment.

Preston would just have to live with him.

And that scent, something earthy and herbaceous like….

Sage?

At least it wasn't mold, and the smell wasn't quite as powerful outside. They could have taken a car, but that would have defeated the purpose of looking for potential magical residue near the victims' homes. Preston needed to cover a wide search area to be sure he didn't miss anything.

It was also nice getting out into the fresh air instead of being cooped up with the others. They were not like the high-society rat snobs Preston had grown up around, where family and tradition meant always, *always* carrying on the line "properly" and didn't leave room for "degrading" behavior like mixing tribes or preferring members of the same gender.

Bari exclusively veered that direction, from what Preston understood, and the others were all… fluid? They were so open and comfortable and free to be whoever they wanted to be, but instead of that making it easier to be around them, all that embraced otherness made Preston feel suffocated, remembering how he'd never been allowed the same.

"Slow down! Where are you even going?"

Preston hadn't consciously been leaving Luke in the dust, though he hadn't done much to dissuade the unconscious desire either. His excuse would be that it was too hot out, even being early September, and moving swiftly allowed a breeze.

"I thought you knew these people," Preston said, not slowing his pace as Luke raced up beside him. "We're going to the first address, then the second, to question the people whose identities we already have."

"But we already *have* their identities and know where they are," Luke countered. "The longer we don't find Jane Doe, the more likely she'll split. We should track her first. I know a few locations she frequents, remember? The others aren't going anywhere."

Preston hated to be undermined, and though he knew he and Luke were technically of the same rank—so this was a disagreement, not a purposeful slight—his fists clenched.

"We're on the same team." Luke gently nudged him, apparently reading Preston as easily as he had Bari, which was… unnerving. Preston had prided himself on hiding his true nature for so long, he didn't like being around someone so good at *seeing* everyone. "Hey, you're magic man, and that's awesome. But I know people. We should look for the lizard girl first. If we don't find any signs of her, we'll hit the homes next. Okay?"

He was also frustratingly nice about it.

"Fine," Preston said, easing his fists and his pace. "Where are we starting?"

"Shaw Street. And the blocks around it. If we don't see her right away, we might still get a lead from one of her friends. Come on." Luke smiled and turned them down a different street.

By the time they were nearing the designated neighborhood, Preston had sweat dripping down the back of his neck. Maybe a car would have been better, since he wasn't picking up on any foreign magic.

"You okay?" Luke asked after Preston tugged on his shirt collar for the ninth time.

"It's sweltering out. Doesn't the heat bother you?"

"I love the heat!" Luke gushed. "If I could—"

"You'd lie in the sun all day?"

"Well, not *all* day."

Cats, Preston thought with a huff.

A twist of guilt churned in his stomach. His parents had always spoken of smaller cat shifters as, well, *vermin*. Like they were undeserving of having a high-ranking status in most cities just because they were related to their larger cousins, whereas rat shifters were seen as smaller and weaker and therefore always at the bottom.

Remember, Trace, we are the ones with true magical potential. Other tribes can't manifest power like a Rat King. You are a testament to our family and our entire race.

Preston hated being called Trace, like his own identity didn't matter and he was just… number three in a long line of expectations—Preston Rathaway III.

Rats being on the bottom wasn't right, but hating other tribes for their lot wasn't right either. Preston didn't want to think like his parents.

Ever.

Luke took the lead, questioning people on and around Shaw Street, while Preston stood back, scanning the area for signs of unusual magical residue. These streets weren't exactly his stomping grounds. There was a reason prostitutes worked these corners; this was the lawless side of town and almost exclusively occupied by shifters, where most of Baraka's illegal dealings could fly under the radar. It wasn't a right or wrong side of the tracks that split the neighborhoods, but there was a single street that marked the line between uptown and downtown where people like Preston's parents never would have crossed.

"Oh, and spread the word, okuy?" Luke was saying to a cluster of street workers already out for the night, despite the sun not having set. "Not only about your friend, but that all pack 'donations' are voluntary now. All work whatsoever is only if you want to. So, ya know… you're free agents now, however you want to handle that."

The two overly thin women and a feminine-looking man in his twenties all exchanged curious glances.

"Seriously?" one of the women asked.

"Because of Bash?" the man added.

"And the new circle." Luke beamed, easing into his role better than he'd let on at the den. "Think about it, and if you wind up needing anything, check in with me. I'll be at the Shelter."

"What if *you* need something, honey?" The man stepped up to Luke and dragged metallic painted nails down the front of Luke's T-shirt, shifting his hips in too tight pants and biting his lip suggestively.

"Like I said." Luke chuckled. "All voluntary."

"Who said it wouldn't be?" The man leered.

"Save it for someone who didn't just turn legal," Preston intervened with a tug on Luke's arm, leading them down a side street. He didn't bother glancing back to see if the slighted rent boy was upset. They didn't need immediate rumors about their reign of debauchery taking precedence over results.

That was definitely the only reason he'd stepped in.

"It's fine," Luke said, not yanking his arm away, which left Preston attached to him longer than intended, and he eventually tore his own grip back. "Joey's flirted with me like that since I was fifteen. He doesn't mean it."

"That's disgusting."

"It's the streets. My streets. What's disgusting was Baraka pimping those people out when *they* were fifteen. If that." Luke snorted. "It's not like any of us chose what he made us do."

Preston's stomach lurched with a furtive glance at Luke.

"Not *me*. I'm not so pretty, like you, that I had to worry about that. Plus, I'm a good runner. No one catches this cat." He proudly patted his chest. "And even fewer can help talk others out of a bad situation. Not one arrest for me or anyone I ever worked with on a job. Best record in the pack."

That *was* impressive, given the amount of laundering, drugs, guns, and who knew what else that went down by pack control, but Preston was a little preoccupied by being so offhandedly called....

Pretty.

Having anything feminine attributed to him had always been a hazard, just one more reason someone might guess the truth. Yet, coming from Luke, it felt... warm somehow, and not oppressive like the blistering heat.

"You, um... told them to find you at the Shelter." Preston changed the subject. "You're not moving into the den with the rest of us?"

"Bash wants me to, but I asked if I could wait. I don't know if I could sleep on that soft of a bed, ya know?" He looked at Preston with a bat of his bright blue eyes, and Preston was tongue-tied by how captivating they were this close. "You do not know. The den's probably a downgrade for you, huh?" Luke was so effortlessly friendly and at ease, hands shoved in his pockets, walking side by side with Preston down some of the worst streets in the city.

"You'll find that university dorm beds are equal-opportunity torture devices."

Luke laughed—and nudged Preston again, like they were fast friends. "You're not so bad. We just gotta work on that sense of humor being a little less mean."

Preston wanted to counter him being *mean* when another wave of sage struck him.

Wait, that wasn't sage. It was more like... mint mixed with bergamot, common scents when more alchemically adept witches cast spells.

After a quick glance, finding no one immediately visible or with too much attention on them, Preston seized Luke's arm and dragged him into an alley. He immediately drew a rune in the air. He wasn't adept enough at this type of magic to make the spell invisible to outside eyes, and he didn't want anyone else seeing what he was about to do.

The rune glowed a soft yellow and flared out as it dissipated with a pulse of light, which would cause any nearby magical residue to glow in kind within a wide radius that, at least this part, was thankfully only visible to Preston as the caster.

"What was that?" Luke asked in a whisper, at least understanding that ducking into the alley had been with stealthy intent.

"I smelled fresh magic. I'm checking to see if there are any recent or active spells nearby." With a peer around the corner, Preston began a scan of everything within eyeline. Most of what he saw was basic and dim, like remnants from glamour magic, probably to make a storefront look less run down, or scars on the pavement from fights with fire and lightning spells. None of it was foreign or too suspicious for streets like this.

"Anything?" Luke asked.

Preston opened his mouth to answer in the negative when he spotted something kitty-corner from their location in the direction they had been headed, like a handprint slapped on a wall inside an alley, and it was glowing....

Prismatic.

He'd never seen magic show every color before.

"I see parts of a rune left behind that's incomplete or... maybe too old for me to recognize. Nell might know. The way it's reacting is like nothing I've ever seen before, and whoever left it is near. I know I smelled magic."

"Maybe it's from our mystery lizard, leftover from what happened to her."

"Maybe."

"Then we'll wait. See if she shows or if anything else happens."

Preston nodded and turned back to Luke. "I'll spread out with additional feelers."

"Feelers?" Luke's brow furrowed, and confusion was even more endearing on his face than a crooked smile.

This was something Preston could feel confident in showing off and was the real reason Bash had asked for him. "Rat King, remember?" He closed his eyes and reached out with his senses to summon his kindred spirits.

There were rats and mice everywhere in these buildings and hidden in corners of nearby alleys, and he called to them like the Pied Piper to heed his will.

Come. See.

"Shit!" Luke hissed as the first of many rodents arrived. Preston heard the thuds of Luke hopping from foot to foot and felt the brush of Luke's arm when he pressed closer amidst dozens of scurrying bodies. But to Luke's credit, he didn't stomp at any or sound disgusted. His next utterance was a reverent "*Sweet….*"

Preston smiled, eyes still closed but able to see through his minions' eyes, several at once, as they hurried out of the alley and branched out along the edges of buildings to check in places where Preston and Luke couldn't see.

Down farther alleys and side streets, Preston discovered other remnants of spells, also common in nature. Nothing was like the prismatic rune fragment or evidence of a spell active enough to explain that smell—

"I hear something!" Luke plastered himself against Preston.

Annoyed by the jolt, Preston severed his connection to the rodents and turned to glare—only to bump noses with Luke.

Luke gasped, sapphire eyes widening to show off a ring of darker blue around his pupils.

There was that sage smell, overpowering any magical scents.

"Wow, you smell good…," Luke said, and Preston swallowed to hear his own thoughts echoed back at him.

There were stories, shifter fairy tales, about finding someone who smelled this incredible to you, and that the right scent meant you had finally found your….

It was nonsense, but having that thought stir in Preston's mind made him instantly panic. "If you think the cat can get any of this rat, think again!" he blurted.

Luke was feline. And male. And a *kid*. Okay, so he was only three years younger than Preston, but three years was a lot at this stage of life, and they were worlds apart in so many other ways.

And similar in one very specific way that Preston knew shouldn't be a problem, no matter what his parents had taught him about "improper" urges, but just because Luke smelled amazing did not mean anything.

Even if it was alluring, the way those stories said shifters should feel about the scent of their one true

A blur ran past them, bringing with it the strongest punch of mint and bergamot yet.

They lurched apart, and both turned to the mouth of the alley.

The lizard! Without sparing each other another glance, they took off out of the alley to give chase.

Chapter 4

"DUDE, WAIT!" Luke hurried to keep up with Preston.

As a runner, he had often, well, *had to run* while doing odd jobs for Baraka and the old circle. He wasn't used to someone outpacing him. Maybe Preston had been in track and field in school or something. Maybe he was fast because he was smaller.

Or maybe Luke was distracted after realizing that someone smelling as good to him as Preston did meant he had finally found his—

He nearly ran into Preston's back as the rat paused, glancing left and right, and finally pushed onward to the left down another alley. These streets were a maze, but Preston must have picked up on something to tell him where to go. All Luke had caught sight of from the blur that ran past and was now, maybe, ahead of them, was a flash of ginger hair, paler in color than his own.

Was the lizard they were looking for a redhead? Luke could have sworn her hair was darker....

"It's her! It has to be!" Preston cried, a stride-length ahead of Luke. "Hurry up!"

Luke was going to say he was trying to, when he felt something tighten in his gut that had nothing to do with nerves about proximity to pretty rat shifters with awesome Disney Princess powers. He glanced down at his body to see orange fur sprouting along the backs of his hands, with his claws extending and eyesight going sharper.

Shit.

"Pres—"

"There!"

They turned another corner, and Preston lashed out with an arm that had seconds ago been empty, releasing glowing blue translucent chains like a character out of a fighting game. Magic wasn't allowed in public any more than shifting, but they were in the absolute bowels of shifter neighborhoods with no one around who would dare get in their way or even acknowledge shouting and running feet for fear of interfering with Baraka's—now *Bash's*—business.

Luke had zero magic himself, and while he had seen various spells done throughout his life, mostly fire to keep people warm in winter at the Shelter, he had never been this close to something so… *cool*.

There was an exclamation of surprise, a thud, and then Preston's spirit chains lifted the figure they had caught and pinned the person to the wall. They were ginger-haired, but this was no lizard—and definitely not a woman.

"Who are *you*?" Preston barked, holding the other end of his chains in both hands and tightening them to make the man hiss. His young, clean-shaven face said he wasn't much older than them, but he was huge, over six foot two, and lean but nicely muscled.

If Luke had met him on the streets under different circumstances, he might have hoped to be sharing breakfast tomorrow. The guy was a *fox*, in both meanings of the word, his ginger hair long and eyes nearly the same warm amber color.

"Where did that scent go?" Preston demanded. "Did you negate it? Did the spell dissipate?"

With a panicked glance downward, Luke remembered the twist in his gut and forced sprouting of fur and other Stage Two attributes, but he was surprised and relieved to find that he was back to human and the urge to shift had also faded.

"Relax, *Fievel*," the man huffed past the pressure the chains were putting on his lungs. "I don't know what you're talking about. I have bupkis for magic affinity. Can't a natural witch like you tell?"

Was this the wrong person? Luke couldn't be sure—the blur had sped past their alley too quickly—but he had thought the hair on the person was ginger. The man was hiding something, but plenty of people had secrets, and it seemed this guy having magic wasn't one of them, because Preston frowned like he could sense that the fox wasn't attuned.

"Hey!" a new voice preceded a second set of rushing feet, and suddenly, Luke was seeing double—at least in coloring. The young woman was the same age and heritage as the fox, and gorgeous, like wow. These two hit the genetic lottery and had to be siblings, if not twins.

Siblings.

"What are you doing with my brother?" she said, confirming the relation and flexing her claws with an instant shift to Stage Two, which managed to be intimidating, even with her wearing a sundress.

Luke hadn't met many foxes, but their midshift was a strange and beautiful mix between what he was used to in wolves and cats. Her ears had an extra orange tuft on the ends as they became pointed, her nose darkening to almost black as a cry sounded from her fanged mouth, like a high-pitched bark blended with a growl.

Pivoting to stand between her and Preston, Luke shifted in kind, feeling okay about allowing the change now that he no longer felt compelled. He wasn't particularly vicious-looking next to most shifters, with whiskers and pale blond stripes in his fur, but he could scrap with the best of them, even if she pushed to Stage Three and grew larger.

"There's no scent on her either!" Preston spat.

"And Tiger too?" The male laughed. "Or should I call you *Kitten*?"

Luke hissed with only the barest glance back. He would not dare look behind him when the fox was obviously trying to make an opening for his sister. Kitten was a common enough nickname thrown at him… but he actually kind of liked Tiger from *An American Tail*.

"Don't try anything," Preston warned. "Now, why were you running?"

"Because someone was chasing us," the female snapped.

"You were running before we gave chase."

"Maybe it was cops." The male shrugged, or as best he could with his arms fastened to his sides. "Why should we tell you? We don't even know who you are to be asking questions."

"Yeah, and I don't know you," Luke said with more hiss in his words and another glance back, catching the male fox in his periphery. "Even if I don't know everyone's name, I'm pretty close to recognizing most shifters in the pack, especially in these streets. You aren't from Centrus. We don't get many foxes."

The female peeked over Luke's shoulder, likely meeting gazes with her brother. As her shift faded to Stage One with only a glow in her eyes, it seemed she was readying to bolt.

"Running would be a bad idea." Preston must have caught the exchange, because a crackling began, and this time, Luke did look all the way behind him. Preston held the chains in one hand, and in the other was a growing ball of lightning like the inside of one of those weird static-inducing balls at Spencer's Gifts.

So cool.

"We can play nice," Luke returned to the woman, releasing his shift and raising his hands. Somehow he and Preston had fallen into good cop/bad cop without even trying. "Assuming *you* can. You're talking to the city's new Magister and Councilor."

They laughed.

"Believe it." Luke met the woman's still glowing eyes. "Centrus just swapped leadership, and we're it. If you're new to town, then you need to check in with our Warden."

"Precisely," Preston followed his lead. "You're coming back with us to the circle's den and answering to her—and to our Alpha."

Luke waited until the fox woman's eyes went human before swiveling to take in everyone fully. Even as Preston released his spirit chains, which blinked out of existence with a spark, Luke could tell Preston was still upset about the spell he'd caught a whiff of and lost.

Maybe they'd followed the wrong people, but until they knew what was going on, any lead out of the ordinary was better than nothing.

"We'll come quietly." The male raised his hands like Luke, and with a sigh and shake of her long hair, the female did the same.

"You better," Preston warned, indicating each alley and side street into the cross section where they stood. In the darkest shadows of those narrow passageways, small glowing eyes could be seen in massive multitude.

The foxes couldn't hide their spooked expressions.

"Trust me, you wouldn't get far," Preston finished and headed toward the main road, leaving Luke and the siblings to bring up the rear.

Seriously—*so cool*.

PRESTON WAS unbelievably relieved that neither of the foxes nor Luke had been able to tell he was bluffing about the lightning spell. He'd never used offensive magic on another person before and honestly wasn't sure if he could. Thankfully, his legitimate annoyance with the situation had made his threat come across as sincere. Luke naturally taking up the role of good cop helped too.

It had almost been… fun.

Siobhan was at the den when they returned, and a quick call to Bash had him and Deanna arriving minutes later to interrogate who they now knew as Jude and Jordana Marley. Preston knew he should take this as a win. The foxes were suspicious, new to town, *siblings* like in Bash's prophecy, and they'd been running from something. If they weren't the cause of the spell Preston had smelled, they might still be involved.

But he hated that he'd lost track of that scent. Anything less than perfection was a failure.

He also hated that he couldn't shake that life lesson no matter how long he'd been away from his parents.

"Hey… did you feel it?"

Nerves churned in Preston's stomach at Luke's secretive whisper. They were poised in the doorway to the living room, listening in while Siobhan and Bash questioned the foxes on the sofa, with Deanna standing menacingly in the doorway across from them.

Now was not the time to bring up pounding hearts after bumped noses and the smell of sage in the air like renewal.

"What?" Preston lied.

"The forced shift."

Shift? Luke wasn't talking about their close encounter, though being this near to him again, squeezed together in the doorway, certainly reminded Preston of that.

"Before we caught them," Luke continued. "I think the spell, or whatever it was, almost affected me. I started shifting without trying."

"You're sure?"

"I think so. I felt all off, and the change started without me thinking about it. Then once we caught the foxes and you said the smell was gone, so was that feeling."

If the same thing had been affecting Preston, he'd been too preoccupied with the chase to notice. "It still doesn't mean they're to blame, but your experience says the spell I picked up on has to be the right one. We need to get back to those streets."

"You can't kick us out!" Jordana's voice rose in alarm, drawing Preston and Luke back to the interrogation.

"We damn well can," Siobhan barked. "I get final say on who stays in this city, and you two are lying through your teeth. Just passing through? Seriously? You think I got chosen as Warden because I'm an easygoing people person? You are up to something, and you're going to tell us what if you want asylum."

Bash had been letting Siobhan do most of the talking, which was smart. If they were going to prove they were a strong circle, he couldn't hand-hold everyone. They all had their specialties, and they needed to prove their autonomy, which in turn would make Bash look strong for having chosen them.

The foxes were quiet after the ultimatum. Sitting side by side on the sofa, they looked even more like siblings, with Jordana merely having a more delicate curve to her cheek and a shorter feminine physique.

"We were on a job," Jude said.

"Jude!"

"We were warned about Bain—*prior* Bain," he pushed on despite her protest, and then turned to his sister for understanding. "This isn't him, Jordy. He's got cats, a lizard, and a Rat King in his circle."

"And a human witch," Bash added nonchalantly, legs crossed as he sat in an armchair. "But do go on with your confession, Mr. Marley."

"We had a job at a museum in Glenwood," Jude continued. "The illegal, 'taking what doesn't belong to you' kind. Some of the goods we dropped off with our fence before leaving town, but several items are for specific buyers we're to deliver to here. We were trying to lay low and get in touch with our contacts, but it seems all chaos has broken loose in this city the past few days. We thought the former Alpha being gone would mean this would be easier, but our buyers aren't being too cooperative anymore."

Bash uncrossed his legs to lean forward with slow, calculating assuredness. "One thing I can say about my father, Mr. Marley, is that business was always business. As long as you played ball, double crosses only meant fewer accomplices in the future. Your buyers are probably thinking the city is lawless in his absence and don't want to pay their bill. Am I right?"

The foxes shared a shifty-eyed glance and nodded.

So that was who they'd been running from—buyers who didn't want to pay.

"If you're willing to give up their names," Bash went on, "I am willing to talk to them for you."

"You *are*?" Jordana sputtered.

"We're not cops. I know some packs in other cities have more legitimate practices, and I might take the opportunity of replacing my father to explore some, but I have no intention of giving up our usual revenue streams, only the methods of maintaining them and how my people are treated. That can include you if you play by my rules."

Preston didn't care about less-than-legitimate practices. It wasn't as if his family had made all their millions through strictly legal means. He understood that living in the shadows as an entire race that most humans didn't know existed required the ability to bend the rules.

He also appreciated smart business even when the methods were illegitimate, and these foxes seemed to understand that too.

"How much of a cut do you want?" Jude asked.

"Standard finder's fee—since my people found you. Ten percent." Jordana scoffed, and both looked about to protest.

"My father would have asked for 35 percent, though he might have simply killed you for not taking this deal through him first," Bash warned.

"We did," Jordana said, and then deflated with a glance at her brother. "Or thought we did. One of our buyers is—*was*—part of the old circle."

"Shit," Luke hissed under his breath exactly what Preston was thinking. Few coups played out smoothly, even if Bash had managed to get the old circle out of the den.

"Then I am going to need a name—all the names," Bash said, "and a list of everything you stole."

The foxes already had lists on their persons for the first of the exchanges they had tried to make. Bash mostly focused on the buyers and frowned.

"I'm going to have to pay a few people a visit."

"Oh no you won't," Deanna called from her post. "You're Alpha now, and you need to delegate. You already did. Those two are investigating, remember?" She nodded across the room at Preston and Luke, and then to Siobhan beside the foxes. "And Shevy's agents can keep an eye on things until the right people can be questioned. You go sticking your nose in every corner, especially corners with enemies lurking who you recently kicked out of their home, you're gonna get that nose bitten off. Don't give them the excuse, boss. If you're needed, they'll let us know. Right?"

Luke straightened from how his posture naturally tended to slouch. "Sure! We got this."

"I can have agents watching every address on that list," Siobhan confirmed.

"And I want to know who's behind this," added Preston, still thinking of the spell he'd sniffed out. "Let us go in first. There's plenty else for you to handle right now."

"All right," Bash agreed with a grudging purse to his lips. "Take the night to plan and go in fresh tomorrow. In the meantime, why don't you and Luke escort our guests to an empty room, since they are going to be staying here until this is resolved."

"What about our things?" Jordana asked.

"Are they secure?"

"Well, yes, but—"

"Then I am sure they can all be retrieved tomorrow. Until then, we can provide any amenities you require. You are not to leave this house alone, understood? Given you committed your crime in Glenwood, I need to give their Alpha a call."

That made both foxes pale.

"You're bringing in Glenwood's Alpha?" Jude asked.

"I need to salvage the situation, so yes." Bash made to stand and leave the room, but Luke stepped in from the doorway.

"Um... aren't you going to tell them what we're really investigating? I think they should know."

In another situation, Preston might have thought Luke's honesty foolhardy, but if they were going to be trusting these foxes, they needed them to know the goal.

"You're right," Bash said, "especially since the public already does, and more will soon."

He went on to explain the forced shifts and current victims, showing the same videos he had the circle—though without admitting his prophecy. The foxes seemed stunned, not having heard anything about this yet. At least, Preston didn't think they had.

He glanced at Luke and thought the cat looked convinced by them too.

"You understand now why you are going to tell us everything you know," Bash said.

"We're not involved in *that*," Jude insisted. "We just took items, artifacts, things."

"Perhaps, but things can be used to smuggle other things or be imbued with spells." Bash handed the lists of buyers and items to Preston before departing, with Deanna close on his tail. "I'll be looking forward to an update."

Siobhan excused herself next, leaving Preston and Luke to their captives.

"Come on." Preston pocketed the lists. "I know where there's an unclaimed room."

He'd already made himself familiar with the den, and he doubted any of the circle would have taken this particular room, since it had two twin beds instead of a king or queen. It was meant for guests or children of circle members, and Preston led them there up the main staircase and to the end of the hall.

"Sorry about the, ya know… standoff earlier," Luke said with a jovial tone. "And the chains! Right, Pres?"

Pres?

He glanced back with what he hoped was a cowing glare and didn't respond.

"It's just all so new for us, and things are crazy right now, and you two are outliers, so we gotta be smart," Luke rattled on.

"How old *are* you?" Jude asked.

"Old enough to probably have more thefts under my belt than you two combined," Luke said. "Not anything cool like a museum heist, but I am the best pickpocket in Centrus. I've done my fair share of moving product and money and things that don't belong to me. Usually for someone else's benefit, but we're not so different. I'm gonna even bet… you're Shelter kids."

"You're good," Jordana said with a tinge of surprise, easing out of the tension she'd held before. "Is that why they picked such a baby-face for Councilor?"

"Yep! Coz baby don't mean innocent."

Preston was glad he was at the front of their train, because he could not hide his smile.

Why did Luke have to be so… adorable?

"You're a Shelter kid yourself, then," Jude surmised. "Be honest, how screwed are we once we've outlived our usefulness?"

"Not at all! Bash is a good guy. And he's going to be a great Alpha. You'll see."

"Unless, of course, you're lying." Preston came to a stop in front of the room and turned on his heels, causing Jude to startle and Jordana to bump into him. Preston placed a hand on the door, and it glowed briefly purple. Then he flung it open and gestured them inside. Luke might be a good judge of character, but Preston couldn't have these strangers thinking they were pushovers.

They gazed inside, apparently amazed at the accommodations, since the rooms were large, well-decorated, and spotless.

Luke looked just as amazed when he peered over their shoulders.

"Each room has its own bathroom, and we'll bring you food and clothing to borrow later, so there should be no reason for you to leave. I placed an alarm spell on the door and extended it to all windows, so if you try to go anywhere without us, I'll know."

The foxes cast him pinched expressions but hurried across the threshold.

"It was nice—" Luke tried, but Preston closed the door before he could finish. "—to meet you."

"Come on." Preston grabbed his arm.

"Okay, jeez! Remember the not-being-mean thing we discussed?"

"That was for my sense of humor." Preston let Luke go and flashed him a sharp scowl. "And I am not mean."

"Where are we going?"

"My room."

"You moved in already? When?"

"Straight from my university dorm the day after Baraka died. I don't like wasting time, so please stop wasting mine."

"I'm coming, I'm coming," Luke said with a raise of his hands.

Preston's room wasn't far, and he stopped in front of it to find his key. The den was basically a safe house, but he didn't feel comfortable leaving it unlocked when he didn't know these people yet, other than Bash. He didn't want just anyone traipsing into his room uninvited.

Luke stood very close to him while he fiddled with the door, and the smell of sage he'd been trying to ignore wafted up around him again, making him shiver.

Not now. They had a job to do that couldn't afford deviations.

Preston threw open his door with as little ceremony as he had Jude and Jordana's and barreled inside, already diving into a tirade of next steps. "Let's start by…," he went on, not looking at Luke as he talked. He went to his computer desk to begin cross-checking the addresses on their list of buyers for the most convenient path of attack tomorrow.

It would also help him see if the locations of the YouTube videos— and the prismatic rune he'd spotted—were near the buyers as well. He should get the address of where Jude and Jordana were staying too.

"At least they're thorough. It looks like they already marked which items they fenced in Glenwood and what they still need to deliver here.

We should—" Preston finally turned his head, and it was only then that he realized Luke hadn't entered behind him.

The cat was stock-still, eyes wide and mouth open in a sort of half-gaping grin that was honestly a little creepy.

Preston felt a wave of embarrassment for not having considered what someone might think of his room. He'd always kept it sparse at home and hid in his closet anything personal, but at school, and here, now, the room was an explosion of, well… *Preston*.

Besides his computer desk with two monitors and a personalized and meticulously designed tower, he had a bookshelf covered in fantasy novels, manga, and action figures, posters of his favorite anime, comics, and movies all over the walls, most of which were cheesy sci-fi or action from decades past, and amidst his geeky paraphernalia was an assortment of holiday decorations—and not from one specific holiday but *all of them*.

Preston's parents had never let him decorate as a kid, and he… liked it, only now he felt the need to burrow in on himself and slam the door in Luke's face, especially when Luke pointed at him and exclaimed: "You're a *nerd*!"

Chapter 5

THE FLINCH and instant tension in Preston's shoulders told Luke that his words probably weren't the best thing to randomly yell at someone.

"I mean in a good way!" he amended, both hands up in surrender instead of pointing dramatically, which also probably wasn't the best way to handle discovering someone had so many of the same interests as him.

Preston remained hunched at his computer desk like he wanted to implode within the safety of his geek cave alone. "*How?*" he bit out slowly.

"Because it is?" Luke realized he was still in the doorway and being way too loud, so he entered and shut the door behind him. "Like, for the past decade or more, because being a nerd is cool, and awesome, and even if some people still think otherwise, screw 'em. *I* think it's cool and awesome, coz I'm a nerd too!"

He wanted to put his hands on everything in sight. He'd never had possessions anywhere close to this. Living at the Shelter didn't allow for many personal items. He had one poster, which was of his favorite anime, *Outlaw Star*, about space pirate cowboys, very *Firefly*-like before *Firefly* existed. Any action figures he'd had were long since broken or had been added to the kids' bucket for the next generation of Shelter dwellers, which was *fine*, but Luke felt a surge of incredible envy, knowing that when he moved into the den, his room would be a sparse joke compared to this.

Luke didn't read much. He *could* read, but slowly and with a limited vocabulary. Manga and comics were easier, because if he didn't know a word, he could still understand things well enough from the pictures. There was a library of sorts at the Shelter, but it too was limited.

In Preston's collection, Luke recognized *Dragonlance* books, volumes of the *Fullmetal Alchemist* manga, and *Death Note*, an Iron Man action figure among tons of anime ones he didn't know—all male characters, never the skimpy sexualized girl ones that were popular—and posters of comics, mostly Marvel, one of the movie *Big Trouble in Little China* and something called *The Ice Pirates*, and then anime ones like—

"*Fruits Basket*!" Luke flew across the room past the back of Preston's chair to a poster of the three main characters, a sweet girl named Tohru, a quiet dark-haired boy who turned into a rat, and a loud angry redhead who turned into a cat. "I loved that one! It's like totally shifters, right? Have you ever gone to an anime convention? I've always wanted to. We could cosplay as Yuki and Kyo so perfect. We look just like them!"

Upon whirling back around, Luke realized his exuberance might be making Preston hunch inward even more than before.

"It's seriously all so cool," he tried to say softer, approaching Preston slowly as he looked around at the other items in the room. "But what's with the mismatched holiday stuff? Chili pepper lights...." He looked over where they were strung near the bed, and then at the walls and corners where other decorations hung. "A pumpkin cutout, Valentine's Day hearts, and... a clover too?"

"I like it," Preston said stiffly. "My parents never decorated for holidays."

"Even for Christmas? Oh, are you Jewish?"

"*No.*" He still wasn't relaxing, and Luke didn't understand why. "It doesn't matter, can we—"

"But look at all this stuff!" Luke spread his arms at the room in general. "It's amazing!"

"It isn't that impressive."

"You have your own TV!" Luke gestured to another corner, where it was mounted on the wall in view from the bed. "And this was all in your dorm room? Dude, the Shelter has two communal TVs, one for adults, one for kids, and you watch what the majority wants, period. When I rented something, I had to stay up until, like, three in the morning to watch it. I know you're a millionaire, but trust me, this is not normal for the rest of us."

"I am not a millionaire." Preston winced. "My parents are."

"Same thing."

"It's not, trust me. Can we focus—"

"It just makes so much sense now!"

"What does?"

Luke hadn't meant to say that part, but his mind was spinning. All these things in the room were like a peek into Preston's soul, especially since he'd been so closed off. Also, since this was his room and he'd been sleeping here for days already, the whole space contained more of that Preston smell that Luke loved, and he felt so....

He didn't know the word, but he couldn't stop smiling as he moved closer to Preston's chair.

"I know we barely know each other, but... *dude*." He looked around the room again. "This is why...." Could he say it? "Why it's you."

"What are you talking about?" Preston turned with a frown.

Luke dropped to his knees to be closer to eye level and put his hands right on Preston's thighs. "You smell it too, being around me, right? Something incredible and unique and totally everything you ever wanted? It's just like in the stories. You and I are—"

Preston's hands plastered over Luke's mouth, halting his confession. "That is an old wives' tale. Just because you think I smell... amazing or whatever, doesn't mean we are anything but colleagues." He removed his hands.

"I smell good to you too."

"Urg!" Preston kicked his chair back, moving out from under Luke's palms. "You don't smell... bad, but I probably only smell good to you because I actually shower every day, unlike people at the Shelter."

"Hey!" Luke jumped to his feet. "We're not plague victims living in muck and disease, ya know. Baraka didn't take care of the Shelter the way he should have, but we always have food, water, and working plumbing, thank you. And I smell more than just 'not bad' to you. Admit it."

"We need to be working—"

"If you're not out yet or whatever, since Bari and the rest of us obviously make you nervous—"

"Stop!" Preston said with more force, his face taking on a light shade of pink that made Luke's insides flutter. "Look, you might be an out and proud gay romantic who believes in shifter fairy tales, but I am not getting pulled into your delusions."

"Bi actually. Maybe pan? It depends—"

"Whatever, same thing."

"It's not the same, like, at all, and—"

"Would you just stop!" Preston yelled—and two rats suddenly hopped onto his desk from somewhere unseen and scurried over to him, as if concerned that he was upset.

Preston huffed loudly and rolled the chair back into place to let the rats reach him easier. They climbed onto him quickly, settling in place with one on each of his shoulders.

"Great, now you've made me worry Bernard and Bianca." He let the rats affectionately nuzzle his neck and reached up to pet them.

"*The Rescuers*?" Luke laughed. "You are such a nerd!"

Preston glared.

The rats took more notice of Luke then and hurried off the mostly calmed Preston to investigate. Luke wasn't sure what to do, so he kept as still as possible to not spook them and allowed the rats to first sniff him and decide what they thought, before they climbed up his body.

They didn't nuzzle him with the same affection as they had Preston, but they didn't seem to mind him and even allowed Luke to pet their tiny heads.

"Aw, you guys are so cute! Don't worry. I might be a cat, but I don't bite. Well, not *you* guys." He grinned and glanced back at Preston, who looked entirely stunned that his pets—friends, minions?—were so easily taken with him.

If they got it, then Luke had confidence he could convince Preston eventually too.

"Okay, Mr. Colleague." Luke moved to the desk and sat on the end, where the rats climbed down and disappeared again, probably to wherever they had a nest to sleep in and food and water. "Let's keep talking shop. Ya know, since there's nothing else to talk about."

PRESTON COULD not be distracted like this. Just because Bernard and Bianca didn't like anyone other than him, rats he'd had since he was fifteen, and suddenly this *cat* was their new best friend, didn't mean Preston and Luke were....

It didn't mean anything!

So what if Luke was sweet and cute and apparently also a huge nerd, which still made Preston feel strange because it was one of the many things he'd always felt he needed to hide about himself. He didn't have friends, not anyone real who liked those same things, because he'd been forced to only befriend other high-society rats his entire childhood, and they were all so… dull.

Such fruitless passions are best left as childish pursuits, Trace. You have obligations to fulfill.

Only he hadn't been allowed childish pursuits when he was a child either. His parents let him buy whatever he wanted, but they still turned up their noses at it, making it impossible for him to feel like he was allowed to be himself.

Luke being all the same things as him and smelling better than good, not that he'd ever admit that, didn't mean shifter fairy tales were real.

And if they were, that only terrified Preston more. He'd never even kissed another boy before.

He'd never kissed anyone.

Luke blessedly didn't bring it up again while they planned the next day. He wasn't staying, since he hadn't moved into the den yet, but he promised to return early the next morning.

DAY 2

RETURN LUKE did, right on time, with a knock to Preston's door.

At least he was punctual—and wearing a *Star Wars* shirt this time, which was better than yesterday.

The foxes hadn't tried anything, but Preston hadn't slept well. He'd been too busy worrying one of his alarm spells might go off and trying not to think about redheaded cats, or how Kyo, the *redheaded cat* from *Fruits Basket*, had always been his favorite.

Jude and Jordana were awake, refreshed, and in borrowed clothing from the other circle members when Preston and Luke went to their room. They were punctual too.

More or less.

"One minute!" Jordana said when she opened the door, mid-brush of her long ginger hair.

The twins seemed to be making themselves at home, semi-serious house arrest notwithstanding. Jordana sat on the end of the nearest bed to finish her brushing, while Jude stood across the room, leaned against the wall with his ankles crossed, smoking, head turned toward the open window.

Billowing out a perfect backlit stream, he looked like a model in a Guess jeans ad, fit and handsome and showing a peek of sculpted abs with the way his raised arm hitched up his T-shirt.

"Ugh." Luke gave a low grunt beside Preston, eyes clearly trained on that strip of skin and picturesque snapshot.

"Could you *not*," Preston growled, and then snapped his head forward before anyone could notice he'd been talking to the wrong culprit, "smoke indoors please? If you'd reached even a single finger out that window, it would have set off my wards, you know."

"I figured." Jude shrugged, and only after taking another sensual, drawn-out puff, did he turn his head. "So I didn't stick my fingers anywhere."

"*Jude*," Jordana chided with a chuckle.

Luke chuckled too.

A blink of Preston's eyes and the cigarette went up in flames, causing Jude to yelp as it scorched his fingers. "Don't do it again," Preston said, and though he was annoyed at the smoking and nothing more, he felt his own heat from Luke staring smugly at the side of his face.

"I take it we're not going to get our things first," Jordana said, munching on a cruller a few minutes later, which Luke had insisted on, for them all to get coffee and something to eat—though the milk-filled latte concoction he'd ordered could hardly be called coffee. "Aren't we planning on handing over the goods to the buyers?"

"Not right away," Preston said, enjoying his much simpler coffee, black, two sugars. They were walking again, since their first potential stops were in the same area where they'd met the foxes, and Preston wanted to be on the lookout for anything he might have missed yesterday.

At least the waning summer heat wasn't as grating this early in the morning.

"Even if some of your buyers *are* willing to pay," Luke added, "no business is happening until after Bash talks with Glenwood's Alpha, and after we know who might be causing these forced shifts. Which of the buyers were chasing you yesterday?"

"First on the list," Jude indicated, when Preston took the paper from his pocket.

"We'll start there," Preston said. Two of the locations were close together, which was why he'd already been headed that direction.

"Um, we were running for a reason," Jordana said with a nervous twist of her hair over one shoulder now that her cruller had been devoured. "They're not going to be happy to see us again."

"They'll recognize Bash's smell on us enough to know we're trusted," Luke said. "Being marked by the new Alpha alone should help, and once they know we're circle members, they'll play ball."

"Ya sure about that, Kitten?" Jude asked with a skeptical head tilt. "What happened to the old circle?"

"The Warden was ready to retire anyway," Preston said, having been briefed by Bash when he was recruited. "The Councilor, while bitter about Baraka being taken down, was as well."

"He was an asshole," Luke muttered.

"From what I hear, both the Shaman and Magister were honestly grateful to have Baraka overthrown," Preston went on. "But the last, Baraka's Second, is also second on your list. He could be trouble."

"Who's that last name?" Luke asked, peering at the list with a close lean into Preston's side. A whiff of sage mixed with faint chocolate and coffee notes made every part of Preston's body stiffen—well, not *every* part. "Payara Northwest? What kind of name is that?"

"No idea." Jude shrugged. "Haven't met him. Just know he's wealthy."

The address for that name was familiar to Preston, but he couldn't recall why. So was the name, strange as it was. Maybe it was someone he had met in passing at one of his parents' parties.

"Sounds like a *Star Wars* name." Luke patted his shirt and then offered what was becoming a familiar nudge at Preston's side. "Do you guys know your *Star Wars* names?"

"What do you mean?" Jordana chuckled.

"You take the first three letters from your first name," Jude surprised Preston by answering, "and first two from your last name to get your *Star Wars* given name. Then for your surname, you take the first two letters from your mother's maiden name and the first three of the city you were born in." He grinned handsomely, and the way Luke beamed back at him made Preston's gut clench. "Marley actually is our mother's maiden name, so I'm Judma Mabro."

"Bro?" Luke frowned. "You weren't born in Glenwood?"

"Brookdale. Then sent to the Glenwood Shelter later."

"So that makes me…." Jordana did the math and smiled with a hop and clap of her hands, a far cry from the vicious presence she'd portrayed yesterday during their standoff. "*Jorma* Mabro. I like it! We'd be smugglers, of course." She leaned into her brother.

"Me too!" Luke bounced excitedly.

"What's your name?" she asked him.

"I don't know my mother's maiden name, or my actual last name. I use Smith, and the other Shelter orphan name is Jones, right, so if I consider *that* the maiden name… nah, even then it doesn't work. You can't say *Luksm*." Luke made a scrunched face, completely contorting his features, and Preston's insides lurched again.

He really hated the way his body had a mind of its own around this… nerd.

"Too bad Skywalker's taken!" Luke laughed.

"Why not drop the 'm'?" Jordana suggested. "Luks. Luks… Jocen!"

They laughed together—everyone but Preston.

"Sounds pretty neat," Luke said, nudging Preston again. "What about you, Pres? What's your *Star Wars* name?"

Pr-Era Yecen. Preston liked adding the dash, so it rolled off the tongue more like *purr-era*.

"No idea."

"*Liar*." Luke mock-whispered to the foxes, "Huge nerd. You should see his room."

"That's not a very nice thing to call someone!" Jordana said.

"Thank you," Preston said pointedly.

"I'm one too!" Luke grinned. "Total dork through and through. So is Bash, and Deanna and Siobhan."

"Did you just call your Alpha a dork?" Jude snickered.

"He knows he is! He donated all his old *Warhammer* stuff to the Shelter for kids to paint and play with, since he doesn't have much free time anymore."

Preston was not going to admit he knew what *Warhammer* was and maybe had some models in his desk drawers that he hadn't set out yet. He'd never known that about Bash, since they hadn't been close in college, more like passing acquaintances due to their families.

"I'm liking you more and more, Kitten." Jude threw an arm across Luke's shoulders, which accentuated their height difference and had the added effect of pulling Luke *away* from Preston.

The urge to slap the fox's arm away was childish and ridiculous, and Preston clenched his fists to be sure no sudden fire or lightning licked free from his fingertips.

"You too, Fievel." Jude peered at him with what Preston took for a *knowing* smirk, though what Jude thought he knew was absolutely baseless. "If you could manage an expression other than a scowl, that is."

Maybe Preston would just kill them all. That would solve these confusing feelings.

"Since you guys know your mom's maiden name," Luke said, changing the subject, seemingly innocent, though making no move to dislodge himself from Jude's hold, "you must remember your folks pretty well for Shelter kids, huh?"

The shared spasm in both foxes' shoulders and melancholy glances said plenty.

"Shit. I know better, sorry," Luke said. "Never ask that question."

Heavy silence lingered for a few tense beats, and then Jude released Luke with a forgiving pat.

Preston was curious what the background for these foxes might be, but for now, they had more important things to focus on. Like how the address they were headed to was bringing them right past where Preston had seen that strange magical residue and rune on the wall.

"I want to check something," he said, pulling ahead to turn down that specific side street. Once the others joined him and were an effective wall to hide him from prying eyes, he cast the same perception spell as yesterday.

Dormant for too long, the rune was faded now, barely even a blip. He'd need to draw it out from memory to see if Nell recognized something he didn't—and ask her what could possibly look prismatic instead of a single-colored aura.

"What did that do?" Jordana asked, since only Preston could see what his spell had caused to glow on the wall.

"Nothing new." He led them out of the alley but noticed Jordana lingering. "Don't fall behind."

"Sorry!" She startled and hurried to catch up to them. "I'm not used to magic."

"Cool, right?" Luke grinned, and Preston fought off flutters.

"Let's get to that first stop."

Isabella Dane, fairly high up in the shifter underground, was someone Preston knew only by reputation. She was a cougar—the feline kind, though Preston had heard rumors of the other meaning—and surrounded herself exclusively with female cat shifters, and not alley cats like Luke.

Definitely not a group whose bad side they wanted to be on.

Reaching a nondescript door down a suspiciously quiet street, Preston took point and knocked, greeted by what was probably the largest woman he had ever encountered in real life.

She towered over him, with broad shoulders and hugely muscled arms like a body builder or professional wrestler, further emphasized by her brightly colored makeup and long auburn curls, like....

A powerful, beautiful *lion*.

"Hey, Lui!" Luke called from behind with his usual cheerfulness. "Can we see Isa? It's about a recent, ahem... attempted acquisition," he finished none too subtly.

"Hn," Lui grunted and stepped aside to allow them entry.

Preston could admit one thing—Luke was helpful to have on their side.

The place was a fortress, with no other exterior doors or windows visible. It appeared like a vast warehouse with staircases leading multiple directions, but again, with no obvious doors leading to separate rooms.

Lui pinched the bridge of her nose, moving to one of the staircases, though not to lead them anywhere. She seemed to be experiencing the onset of a headache and leaned against the railing with a grumble.

"Uh...," Luke attempted, but a separate voice called from the top of another set of stairs.

"Is that the little runner kitten? And what brings you here, dear, accompanied by the very foxes I've been looking for?"

Isabella was middle-aged and ravishing, with hardly any wrinkles on her brown face and thick brown hair left loose down to her waist. She wore a white pencil skirt and blazer with no undershirt, revealing an ample bosom from the *V* nearly to her navel.

"Hi, Isa!" Luke waved. "It's Luke, yeah. Um, we were actually hoping to talk to you about these foxes and the deal you made."

"I see." Isabella smiled dangerously and slowly curled her long-nailed fingers around the railing. Her eyes raked over Jude and Jordana. "I was about to send Luisa out to look for you to retrieve what you owe me."

"Be on guard," Luke whispered.

No shit, Preston thought, but if Luke was reading the threat from this woman, then it was very, very real.

"What about what you owe us?" Jordana called back.

"No one is owing anyone anything until we talk," Preston said. It was four against two if things got ugly—assuming no other large cat shifters appeared. "We're here on official business from the new Alpha."

"The son?" Isabella scoffed.

"Your *Alpha*, and we are your new Magister and Councilor."

"Really? And does the… *Alpha* know where you are this very moment?"

Preston knew better than to answer, but they hadn't specified to Bash which contact they'd be going to first.

Isabella grinned like she'd seen in their expressions everything she needed. "How beneficial for me to have you all here to bear witness to my experiment. As you will, Luisa. We can find the merchandise on our own."

If her words hadn't pulled their attentions to Lui, the lion's roar would have.

She was shifting, seemingly out of her control, not suffering from a headache, and cycled through the normal stages to the largest Stage Three rapidly—only she grew much, *much* larger than any version Preston had ever seen.

Even for a woman of her size, and a lion at that, she doubled in height and mass with a rippling of her muscles as reddish fur grew to cover her and her clothing tore away in tatters. Her claws were massive, jaws large enough that she could have snapped any of their heads off in a bite. Once she lifted her head with another roar and turned her glowing eyes on them, she stalked forward with the determination of a starving predator.

"Run!" Luke cried.

Chapter 6

RUN WHERE? Luke answered his own frantic shout, because when they spun to return out the door they'd come in through, it was gone.

Shit. He knew Isabella wasn't a witch, but some of her people had magic, and they had clearly warded this place in the weirdest way possible. What sort of building only had stairs and no windows or doors, like some painting done by that… whatever his name was!

"It's a fucking M. C. Escher painting in here!" Preston yelled.

Yeah—him!

They scattered at the not-there door, and the only place to go was up. Preston was fast and reached the top of the nearest staircase first, just in time for Lui to grab hold of the railings below them and *shake*.

The whole thing trembled, and Luke nearly toppled backward into Jordana, which would have turned into a hilariously not funny domino effect.

"She's going to tear the fucking stairs apart!" Jude said as they hurried the rest of the way up. "Shock her!"

"Throw a fireball or something!" begged Jordana.

"Swarm her!" Luke finished, all directing their pleas at Preston, since he had the real firepower.

Only he stood at the top of the stairs looking petrified.

"I-I can't think!"

Lui roared, eyes wild, as her immense form started to ascend the stairs. They could barely hold her weight, causing even the platform above to tremble. While a male lion might have had a true mane about its head, Lui's hair acted close enough to one, making her almost mythical in appearance—and seriously terrifying.

"Pres!" Luke hollered.

"There aren't any rodents here! And I've never used offensive spells on another person! I was bluffing yesterday!"

Lui's jaws snapped with prominent fangs that looked very eager to clamp on to them, and there were no connecting stairs up here. If she reached them or caused the whole thing to collapse, they were toast.

"Shift to Stage Four! Now!" Luke ordered.

They stared at him.

"Do it!"

Isabella watched from her own second-floor landing, completely at ease and enjoying the show.

Luke flicked her off with both hands before allowing himself to shrink.

So much for his "Han Shot First" shirt.

Shifting straight to animal form was a little like the feeling of freefalling when trying to sleep. One second, Luke was growing into Stage Three with senses sharpening, the next, he was shrinking, engulfed by his clothing, and a moment later, he leapt from their confines as a medium-sized tabby cat.

The foxes were right behind him, almost identical, aside from Jordana being smaller. What surprised Luke was that they weren't typical in coloring. Their paws were black, as well as their noses, but they were white almost everywhere else, like a mimic of their pale skin tones, only having orange around their ears, the fronts of their faces, and down their legs.

The unique pattern was gorgeous, but Luke had little time to admire it, as Lui's maw reached the top of the stairs and chomped.

He sprang backward with a hiss, frantically searching for Preston. There! A dark gray, almost black rat scurried out from under Preston's clothing, squeaking in distress. Luke pounced, scooped him up into his mouth, and leapt right into oblivion back to the first floor.

As a cat, he had no trouble landing on his feet and quickly set Preston down again, looking at the platform to be certain the foxes got the idea.

One after the other, Jude and Jordana executed their own great leaps, not quite as effortlessly as a cat, but better than a tiny rat could have managed.

Luke hoped Preston wasn't too mad at him later.

A quake alerted them to Lui having followed before they'd even seen her jump. She roared ferociously, on all fours like a charging bull, causing them to skitter outward in a frightened shock wave.

As Luke did so, he shifted out of cat form, and the others followed his lead—which was like, wow, okay, they were following *his* lead, so he better know what the hell he was doing.

He continued the reverse shift until he hit Stage Two, with fangs on his canines, claws extended, a rosier hue to his skin, and striped ginger fur edging his cheekbones and the lines of his body. He didn't want to lose speed by becoming too large.

Wait.... He was in control! He didn't feel that weird twist like yesterday. Why was Lui affected and no one else? Was this even the same thing?

"What do we do?" Jude cried.

Right. Shit. Lui readied to attack, and them being spread out only meant one would get mauled to death first before she turned on the others.

"Don't let her corner you!" Luke called and took a deep breath as he charged before Lui could charge him.

He sprang upward as she launched forward, twisting in the air with an acrobat's grace. After swiping once with his claws, he landed facing the direction she had gone.

If only a tiny cat scratch was enough.

Jude and Jordana leapt in to follow Luke's example, taking swipes of their own, and immediately darted out of harm's way when Lui tried to swipe back.

Luke knew how to kite in a boss fight.

"Pres!" He realized the rat shifter was frozen, also stopped at Stage Two, with sleek black fur and missing his glasses, but he seemed transfixed on Luke instead of the lion aiming her next charge at him. "*Preston!*"

Snapping to attention, Preston launched a ball of concentrated lightning without having the luxury of second-guessing.

It hit her—and then fizzled around the fur of Lui's great maw like an annoyance that made her nose twitch and fangs snap with intent to rend Preston apart.

He dove, rolling out of the way just in time, and launched another magic missile, this time fire, which shot out more like a line of flames that struck her and then spread outward, creating a blazing square to encapsulate her.

Wow, that was cool. Or would have been if Lui didn't shake it off like another annoyance and walk out of the fire with only a few singed tufts of fur.

"She's too strong!" Jude shouted.

He was right. It would take forever to chip away at her like this, causing a few scratches and magical burns that barely slowed her down. Luke didn't know what to suggest next. He wasn't a combat strategist. He was a talker, a negotiator, not the Warden, Second, or Alpha!

"I got it!" Jordana called with a gleam in her amber eyes. "Follow my lead!"

At first it seemed she simply continued what they'd already been doing—slashing and running while inflicting too little damage. The rest of them did the same anyway, always keeping separate from one another to avoid giving Lui too large of a target. Eventually, Luke realized Jordana was leading them in a very specific direction—closer to one of the walls.

Of course! She couldn't say her plan out loud or Lui might realize, but Jordana must be a gamer too, because this was exactly how you took down a large opponent in *Batman: Arkham Asylum*.

Luke used the many staircases to his advantage, swinging around railings to add momentum to his kicks and slashes and making sure Lui was guided the right direction with plenty of room to build speed. He couldn't be sure if Jude and Preston got the idea, but they echoed what he and Jordana did, swiping where possible, with Preston adding an occasional fireball or burst of lightning.

Then Lui stopped, and before Luke could call out in warning, Jude went in for his next strike. Lui snatched him by the arm right out of midleap and swooped her head around so fast, Luke didn't know which sound was worse—the cut of the air or crunch into bone.

"No!" Jordana shrieked.

She dove forward, digging her claws into either side of Lui's neck, and then flipped backward again. Retreating after landing, she taunted Lui to pursue her instead.

Lui tossed Jude aside, galloping forward on the same trajectory as before, and Jordana didn't dart out of the way. She held her ground, waiting, *waiting*, and then, at the last possible second, a hair's breadth from having Lui tear into her, Jordana sprung upward with a great Hail Mary leap.

Leaving Lui to barrel into the wall.

Lui dropped, knocked unconscious by her own enhanced strength— just like an enemy in the video game.

"Jude!" Jordana ran to him.

He hadn't gotten up from where he'd crumpled, bleeding, with his arm clearly out of the socket, but at least he looked conscious.

A blur above drew Luke's attention.

"Isa!" he cried at her attempting to flee across the platform.

Preston's spirit chains launched after her, wrapping around her body, and sparked with lightning as he yanked her to the first floor. His cheeks were flushed—and other places, since he *was* naked—but even panting and guarded, he wore an expression of triumph.

"Nice!" Luke cheered.

"Let's start over," Preston snarled at Isabella, before sending a second length of glowing chains at Lui's thankfully shrinking form to pull her closer too, "so you can tell us exactly *what the fuck that was.*"

To Luke's dismay, Isabella grinned.

The M.C. Hammer, or whoever, spell fell away, revealing only a couple remaining staircases and the doors and windows that had been missing. Out of those doors and down the stairs came the rest of Isabella's crew, more than half a dozen very powerful cat shifters.

So much for a win.

The building rocked with a thunderous tremor, and Luke thought it was whatever creative way these women were going to end them, only for a literal bulldozer to come crashing through the wall where the front door had been.

A horde of other shifters poured in through that hole, snarling and shifting to Stage Two or Three as they formed a protective wall around Luke and the others against Isabella's now very defeated-looking underlings.

"Stand down in the name of your Warden!" called a familiar voice as Siobhan jumped down from the driver's seat with a shimmer of lizard scales across her skin.

Hell yes.

"Did you know the building next door is being demolished? Good thing I have my CDL. Plus, sometimes it's just fun watching something go boom." Siobhan eyed Luke and Preston with a proud gleam of fangs. "Told you I'd be watching these addresses."

PRESTON WAS glad to be back in actual clothing. His glasses hadn't been recovered, but he had several extras on hand. He'd rather be in bed, though. After all that expulsion of magic, he felt like he hadn't slept for a week. He was going to have to train—hard—to be an effective Magister if this sort of free-for-all fighting was in his future on the regular.

And it might be, because there was no way this was over.

Something had been very wrong about that encounter, and not only Preston's fumbling.

At least Isabella and her crew were detained. Jordana was with Jude while his injuries were being treated by Nell, and Siobhan's people were searching Isabella's stronghold and gathering everything from where Jude and Jordana had been staying to finally bring the stolen artifacts to the den.

Everyone was scattered throughout the house, giving Preston a few minutes' reprieve to collapse on the sofa. They were mostly waiting on Bash and Deanna to discuss next steps, since those two were ensuring the destruction near Shaw Street wouldn't draw unwanted attention.

Thankfully, with the building next door already scheduled for demolition and the general state of those neighborhoods, it wasn't a difficult cover-up for a second building to require demolition too.

Isabella's going to need a new place, Preston thought snidely.

"Wow, am I sore!"

The silence was broken by the arrival of Luke, rubbing his shoulders. He was dressed again too, in a long-sleeved T-shirt and jeans, but when Preston looked at him, all he could think was, *I know what you look like naked.*

"I also feel super gross. I hate putting on clean clothes when I'm dirty." Luke plopped down beside Preston and sniffed none too subtly at his armpit.

Slightly less charming.

"Did you not rinse yourself off first?" Preston asked.

"I didn't know where! I just put on the clothes Siobhan gave me."

Preston sat up with a sneer and waved a hand at Luke, performing a tidying spell, which could pick up clutter and put it away, throw out trash, or mildly clean and straighten a person's appearance. Not quite as good as a shower or grooming routine but close enough.

Luke looked and smelled better now. Much better, like a fresh sprig of….

Fuck.

"Prestidigitation!" Luke flew into a sitting position.

"What?"

"You know, how you can go poof and make something all clean again?"

"That is not what that word means."

"It is in D&D!" Luke insisted. "Or, like, one of its uses."

Preston had never played *Dungeons & Dragons*—that required friends who also wanted to play—but he'd always hoped to.

"Sounds stupid," he said.

Luke didn't look like he was buying it. "You were amazing back there, ya know."

"What? I completely froze. I even know portal magic, but it can be complicated and dangerous, and I was afraid if I tried porting us out of there, I'd cut someone in half—"

"You helped." Luke stopped him with a firm and very warm hand on his wrist. "You just need to feel comfortable defending yourself. In case you weren't aware, when someone's trying to hurt you, you are allowed to fight back."

That was something Preston had never felt he could do, not when most of the hurt came from the two people in his life who he least felt like he could stand up to.

"Hey, if you're wary of the lightning or fire or whatever, what about a machete with your spirit thingy? Oh! Or a lightsaber! Though I guess that's all still pretty offensive...."

Preston swallowed against the dryness in his throat. Luke hadn't taken his hand away, and he didn't think he wanted him to. He met Luke's shining eyes and said, "Pr-Era Yecen."

"Huh?"

"Pr-Era Yecen... is my *Star Wars* name."

There was literally no light in the world, from sunshine to Preston's own fire or lightning sparking from his fingertips, that was as bright as when this cat's face lit up.

"All's well!" Nell's voice announced her arrival, causing Preston to lurch his hand away. To Luke's credit, his smile only twitched a little to betray his disappointment. "Or all will be well eventually."

She came in, accompanied by Jude and Jordana, the former of which had his shoulder bandaged and in a sling. Both foxes looked pale and exhausted, and Jordana had an arm around her brother's waist to support him.

"Mr. Marley just needs rest," Nell finished.

Commotion at the front door alerted them that Siobhan and her agents had returned, and a parade of people carrying boxes behind Nell made her spin in excitement.

"Wonderful! Yes, right this way." She left, hurrying ahead to show them exactly where she wanted everything.

"Sit down, you two," Luke called. "Or did you want to go straight to bed?"

"Maybe sit for a sec," Jude said, slumping into a chair, where Jordana sat on the arm. "Even climbing those basement steps has me wiped. I'll catch my breath, then head up."

"I'll admit, you two were pretty fearless," Preston said. "Without you, I don't think we could have made it."

"Without *all of us*," Luke added.

The siblings smiled, and Preston tried to take the compliment.

"Oh *my*!" a new voice cried. "What have I done to be in the presence of such beauty?"

Bari entered, looking as fashionable as usual—though seriously, who wore a pink floral-patterned blazer to mull about the house—all smiles and flirtation with a perfectly polished persona. It was both a testament to Bash's attractiveness and a complete contrast to how the Alpha presented himself.

Crossing the room to the foxes, Bari dragged a hand along the back of the sofa. "And equally intended, goodness! You two are ravishing!"

"*Bari*," Preston chastised, partially because he knew this was only a precursor to Bari's sexual charisma oozing off the walls and so the pair could lose their shocked expressions, having previously met a very different person with that face. "This is Jude and Jordana Marley, suspects in our assignment—or at least they were."

"Unintentionally involved," Luke said. "Bash doesn't want them going anywhere alone."

"I see." Bari stopped in front of their chair with a steeple of his expressive hands, like he was plotting something devious. "Under house arrest here at the den like poor *moi*? Let's be prisoners together, then and fast friends, because you two are fabulous."

Jordana recovered with a dismissive giggle. "Hardly. More like fatigued and a bit roughed up at the moment."

"All easily remedied. Although my mind is awhirl with ways you could be even more fabulous. You're related, I assume?"

"Twins," she affirmed.

"I too am a twin!" Bari gushed the obvious. "And let me tell you, while my brother can also pull off the effortlessly cool look in off-the-rack basics—"

Jude blinked like he knew he should be offended, since the comment was directed at him.

"—I require a more stylish ensemble, and you are no exception, darlings. You must let me make you over sometime. Both of you."

Jude seemed to recover from his initial shock and eyed Bari with a scan of appreciation.

"I've never owned anything full price in my life," Jordana said. "You're in fashion?"

"Only as a hobby, but it's one of my great passions. And I never pay full price. I rent a studio apartment, work three jobs off and on to pay rent and tuition, and I still never walk out of a store without a discount."

"Hard to say no to someone offering to dress me," Jude said with a leading lilt. "Though I assume being son of an Alpha helped your wardrobe?"

Bari leaned much closer than most would infringe upon another's bubble. "It might have if I ever accepted that man's money." He stood up straight again and reached to take Jordana's hand without so much as a pause in subjects. "I always thought Barbie would be far hotter as a redhead. And Ken for that matter." He winked at Jude.

Jordana glowed. Bari did have a certain effect on people.

Seeing Jude's attention on Bari also eased some of the tension in Preston's gut.

For some reason.

"Actually, brother," a similar yet very different voice broke in, "why don't you keep those two company upstairs so I can discuss a few private matters with my circle?"

Bash and Deanna had finally arrived.

"I'd be honored!" Bari said. "I was going insane with boredom, cooped up in this house with everyone talking business all the time. Let's say we talk pleasure." He hoisted up Jordana and then reached more gingerly to help up Jude, who he then looped arms with and pressed close against his non-injured side. "*Whatever* direction that takes us."

Jude smirked with interest too. It seemed so easy for them, expressing their desires.

Preston caught Luke smiling at him and quickly looked away.

Not much later, Siobhan and Nell joined them, having deposited everything downstairs in Nell's workshop, inherited from the previous Shaman.

"I've decided to banish Isabella and her crew for going against the circle," Bash said once they were gathered in similar placement as the other day. "We need a show of strength, and it works as an exchange with Glenwood. Their Alpha agreed that we can do as we wish with the Marleys and their stolen merchandise, so long as we keep him informed, and Isabella promised to be an asset to her new city. It's a fair exchange, and we get rid of some troublemakers."

"Works for me," Siobhan said. "At least all this is solved now."

"Actually, it isn't," Preston said. As much as he wanted to rest, it had to be stated. "Isabella can't be the cause of the forced shifts. What we experienced with Lui was entirely different. The others always went straight to animal form, but Lui didn't, and she was partially in control. I didn't smell magic either."

"He's right," Luke said. "Yesterday, when Pres first sensed that magic, I totally felt like I was going to shift without trying. But today, I didn't feel any of that around Lui."

"You think someone else is involved?" Bash asked.

"I think someone else started things," Preston clarified, ignoring that Luke had once again called him *Pres* in mixed company, "and Isabella was merely the next person experimenting with its effects."

"That makes sense," Nell said, pulling a small vial of white powder from her skirt pocket and holding it up.

"What's that?" Deanna frowned.

"What I was going to tell everyone next. This is a sample of something Siobhan's agents brought back from Isabella's. There were several vials of the same substance, which is something a quick perception spell also found all over the stolen artifacts. They're *shifter* artifacts, all related to shifter culture."

"You're sure?" Preston asked.

"Definitely. Because even without a detailed investigation, I can tell you that *this*… is mostly made of bone dust from ancient shifters."

Chapter 7

THE ROOM was silent. Even the least educated among shifters knew the old stories of their kind. Preston had recently referred to them as fairy tales because the lore surrounding their ancestors was shrouded in mystery, including lost creation tablets that depicted how shifters were the first sentient denizens on Earth, and humans were a corruption of their purer blood.

Not everyone believed that to be the case, but befouling shifter burial grounds was one of the biggest affronts to their people, not only because it was grave robbing, but because it increased the chance that normal humans might discover what they were. Artifacts uncovered by accident or from human excavations was allowed, but just where had these items come from if there was bone dust encasing them?

"You're certain it's that old?" Bash asked.

"Thousands of years, in fact," Nell said. "Age is easy to discern from a perception spell, but even more curious was the rune and aura Preston described to me from Shaw Street. A *prismatic* aura… I had to wonder, and this bone dust confirms my suspicions. This too shows every color, because it isn't merely one type of shifter's remains but a mix of dust from every tribe, every *type* within each tribe, of varied gender, ages, and from more individuals than I can count."

She drew a quick perception rune in the air, and as the rune passed through the vial and disappeared, it left the powdery substance inside glowing with that same prismatic spectrum.

No wonder it was a rainbow—it was a chimera of shifter remains.

The glow also helped illuminate a word written across the vial.

Moondust.

"Now we have two mystery spells?" Siobhan barked.

"Maybe," Preston said. "This is all happening at the same time, so it must be related. My guess is someone has been experimenting with that Moondust for a while and needed more artifacts with shifter bone residue to keep going."

"Which means it's likely one of the other buyers who started this," Bash deduced. "Nothing changes. You and Luke are still investigating and going to talk to the other buyers and to the original victims of the forced shifts. Take the remainder of the day to rest and let Nell finish looking into everything else, but I need you back on the streets tomorrow. The days are ticking by, and someone is going to push this too far with no idea how dangerous it's going to be."

"You got it, boss," Luke said.

"I don't know if this will help or not, but...." Nell crossed to the sofa, repocketed the vial, and removed instead a small slip of paper that she handed to Luke, who frowned at it and then handed it to Preston. "It was with the artifacts, a donation report. It seems they were all given to the Glenwood Museum by the same benefactor, only it doesn't include a name."

Preston frowned at the slip too. The notes were in a very clean and handsome script, but all they stated was: *To be kept in the same display, especially item number eleven.*

"I'll finish cataloging everything using the Marleys' list and let you know which one eleven is once I find it. What I know now is that the residue on the artifacts is pure, but the vials from Isabella's have additives. Maybe that's why Lui's shift was different."

For now, Preston pocketed the slip. "Thanks."

"Such long faces!" Bash called with the hint of a smile. "I know this isn't an ideal first week, but you have all been doing exceptionally. Keep it up and we will solve this. Siobhan, I expect your people to still be watching every place of interest."

"You got it." She saluted.

"But first, let's see our *guests* to the border." Bash dismissed them with a nod, and he, Deanna, and Siobhan headed to where they were holding Isabella and her crew.

Nell offered a supportive smile before retreating to her workshop.

All Preston wanted to do with the weight of this yet unsolved mystery hanging over them was to have Luke's hand on his wrist again, warm and encouraging, or to maybe reach for that hand himself.

It was probably just his exhaustion talking, and before he could do anything foolhardy, he stood. "I'm going to get some rest."

Ignoring the heat from Luke's gaze following him out, Preston collapsed the moment he reached his bed.

DAY 3

THERE WAS the strangest, soft… whimpering sound? It was almost like a child's snore, and it roused Preston to blink hazily at his window.

At first he thought it was getting dark, given the dim light filtering in from the window, but then he blinked at his clock—less bleary than usual since he hadn't removed his glasses before dozing off—and saw that it was 5:00 *a.m.*, meaning he'd slept for over twelve hours.

Fuck.

He really had collapsed and passed right out, more exhausted than he realized after the ordeal of battling a giant lion while pelting out more spells in a few minutes than he'd ever used in a week.

His neck throbbed when he pushed up onto his hands to twist it straight and then the opposite direction of how he'd been sleeping— when he nearly yelped and flung himself off the bed at spotting an orange cat sleeping beside him.

Preston's initial thought was worry for Bernard and Bianca. Had some stray moved into his room and found *snacks*? Then he allowed himself to exhale, and when he took in his next deep breath, he knew.

This cat smelled like *sage*.

Preston was so tired that he hadn't even locked his door. Either that or Luke busted in anyway, which he wouldn't have put past the alley cat. And he *was* in cat form, with a pile of discarded clothing on the floor to solidify his identity.

The appropriate response should have been annoyance, even a sense of violation and fury that someone who was still mostly a stranger had come into Preston's room uninvited to *sleep with him*.

Luke was just so sweet-looking as a slumbering tabby cat, curled into the tightest ball, with his eyes moving behind his lids like he was dreaming. The tip of his tail twitched to the same rhythm while he gently snored.

A cat's snore was more like a see-sawing sigh than the grating rumble of a human. Luke was also the prettiest cat Preston had ever seen in person. He'd only gotten near a couple strays before, which were usually dirty and unhealthy-looking.

Luke was pristine as a cat, his fur clean and luxurious in its mix of orange and white like the softest of plush blankets. His tail was fluffier than the rest of him, and he looked so inviting to touch that Preston reached to stroke his fur before he could think better of it.

The end of Luke's tail flapped faster, but his snoring continued, prompting Preston to pet with his whole hand along the grain of Luke's side, and farther over his tail to feel its extra fluff. He petted Luke's side again and then scratched up the back of Luke's neck to the top of his head, where Luke's ears twitched.

He really was so cute like this, something Preston hadn't been able to appreciate when Luke had him in his mouth yesterday—and wow, he should not think of it like *that*.

What would Preston's parents say if they knew he was petting a cat shifter? What would they think of one being in his bed? Or that he maybe… liked this cat, a lot, and didn't mind finding Luke beside him.

Until the snoring stopped and a naked *man* was beneath Preston's hand instead.

"THAT'S NICE…," Luke mumbled, waking to the pleasant sensation of someone's hand along the curve of his hip, only for it to violently lurch away right when he was about to lean up into the touch.

He rolled onto his back and stretched his arms up, his feet turning into points off the end of the bed. Blinking the haze from his eyes, he opened them to see Preston on his knees beside him, gaping in apparent horror.

Oh shit.

"I didn't mean to fall asleep!" Luke flew upright, looking around at the light bleeding into the room and seeing the time on the nearby clock—which had a glowing orange dragon ball atop it from the anime of the same name.

How could Luke not have wanted to stay here until morning? There was no other room in the den where he felt as comfortable, and when he'd explored and considered Bash's order to pick one for himself, the only place he wanted to be was here.

"It was an accident, seriously!" he insisted.

Although curling up beside Preston had been on purpose.

Preston's cheeks were bright red, his body stiff and eyes glued to Luke's face like he didn't dare blink. He must be super pissed.

"I'm sorry!" Luke scrambled off the bed to get to his feet.

Preston faced the headboard with how he was kneeling, and only slightly turned to follow him.

"Crap. *Crap.* I was just helping Nell in her workshop, and then I looked around the den a while, but I didn't want to leave and go back to the Shelter. Then I was worried when you didn't come down for dinner or anything, so I came up to check. You looked so cute and cozy all passed out that I couldn't resist lying down too. I figured being fun size would make it less likely to wake you. I'm *sorry!*"

Gradually, Preston turned to stretch out his legs and drop them over the end of the bed, only now his gaze was glued to the floor. He didn't speak.

"Uh… Pres? Is something else…."

Oh, Luke was a goon. Preston wasn't mad—or at least that wasn't why his face was so red. He was *blushing* and trying not to look at Luke while he was naked. Which was crazy! Shifters didn't care about that sort of thing. None Luke knew anyway. Little rich rat boy must have had a totally different experience growing up.

And that was kind of… fun actually—and way too tempting not to take advantage of.

"You slept well, though, right? I did." Luke languidly stretched in the wake of Preston's silence, arching his chest forward with a bow of his back and running his hands down his pecs and stomach and lower along his hips where Preston had so recently been petting.

He caught the flash of dark eyes on him.

"Maybe a soft bed won't be as bad as I thought. Kinda warm in here, though. I'm almost sweaty. Probably coz I just woke up."

He proceeded to rub the back of his neck and stretched his body in every way a body could stretch, with sighs and grunts of pleasure in each act, always making sure to stay facing Preston, and even widening his stance to better show off between his legs.

Preston still didn't speak but kept sneaking glances.

Luke had never thought he was that special to look at, but he liked his ginger hair and the freckles that had never migrated to his face but could be found along his shoulders. He was trim, with slight muscle and smooth pale skin, and while he didn't have a huge ego over how he was hung, he knew he was decently sized and not too shabby overall.

Preston certainly seemed to think so.

"Mm," Luke hummed, more obviously lewd, running one hand down his right thigh purposely close to *center* to see if Preston would bite—though if Luke wasn't careful, his half chub from teasing, and it being morning and all, was going to reach full mast very quickly.

"I-I know what you're doing!" Preston blurted, eyes darting to the thumb on Luke's thigh that stretched outward to graze his length.

"And what am I doing?"

"Being indecent."

"Yeah? Is this one of those Shelter kid, uhh… fop things?" Luke feigned innocence while lightly running his thumb up and down the edge of his cock, making it twitch.

"Fop?" Preston huffed in confusion.

"You know, when something is, like… bad manners, or whatever."

"*Faux pas.*"

"That. Guess I don't think of being naked as a big deal. Plus… I think you kinda like it."

"I-I'm just—"

"Tongue-tied?" Luke bit his lower lip and grinned when Preston met his gaze. He was curious how far he might push things before Preston told him to stop.

Moving a step forward, then another, Luke brought himself right between Preston's legs with as slow a pace as possible to give plenty of time for dissent. When none came, he leaned forward to place both hands on the mattress, framing Preston's thighs.

Preston leaned away with a small exclamation of air, but even with Luke's length close enough to press into his clothed hip, he didn't say stop. His face was flushed, chest heaving, and eyes wide that kept switching from Luke's gaze to his lips.

"Your family isn't the 'frolic in the woods, roll in the grass' kind, huh?"

"N-no. Who does that?"

"Everyone? Everyone I know. Is that why you were staring during the fight?" Luke flicked his eyes down and back up Preston's rumpled form. "Coz we were all naked? Here I thought it was my mad flipping skills."

"That was also… impressive." Preston was clearly trying to not lean upright and touch Luke any more than he was, while failing at keeping his eyes from straying between them at where their bodies connected.

"You were impressive too. And ya know, maybe being a bit of a prude has its benefits, coz I didn't even pause to appreciate seeing *you* naked. Though if I close my eyes…." Luke did just that, still looming, as he hummed approval. "I can picture—"

"Stop that!" Preston protested, though there was too much laughter in his words for him to mean it.

"My brain. You don't get a say. And *wow*, you have a really nice—"

Familiar palms pressed to Luke's mouth, coaxing his eyes to open again. Preston's cheeks were aflame, but he couldn't hide the smile fighting for purchase on his prettily curved lips. He lowered his hands, keeping them awkwardly beneath Luke's chin as if unsure where else to put them.

Luke shifted closer with a firmer press of his naked body, and Preston gulped. Even so, rather than push Luke away, he followed the momentum, until he was laid out on the bed, permitting Luke to climb atop him.

"You don't have to be embarrassed," Luke said. "Of anything. Not your body. Seeing mine. Having feelings you keep trying to pretend you don't. I don't get why you won't let yourself feel them, though. You're Centrus City's Magister. You can do whatever you want."

"Not… whatever I want." Preston heaved a breath, dropping his hands to his sides to allow Luke closer.

"Within reason."

"M-my parents wouldn't think it within reason."

"Liking a cat?"

"Or a man."

"Oh…." Luke had guessed that might be part of it, but he'd figured Preston just wasn't ready to come out publicly, not that he was forced to feel that way. "Sorry. Guess I take for granted how much freedom I had at the Shelter. It really is okay, though. Whatever other people think, it doesn't matter if it's what *you* want."

Luke had had this type of talk with friends, but younger friends. Preston was three years his senior, yet in this, Luke was the experienced one, leading them along. Like how he bent that last bit closer to capture a kiss.

Air huffed between Preston's lips. Luke held still, merely resting his lips on Preston's to let him decide their next course.

A lift of Preston's head connected them firmer, so Luke pressed down to meet him.

A gasp opened Preston's lips to test with his tongue. Luke opened his mouth to meet that too.

When Preston laughed in his uncertainty, Luke took control, guiding a deeper taste with a boldly exploring tongue, until the tentative rat kissed him back, matching every stroke and tilt of their heads.

Luke could feel himself twitching to hardness, already worked up from teasing Preston—and himself—and not having expected to get this far. Now that he was here, now that he had Preston beneath him, squirming and kissing back with increasing passion, their sloppy, unhurried make-out session was like embers stoked into a bonfire.

Preston smelled like pie and summer and *home*, and the slide of their tongues was a communion of all three.

Eager for what else might be allowed, Luke pushed a hand up Preston's shirt. "Wanna even things up?"

Preston's eyes glimmered with the stirrings of a Stage One shift. *Win*.

Three sharp knocks sounded at the door.

"Preston?" Nell called. "Sorry to wake you, but I have news, and Bash wants everyone to gather downstairs."

Preston sagged into the mattress with a mesh of disappointment and relief on his face. He wanted to say yes, but he was nervous, uneasy. Luke got that, but he also knew he could get Preston past it.

"Down in a minute!" Preston called back.

"Um… is Luke in there with you? We can't find him, but everyone was certain he stayed."

Preston's face flared with color.

"Just burning the midnight oil like you, Nell!" Luke answered, which was close enough to making his presence in the room seem innocent. "We'll be there!"

Nell retreated to knock on the next door, and Luke chuckled before rolling off to lay beside Preston. Both their legs dangled off the bed, one set clothed, the other not, as they stilled their pulses, though Luke would swear he could hear Preston's hammering.

He caught sight of a pair of onlookers from the edge of Preston's desk.

"Little pervs." Luke nudged Preston and pointed at Bernard and Bianca. "I think they approve." He turned his head to look at Preston, waiting for dark eyes to meet his, even if they were a little bashful and unsure yet. "To be continued?"

Preston worried his kiss-bitten lips, but he didn't say no.

"How about I remain… cautiously optimistic?"

A smile tugged at Preston's mouth, which Luke counted as another win.

LUKE REDRESSED in the same clothes, since they had been borrowed from one of Siobhan's agents halfway through yesterday and were still mostly clean. He wasn't much of a band shirt guy, but Goo Goo Dolls were okay.

The living room was becoming their standard circle meeting place, which would have been nice and comfortable if what they were meeting about wasn't constantly crappy. And if Luke wasn't feeling more and more like he should have known about all this before it escalated.

Forced shifts posted online, secret dealings of a drug called Moondust, a whole conspiracy under their noses. He'd never felt so out of the loop.

Both foxes and Bari joined them this time, with Jude already looking better despite his arm in a sling, and both siblings looking, well, like Bari had had a hand in their grooming.

They did have their things now. Maybe Jordana had one really nice dress. Maybe she'd borrowed one from Nell. Maybe the addition of accessories like bangles, a necklace, and an opal ring glittering on her finger made all the difference, as well as a slight curl to the ends of her ginger hair, with subtle makeup accentuating her already gorgeous features, but damn, she looked even more like a bombshell than before.

Jude too. His own longish hair was almost like that Hemsworth guy in the *Thor* movie, and he wore snugly fit jeans and a shirt that had to have been borrowed from Bari because it was bronze paisley, and seriously, who wore stuff like that?

Bari—Bari wore his own richly patterned button-down in bright teal and purple.

Luke could never pull that off, though he wondered if the exchange of smirks between Bari and Jude meant either of them had pulled anything off each other last night.

Lucky bastards.

"I hope this is worth it for not even six in the morning," Deanna groused and flopped onto the floor beside Siobhan like she couldn't be bothered to make it to her usual cushion.

"I'd say so," Nell said, standing beside Bash. This time what she held was the original list of stolen items. She looked wearier than the rest, clearly not having slept. "I finished cataloging everything that was brought in, but it seems there's one item unaccounted for." She looked pointedly at Preston.

He pulled out the small donation slip she'd given him yesterday, which called out one specific item.

"Let me guess," he said, "item number eleven?"

Chapter 8

THIS WAS serious. The one item that might have given them the biggest clue was the one thing missing, and they still didn't know who all was involved or why someone would want to do this in the first place. To create more powerful shifters, clearly, but the danger in experimenting was putting the entire species at risk.

Yet all Preston could think was—*oh God, his dick was on my hip, and we kissed, and Bernard and Bianca are complete and utter traitors!*

"We swear!" Jude insisted, bringing Preston back to attention. "Everything was accounted for on that list. We didn't fence it with the other items in Glenwood. It should be here."

"It would seem it is not." Bash eyed the foxes with renewed distrust.

"They wouldn't lie," Bari defended, given he had bonded with them yesterday—and dressed them, apparently. "I'm sure they're telling you everything they can."

"If that's true," Bash continued, "then it means someone else broke into your stash while you were away and took it. To claim that item and nothing else, it had to be one of your buyers, and they must know, just like whoever donated these artifacts, that number eleven is essential. If only we knew why...," he mumbled, a bit gruffer.

"I'm sorry," Jordana said, "but I can't explain any other possibility."

The early hour had all of them surly, and Bash rubbed his eyes, almost betraying his full frustration. A deep breath later, he wore his usual façade. "Five days. There are less than five days left until the Harvest Moon. We need to track that item down through any means necessary. You never spoke with the victims?" He turned to Preston and Luke.

"Kinda got sidetracked," Luke admitted.

"Start there. Find out if they remember encountering any strange items. See if they know about the Moondust from Isabella's. Then go see McDonough."

Preston sat up straighter.

Sean McDonough—Baraka Bain's Second.

He was on the buyer list and had already been a person of interest. Preston had even met him before, as an honored guest at one of his parents' parties, where only other rat shifters or people of high influence were ever allowed to attend.

Like Baraka, Sean was the sort of man who left anyone in his wake feeling small and lacking.

"Isabella swore she only had access to the Moondust through him and doesn't know its initial origin," Bash said. "After my father's death, she thought she could experiment and corner the market herself. We need to know what that *market* is."

"You don't expect us to go along this time, do you?" Jordana asked, clinging to Jude as she hovered beside him. "My brother's injured, and I don't want to leave him. Surely someone else would be better backup."

Bash looked to Siobhan, who grinned.

"All points of interest are covered, boss," she said. "My agents got this."

Preston wished he could feel as confident about him and Luke confronting a previous circle member who had decades of experience, considering how the encounter with Isabella had gone down.

"I can keep our guests company," Bari said, standing behind the foxes' chair like a guardian and twirling his fingers through Jude's long hair.

"No, you can help Nell with anything she needs so she can get some rest," Bash argued.

Bari was clearly going to protest—until he glanced at Nell's exhausted expression and crumbled. He was a decent sort, if a little... horny.

On the sofa, Preston's knee knocked against Luke, who winked at him.

Fuck.

"Those who can rest, do so," Bash ordered. "Everyone else, get to work."

At least Preston's marathon slumber meant he was wide-awake, and Luke appeared to be too.

"You hang tight today, okay?" Luke offered the foxes. "You look really nice, by the way. Totally over-my-head chic, which I'm guessing is a good thing?" He laughed and then scrutinized Jordana a little closer. "You weren't wearing that kinda makeup before, right? Wait, did *Bari* have makeup to put on you?"

"Just the eyeliner." Bari shrugged and then placed a hand near his mouth to mock-whisper, "And a little concealer, but don't you dare spread that around." He shared a smile with each fox and headed off to join Nell.

"He is a wizard," Jordana gushed. "You two be careful now."

Preston planned on it and would do his best to conserve magic, should he need to use any later. For now, he focused on just how one was supposed to act around someone whose tongue had been in his mouth a few minutes ago.

Five blocks in, he still hadn't figured it out.

"So, um… everything okay?" Luke asked, after their mostly one-sided conversation had dwindled. "Did I cross a line? I mean, I did, but then you seemed pretty into it, so…." He blinked those beautiful blue eyes at Preston for some sign that he wasn't being shunned.

"You did cross a line."

Luke frowned.

"And I was into it."

Then brightened again.

"*But*… I'm not like the rest of you. Bari can throw himself at a tall handsome fox like it's nothing. The others are all open and easy with casual touches or… *being naked*, and I… wasn't raised that way. My parents have no idea I have feelings like… this." He gestured vaguely. "That was my first kiss."

"With a guy?"

Preston glared at him.

"Oh! Wow. Then… can I ask you something?"

"Yes."

"Do you think your first kiss being with a guy is a bad thing? Or that liking guys is bad?"

"I… would have, for a long time."

"And now?"

Preston closed his eyes for a few steadying beats. "My parents did know I felt this way once, when I was younger, but they thought it was a phase. Those feelings never went away. Limbo seemed like the best compromise to avoid disappointing anyone."

"Like *celibacy*?" Luke squawked, but when Preston glared at him, at least there wasn't anyone nearby to have overheard. "Sorry, it's just… that sounds super extreme if you're not the type who actually, ya know, wants to be celibate."

"What was I supposed to do? Everything my parents ever planned for me were the reasons I succeeded. I quit college to be part of this circle, but a little time spent online and I can probably still get my degree a semester earlier than most. Why? Because they pushed me to be better. Always, always better. The reason I know so many spells, even if my stamina could use improvement, and just how much I worked to be perfect at using my abilities as a Rat King, is all because of them."

"Okay," Luke said with a cautious, patient tone, "but end of the day your life is still yours. All that awesome stuff in your room is not something you should feel shame over, or a kiss with me. When do you relax? Have fun? Be you?"

Preston stopped at the next street corner but didn't answer.

Luke didn't push for one. He smiled and, as cautiously as he had spoken, grasped Preston's hand right there in the open.

"No time like the present."

Preston squeezed back but then let go, since across the street was one of the victims' homes. "Work first."

"Play later?" Luke grinned. "After all, you are my ma—"

"*Maybe*." Preston slapped his hand across Luke's mouth. "Later."

He wasn't ready to say the other word yet.

They still had no idea where to find the lizard woman they had first been searching for, but whatever leads they could find would be better than none.

And find them they did, since Sydney Hyland, the wolf who'd experienced a forced shift, had heard rumors about a shifter drug going around from a couple of the social cases she helped with at the Shelter, but she hadn't seen either of those clients since. She described what happened to her like being in a dream she couldn't wake up from, totally aware mentally but unable to stop her shift or where she went and what she did until the feeling faded.

George Lien, the hawk shifter and fellow runner Luke knew, was visibly spooked when they went to see him, packed and ready to head out of town as soon as he was allowed.

"What's going on, man?" Luke asked. "There's some weird drug, missing people, and I'm pretty sure the reason I hadn't heard about any of it yet is because anyone who knows anything is gone or in on it. If you know something, you have to tell us. This could be huge, like, 'tons more shifters experiencing what you did in the middle of downtown' huge."

George had the sharp eyes of a bird of prey, constantly darting them around his tiny apartment for anything unwelcome, like he expected an ambush. He also had to be on something because he was especially twitchy, and Preston seriously hoped it wasn't the Moondust.

"This is big," George said with a rock forward and rub of his hands. He had greasy brown hair and scruff that went too far down his neck, like he hadn't shaved or bathed since his incident. "Bash taking over the pack kinda big. Blood in the streets big—"

"We know," Preston interrupted. Luke had sat beside George on some worn-out sofa, but Preston had no intention of touching anything. "What we need are details, the who, what, where, and *now*."

Luke flashed hinting eyes at him to pull back, but they didn't have time for a soft hand.

"Okay." George rocked again. "But I want out. Permission to leave on a train for Brookdale *tonight*."

"Okay," Luke agreed. "We'll make it happen."

If this led anywhere, Bash would probably drop the hawk off himself.

George stopped rocking and lowered his voice to a whisper. "McDonough's involved."

Or not.

"We know that already," Preston spat.

"About Connie?"

"*Conrad* McDonough?" Luke looked between them. "We thought just Sean. Aren't they on the outs? Connie was always pissed his brother got to be Second and he didn't even get a seat at the table."

"Siblings?" Preston stressed.

"Yeah," George said, clicking his teeth like the clack of a beak, but Preston had to assure himself that the man was not shifting, just fidgety. "The drug thing, Moondust, a few missing people, yeah, just the right amount and the right people who no one would notice being gone. Sean promised his brother a seat this time if he helps him take the pack back from Bash. That's what the drug's for, supposed to make shifters stronger, like, back-to-our-roots stronger, ancient shit, ya know? I did a few runs for it."

"For the drug?" Luke asked. "For McDonough?"

"For Baraka! He started the whole thing, wanting to prove his strength to other cities or some shit. Kept it super low-profile, barely any runners involved. I don't even know if the others are alive, let alone around anymore. After Bash offed his dad and took over, McDonough started changing focus. He was almost giddy. But that drug… it's scary stuff."

"Sorry for having to ask, then, Georgie, but… why'd ya take it?"

George stared at Luke in dismay. "I didn't."

"THIS IS *fucked*." Luke stared at the list of addresses for both victims and buyers, all of which they'd crossed off except the lizard chick, who didn't have an address to check, the weird-named guy, Payara Northwest, and the address the foxes had for Sean McDonough   which Luke totally should have recognized. "This is Connie's place, speakeasy type bar, shifters only, limited hours, and definitely should have been a red flag. And now we have another set of siblings? Urg!"

He thrust the list back at Preston, who pocketed it, since they didn't need an address to a place Luke knew. They were already almost there.

Preston hadn't said much, deep in thought it seemed, and then quietly mumbled the prophecy Bash first told them.

"It begins with an exodus of siblings and charm,
Neither knowing the extent of their greed's lasting harm.
All beasts will howl on and rage, none immune
If the source is not stopped by wane on Harvest Moon."

"I guess Connie and Sean are kinda charming." Luke shrugged.

"But what would exodus mean for them? From loyalty to the pack, to Bash?"

"Bash said it's not always crystal clear, right? Maybe."

"Let's find Siobhan's agents around the address first," Preston said. "Have them go in with us. You'd recognize them, right?"

"Should. Hadn't really been looking when we went to Isa's, but I know most of the people Shevy tapped, either as previous enforcers or Shelter kids."

"Do the McDonoughs have magic?"

"No, but they'll have muscle, the kind who'll be real loyal. Maybe we should call Siobhan directly. And Bash and Deanna, coz…." Luke trailed off as a very potent scent struck him, overpowering everything else nearby.

He was used to this scent in these streets—fights could break out from the speakeasy often—but it wasn't operating hours, and the smell was too strong to be the usual cuts and split lips.

Blood. A lot of it.

Preston grabbed Luke's arm. He'd obviously picked up on the scent too. No shifter could have missed it.

"How close are we?" Preston hissed.

"About ten paces. The entrance is right around the corner."

A quick glance around showed way too little activity, like no people at all, which meant any other shifters who'd been around must have smelled the same thing and bolted—or investigated.

Where were Siobhan's agents? This wasn't Shaw Street, but it was close, in the depths of shifter territory, which meant cleanup didn't have to happen immediately if something shady had gone down. But whatever had happened must have been recent because the blood smelled fresh, and the streets were too quiet.

"Stay behind me," Preston said and began to approach the corner.

"You gonna be okay blasting off those offensive spells?" Luke asked.

"That's not going to be a problem anymore."

One brush with death was enough, Luke figured, and gratefully stuck close behind Preston as they turned into the alley where the door to the speakeasy looked nice and benign to anyone who didn't know what lay inside.

Or would have on a normal day—if the door wasn't flung open, with a trail of blood leading out from the inside and splattered garishly over the pavement and opposite wall.

Three bodies lay unmoving in a heap of ravaged remains.

"Shit…." Luke lifted a hand to his mouth to keep from retching.

Preston advanced, slow but seemingly collected, with an outstretched arm and lightning sparking at his fingertips in wait for an attacker.

None appeared. The wounds looked like claw marks as they drew closer, but it was too brutal to tell what kind. The open door showed an empty building, and there were footprints in the blood from others having rushed out, as well as a large Stage Three type footprint from what had likely done this and might be on the loose.

"What the hell happened? Who are these people?" Preston posed the obvious questions, and the quake in his voice betrayed that he wasn't as collected as he looked.

Luke moved around him, still trying to keep from breathing in too deep, and studied what remained of the victims' faces. Two he could see easily and recognized just like he'd told Preston he would.

"Siobhan's agents." Then he turned over the third body with a gentle nudge of his foot and recognized that face too. "And our missing lizard. *Fuck.*"

Preston's phone rang, making them flinch. They hadn't expected to be in a horror movie today.

"What?" Preston answered.

The widening of his eyes didn't make Luke feel better.

Preston pulled the phone from his ear and hit speaker. "Say that again. Then we have something to report too."

"It's bad," Siobhan said. "I need your help glamouring and with crowd control off Spencer Ave."

That was only a few blocks away.

"A werewolf just attacked a convenience store."

THE GOOD news was that Siobhan and several of her agents had intercepted the raging wolf before anyone else could get hurt, and Luke helped Preston convince the eyewitnesses that it had just been a crazed junkie wearing a costume—aided by a quickly placed glamour spell—before the authorities arrived. This type of thing was their job, protecting the pack, and their entire species, from exposure.

The bad news was that another video got posted from the ordeal, went viral, and made the local news. Even if most people were calling it a hoax, it didn't make Centrus City's leadership look all that competent.

And three people had died.

Luke couldn't help feeling responsible, like he should have known. He should have known something before things got this bad. What other use was he when knowing people and having insider info was why Bash chose him?

Jude looked especially agitated back at the den, but then, all of them were antsy. They hadn't found either of the McDonoughs, and with the wolf returned to human but in police custody, they had no way of asking if he'd taken the Moondust or if something else had happened.

Jordana was quiet too as they gathered in the living room once more, with Bash pacing behind the sofa.

"Nothing? Your people can't find any sign of the McDonoughs?" Bash demanded of Siobhan.

"I'm sorry, boss. We're looking, but some of them are still green, and they're spooked. Those bodies…. Plus, the McDonoughs know how to make themselves ghosts."

"The fuckers were probably experimenting like Isa," Deanna muttered.

"What else do we know?" Bash stopped his pacing to look at Preston and Luke.

"Georgie said he didn't take the drug," Luke offered. "Whatever that's worth. He told us Baraka started the whole Moondust thing, but the McDonoughs continued it after he died. Oh, and we didn't get to the final buyer. Kinda had to focus on damage control."

Bash sighed with both hands planted on the back of the sofa. "Of course my father was behind this. He never could see the big picture if it interfered with his ambitions. We need to all be out there. Check out the final buyer, discover everything we can. We have to find Sean and Conrad McDonough today."

"Why, Bashir, I'm flattered."

Everyone jumped to their feet or spun around to face the main entrance into the living room, where Sean McDonough himself entered, followed by his brother, Conrad, and several large shifters who all smelled like wolves.

Sean was a beast of a man with a reddish mustache, dark hair speckled with gray, and wearing a black turtleneck and long leather jacket like a mob boss—which he had been as a member of Baraka's circle.

His brother had the same imposing height and girth, sans the mustache, but similar in appearance, and though their numbers were even against those on Bash's side, Luke had a sneaky suspicion that everyone with the McDonoughs had already taken Moondust, because they were twitching.

"No need to go looking. We're right here."

Chapter 9

EVERYONE ON their side of the room was on their feet and shifted to Stage Two in seconds—except Bash, who stood his ground, opposite Sean.

Preston was not feeling up for another rumble, but it seemed they might not have a choice.

"Bold move, coming here now," Bash said with nary a waver in his voice. "One coup, and done by a family member, is respected. Another this soon will look like chaos to neighboring cities and invite a pack-wide takeover.

"So why don't you rejects from *The Sopranos* turn around while you still can—oh, and hand over all the remaining Moondust you've been peddling that started with my father."

Conrad and several of the others laughed, flexing their hands into the start of claws and cracking their necks with a crease in their brows, just like Lui had done before going She-Hulk and charging at them.

Sean, like Bash, kept a steadier facade. "Honestly, Bashir, you did me a favor. I probably would have taken Baraka out myself before long.

"As for the other cities getting trigger-happy and coming for the throne I earned after years of working under your father's thumb, I think we can handle it." He grinned, and there was no doubt that his crew, Conrad included, had taken the Moondust. They'd come prepared to fight, most wearing minimal clothing that they now discarded as they began to grow well beyond a normal Stage Three.

Bash held out his arms to keep their side back, still vying for diplomacy. But as their finest at reading people, Luke and Siobhan, continued to shift to their own impressive Stage Three forms, Preston had little faith that diplomacy would work.

He remained behind the sofa. He was a rat, not meant to be frontline, even if he did have magic. He couldn't call on Bernard and Bianca. He would need dozens, hundreds, thousands of rodents to make a difference against these brutes, and that would take minutes they didn't have.

"This isn't controllable," Bash warned, eyeing the multitude of werewolves like the most fearsome horror adaptations of their kind.

They were practically prehistoric-looking, like dire wolves from a fantasy novel on two legs. Their varyingly colored fur flared, making them appear even larger, with fangs and claws as long as Preston's forearms and spittle at the corners of their gaping maws.

"Controllable enough," Sean said—and looked at *Nell*. "All I need now is someone to mass-produce the Moondust and keep a steady supply on hand. Seems you've provided that for me too. Grace period's over."

The first of the wolves struck an invisible shield that made Preston gasp. The air rippled with bluish color, as Nell, their lone human, looking dangerously frail in comparison to present company, had the foresight to throw up a barrier. Her hands emanated the same bluish tint from glowing runes on her palms.

"Get them out of here!" Bash ordered his brother, and though Bari, Jude, and Jordana were all snarling at Stage Two like the rest, Bari grabbed both foxes and sprinted toward another exit—

Where two more wolves burst inside, and one nearly took Bari's head off with a massive swipe.

"Down!" Preston cried, firing off a concentrated ball of lightning that exploded across the werewolves' chests. It made them flinch and withdraw out the doorway, but only for a second. Preston knew he could cause more damage if he truly let loose, but at the cost of staying conscious, and maybe risking the others getting caught in friendly fire.

Offensive magic wouldn't be enough, even if he did go all out. It had barely helped against Lui.

A howl escaped Nell as she extended the shield she was struggling to maintain to encompass where Bari and the foxes had fallen. It was her at the far end beside Bash, then Deanna and Siobhan, having vaulted the sofa, and Luke, who'd raced around it. Bari and the foxes were farther back, but Jordana leapt to her feet to guard the others, since her brother was injured and Bari didn't seem the fighter type any more than Preston wanted to be.

But he had to be. They all did.

Springing over the arm of the sofa to land behind Nell, Preston clapped a hand on her shoulder, imbuing her with added magic to boost the shield as much as he could. It glowed with every swipe and clawed fist against its bubble of protection.

They were the circle now. They were the adults in the room with the supposed power and responsibility to fight. Even if Siobhan had a coterie of agents outside, they must have already been incapacitated, because Sean and his goons had made it in here.

Deanna was at Stage Three like Luke and Siobhan, clothing torn and jaws snapping at their would-be attackers. But even in their largest forms—with Deanna a beautiful all-black werepanther that would have been imposing if not contrasted against the doubled size of the wolves, Luke smaller with orange and creamsicle-colored stripes but needle-point claws and fangs, and Siobhan covered in platinum scales to match her hair, and head elongated like a dragon—there was no way they stood a chance against so many if the barrier broke.

It stretched across the room like a divider, but the wolves were pounding on it, all of them, spread outward around Sean at the center, pummeling with constant flashes of blue impact points in their wakes.

Bash still hadn't shifted beyond a flicker of golden eyes, glaring at the equally human-looking Sean for daring to try this.

"Reconsider," he advised.

"No," Sean said.

The next strike left a blue fissure in the barrier.

"This pack is mine."

"*Preston.*" Nell's voice cracked like the shield. He could feel his own strength waning, failing to help her keep more fractures from forming, until they riddled the translucent partition like lightning scars. "Your portal magic!"

His eyes snapped to hers. "I...."

"You have to. The others aren't safe."

"What about you?"

"Sean won't risk losing the one asset he needs. *Go.*" She turned her head the slightest bit farther, her eyes glimmering with pleading.

Preston hardly knew Nell, yet she was playing martyr, asking him to be the hero who would carry her passed torch.

The first fissure in the barrier grew so long and large, it split, allowing one of the wolves to dig his claws into the opening and start tearing it apart like paper.

"To me!" Preston cried and leapt away from Nell, back between the sofa and coffee table, urging the others to climb over whatever necessary to reach him. "*Now!*" he roared when some of them hesitated.

As more cracks turned into craters along the failing shield, everyone but Nell scrambled to reach Preston, who formed the clearest image of a location in his mind where he could safely bring this many people and opened a portal right beneath their feet.

LUKE'S STOMACH plummeted, and not only because he'd never traveled by *Dimension Door* before—or at least that's what he planned to call it. He found his feet without having to catch his balance, unlike some of the others, who toppled onto their asses in what looked like an almost empty room.

A dorm room, with a bed stripped of blankets, a vacant desk and chair, and sparse walls with traces of tape where posters must have hung until recently.

"Those *fuckers*!" Deanna boomed, shifting human as she paced the new location. "Drugs? An ambush? *Now*? I swear I am going to—"

"Hey!" Preston grabbed her arm as she reared it back, even as he was panting from the exertion of his spell, to prevent her from putting a hole in the wall. "I still need this room signed off on at the end of the semester, so if you could maybe… not."

She huffed but reeled in her temper to be redirected where it belonged, promising, "I am gonna knock Sean and Connie's heads together like a goddamn Stooges skit until their ears bleed."

Luke snorted. Shelter kids often had outdated references, given there were more VHS tapes on hand than DVDs or Blu-rays.

The flicker of a smile on his face couldn't last, however, not when the entire reason they'd had to run and leave Nell behind was because of him.

He should have known. He should have seen this coming.

"Quick thinking," Bash said to Preston, unbuttoning his shirt to hand to Deanna.

She, Siobhan, and Luke were all mostly naked, having shifted to Stage Three, but since they hadn't fought or moved much in that state, their bottoms weren't as shredded as their tops. Luke ripped his own mess of a shirt from his body to fall to the floor.

Bari followed his brother's example and handed his button-down to Siobhan, who eyed the colorful article with a wry expression but still donned it. The Bains looked even more identical wearing just jeans—until one of them moved, gestured, or spoke.

"It was Nell's quick thinking," Preston said, "but at least I knew this room would be empty, and the McDonoughs shouldn't know of it."

"What are we going to do now?" Jordana asked, moving to sit on the bed with Jude, who still looked more agitated than anyone else, but then no one else had an arm they couldn't use.

"We retake the den before they make more Moondust," Bash said.

"And Nell?" Siobhan asked.

"She told me she wasn't worried," Preston said, "since Sean wants use of her skills. I think she's right. He must already be running out, which means if we can stop them before more is made, there won't be as uneven of a fight next time."

"I hate to ask this, but…," Luke posed in a small voice that he wished didn't draw everyone's attention when he already felt bared open, "does this mean you're not Alpha anymore until we take Sean down?"

The tension that tore through the group said most of the others weren't sure either, but Bash spoke firmly. "As long as I'm alive, no new Alpha can appoint themselves—unless we are officially ousted from the den for a full seven days. Lucky for us, we only have five anyway." He smiled in a strange, cold manner he had of curving his lips without an ounce of goodwill or humor.

Five days. Only five days until the Harvest Moon and the apparent end of shifter civilization.

"This is my fault…," Luke lamented.

"How is that?" Bash asked.

"The whole reason you wanted me in the circle was because I'm supposed to know everyone and everything that's going on, and I didn't know shit about any of this."

"Luke…." Bash's low voice brought Luke's eyes up from staring at the floor, and the whole scene before him felt more futile than ever with half of them undressed or in tatters or both. Luke wasn't supposed to be facing down his half-naked Alpha in an empty dorm room while he was barely covered himself, feeling like a failure. "I wouldn't have expected you to know these things, when my own father and his Second were the ones keeping things quiet."

"I know, but—"

"Regrets are a waste of time we don't have. I will not look down on you for what you can't or don't accomplish. All that matters is the actions you do take with the conviction to make things right again. That is what we need now. That is where our focus must be—on what we do next.

"Seeing as how we don't know how much of the Moondust they currently have, or how long Nell can stall creating more, we need to amass a large enough force to take back the den as efficiently as possible. Not quickly, *efficiently*. We cannot afford to get this wrong."

Bash turned from Luke to accept suggestions, and Luke tried to take his words to heart.

He couldn't feel sorry for himself when they had work to do.

"I still have agents I can call in," Siobhan said, plopping down in the middle of the floor, "seasoned ones."

"I know a few retired enforcers who'll step up for a cause like this." Deanna joined her with a heavier slump.

Bari had taken the chair at the desk and offered, "I might know a few people if we're talking in a day or two. From out of town, though."

"I'll take them," Bash said, "so long as they keep their involvement quiet. Tell them the Alpha of Centrus City will owe them a favor."

"Uh…." Luke forced himself to speak up too. "There's people at the Shelter I can ask, either a little older or just passing through town, who have strong enough magic or are the right kind of muscle for this."

"Good." Bash glanced at the foxes.

"Sorry, we can't offer much." Jordana shrugged.

"It's all right. A couple of the old circle members who weren't fans of my father or Sean McDonough might help. Preston?" Bash turned finally to the rat, who'd leaned against the wall that Deanna nearly punched, and now looked startled.

"I… can't think of anyone."

"Not even with the resources of the Rathaways?"

"They're my *parents'* resources, not mine. I can't go to them."

"Preston—"

"I *can't*."

Luke wasn't the only one who didn't want eyes on him. Preston wasn't meeting Bash's stare, which was now everyone else's stare too. Preston didn't have a good relationship with his parents. Luke used to think any family would be better than none, but what he knew of Preston's said otherwise.

Slowly and exuding his powerful presence, Bash approached Preston, who squirmed against the wall and tentatively looked up.

"Everyone knows about me becoming Alpha and that I have chosen my advisors, meaning it is highly likely all your identities have spread as well. A circle is not meant to be secret from its pack."

"I know," Preston said with a cringe, "but my parents haven't learned I'm Magister yet. If they had, they'd have blown up my phone by now. I can't go to them with a disaster on our hands. I just... can't."

Bash sighed. "I won't push, but I hope you reconsider. We may need every able body we can get. For now, stick with Luke. Priority one is backup once we have a solid plan to retake the den, if not by tomorrow, then the next day, maybe one day more, but no later. Beyond that, anything else you can discover about what's been going on...." He glanced at Luke. "I'll take it. There's still too much about this we don't understand, like what happened to item number eleven. Unless it's currently in Sean McDonough's pocket," he finished with a grumble.

Because the Moondust and what caused the forced shifts couldn't be the same thing. Luke had felt the effects himself without taking anything, George never took it, and although they hadn't gotten the chance to go back and ask Sydney, Luke knew she wouldn't have either.

"Start making calls," Bash ordered. "Use the landline instead of cellphones. For what we'll need to do in person, that waits until morning. Sean is going to be looking for us, and we cannot risk giving him easy targets until we're ready."

Luke's part in this would all be in person. The Shelter had a landline, and some of the people he had in mind had cells, but he couldn't ask for this sort of thing over the phone, not from people like him, who'd already fought tooth and nail to survive.

He sat down right where he was and leaned against the door at his back. He was used to being alone with his thoughts in a crowd. He didn't mind, however, when even his thoughts were crowded in on, as Preston moved from where he'd been standing to sit beside him.

"Guess neither of us have calls to make, huh?" Luke said, watching the others take turns on the landline and conferring with each other about options.

"My parents...," Preston started, but his words faded.

"It's okay." Luke nudged him and then let himself stay there, leaning against Preston's side.

"It's okay for you too. You really couldn't have known any of this would happen."

"I *could* have… but I guess I might be one of the victims by now if I had." Luke still couldn't shake how he'd felt that day when the shift came upon him from an outside source, and nothing since had felt the same as that strange twist inside. "We gotta be missing something. What was different about that first day? You smelled magic. I felt it."

"The rune and residue I saw was a leftover," Preston said, "not the cause of the spell."

"Like tire tracks after a getaway?"

"Basically." Preston huffed a laugh. "I just don't know from what."

Bari was on the phone now, animatedly talking to friends from his city. Jude and Jordana were still on the bed, but Jude had wriggled free of his sister's hold and sat apart, giving her occasional and what he thought were furtive glances, but Luke saw, while Jordana seemed to be up in her head, wringing her hands in her lap.

Hands with scratches on them. She must have gotten caught by some of their attackers' claws.

"I hope they're okay," Luke said with a nod in their direction. "They seem off. Jude especially."

"He's hurt," Preston reasoned, "and they're probably wishing they had better protectors." He huffed again and turned to look at Luke.

Luke stared back at him, almost bringing them as close as they'd been when they bumped noses that first day. They had done more since, but a crowded room wasn't the best place for a second kiss or deeper exploration—not that Luke had never sneakily fooled around. Shelter kids had to get creative sometimes.

He licked his lips at the thought and watched Preston's cheeks flush as he followed the movement. Luke did it again, and when Preston looked down as if to avoid blushing darker, he failed miserably and quickly snapped his gaze forward.

"What?" Luke chuckled.

"You're, um… mostly naked again."

"Strategically," Luke argued, but when he glanced at his lap, maybe it wasn't so strategic anymore after sitting, 'cause his torn pants had shifted so that a prominent hole was exposing his crotch—and he wasn't wearing underwear. "Oops!"

If they'd been alone, Luke might have played it up again, but for now, he adjusted so the hole wasn't offering a peepshow.

He liked when Preston's cheeks got rosy over him, though. There was a bit of five o'clock shadow on those cheeks too, dark and even instead of pale and patchy like Luke's would have had if he hadn't shaved. Although he could go weeks and patchy would still be as good as it got.

On Preston, stubble was really hot, and sitting so close to him surrounded Luke with that pie- and homelike smell.

"You were great again, ya know," Luke said.

Preston's lips twitched. "Guess I'll have to get used to saving the day. And seeing my friends in partial to full nudity."

He clearly meant the others as much as Luke, since his eyes strayed to the shirtless twin brothers, standing together now, while Deanna was on the phone. Preston's eyes raked over them with far less subtlety than when he'd glanced at Luke.

"*Hey*." Luke nudged him harder.

"It's a nice view." Preston shrugged.

It was—Bash and Bari had the chiseled physiques of two bronze Adonises—but Luke preferred being the one Preston gawked at. "While I am glad you can admit that, and it is nice, *stop it*."

The grin Preston flashed at him said he may have been staring on purpose. "As if you weren't checking out Jude yesterday. You can dish out the teasing but not take it?"

Damn, he was pretty when he smiled.

"There are some views I like better," Preston added quietly.

"Me too." Luke licked his lips again. "And maybe some people who smell better than anything ever has?"

"Maybe."

Luke couldn't resist leaning closer—

When a nudge at his back made him jerk from the door, since the door was the only thing behind him, and *how was it nudging him*?

Preston yelped, and they both scrambled to their feet, drawing the attention of the others, who immediately readied to defend against....

What turned out to be two rats squeezing into the room through the space between door and floor.

"Thank goodness." Preston bent to scoop them into his hands. "I forgot I called them. I couldn't very well leave Bernard and Bianca at the den with those traitors."

Siobhan and Bari seemed especially amused by the sudden arrival of furry friends, but Bash stepped forward with his usual seriousness.

"How many rodents can you control at a time?"

Right. Preston did have "friends" he could call on.

"As many as we need," Preston confirmed.

They took turns sneaking out to the bathroom so as not to alert anyone who might question the presence of so many people in one room, and eventually ordered pizza. Before long, they had the start of a gameplan, just not much space for everyone to comfortably sleep.

It was Luke's suggestion to shift to Stage Four. It was an old Shelter trick if there were more people than beds, or when winter got cold and the heater wasn't working the best—dogpiling in their animal forms could fit almost a dozen people on one mattress, depending on shifter type.

Eight was easy.

Having two wolves, two foxes, a panther, and a Komodo dragon cuddled around him was sort of a dream come true for Luke. He loved snuggling, but he could tell that Preston wasn't as comfortable, even with Bernard and Bianca to keep his tiny form company.

Luke gently booped Preston's nose, encouraging him to snuggle closer against him. Bernard and Bianca followed, but Luke didn't mind. Before long, he was dozing off with the pack's inner circle, several new friends, and the best smelling rat in the world keeping him warm.

DAY 4

WHAT WOKE Luke wasn't the sun shining in through the thin curtains but the gentlest jostling of the bed that he might have ignored if he hadn't defied death several days in a row. He stirred, blinking his eyes open to see who had changed positions or was getting up to use the bathroom.

It was Jordana, slipping out the door as a human. Luke wouldn't have questioned it, and almost snuggled back to sleep, when a few moments later, Jude followed.

He turned his head to nudge Preston, but he was already awake, staring at the door—and Bash, Bari, Siobhan, and Deanna were all awake too.

"I don't know anything!" Bari asserted, after they'd shifted human and were hurriedly dressing.

"You're the one who's been getting all cozy with 'em," Deanna said.

"But I had no idea they'd…." He trailed off and worried his lip. "Although…."

"What?" Bash demanded.

"When I checked on Jude at one point yesterday, before everyone got back, there maybe was a period of time when I couldn't find Jordana. But then she showed up!" he defended at a frustrated eye roll from his brother. "I figured she'd been exploring!"

"Weren't they warded against leaving alone?"

"Only in their room," Preston said, "which I didn't feel the need to reapply yesterday. We'll follow them." He grabbed Luke's elbow and led them to the door. "I already have Bernard and Bianca on their tail."

"Find out what they haven't been telling us," Bash called. "The rest of us will continue working on how we're going to keep my prophecy from ending the world as we know it."

Luke really wished he hadn't put it like that.

Chapter 10

"I KNEW we shouldn't have trusted them," Preston said as he and Luke hurried after where Bernard and Bianca were hot on Jude's tail—who was hot on his sister's tail, which was strange, since it meant they hadn't met up yet and maybe weren't in on this together.

Whatever *this* was.

"No way." Luke kept dissenting every time Preston tried to call foul. "They weren't lying after we bonded."

"You talked *Star Wars* and survived a fight together. You're not suddenly besties."

"But they bonded with Bari too! Jude looked really good in that shirt. I'd look ridiculous."

"You still look ridiculous," Preston muttered.

It would eventually be another hot day, but for morning, it was tolerable enough that going shirtless had to seem excessive to the average passerby. They'd been getting stares, considering Luke's current lack of attire, and wearing pants with *strategic* holes.

Who didn't wear underwear? Thankfully, Luke had situated the garment so as not to get them stopped for indecent exposure.

Even though Preston's clothing wasn't likewise torn, it was still rumpled from being worn yesterday, and he could really use a shower. And coffee. And food that wasn't delivery pizza.

"I know where we're headed!" Luke exclaimed, either ignoring or not caring about Preston's comment. "I can stop at the Shelter for clothes."

"We are not detour—" Preston cut himself off, recognizing that Bernard and Bianca had turned toward the Shelter as well.

It took extra concentration for him to see where he was going and to see through the eyes of the rats, but they'd just lost Jude around a corner, and once it was turned, the only place he could have disappeared to was inside the Shelter.

"We better hurry." Preston picked up the pace.

"Why?"

"Bernard and Bianca aren't going to be able to help when dozens upon dozens of shifter scents just swallowed our leads."

They weren't far from the streets where all the other terrible things had gone down. Shaw Street was close, as well as Isabella's and the incident from that speakeasy that had spilled into a nearby convenience store. Everything seemed to be centered around these same neighborhoods, and the Shelter was right amongst it all.

Preston rushed in through the first door they came upon to scan for signs of Jude or Jordana and immediately froze. His stomach plummeted with a wave of coolness washing over him as the blood drained from his face to his feet. He'd never been inside the Shelter before.

How did people live like this?

It was clean, but there was occasional litter in several corners, despite nearby trash cans, and there were so many people: children, the elderly, and every age between. While most of them looked clean enough too, their clothing wasn't in the best state, and the entrance Preston had used brought him within view of several rooms, all of which were packed with so many beds that he had no idea how anyone could traverse the rooms without stepping on people during the night.

"What's up? Can the rats not find them?"

Preston looked at Luke with a new sense of wonder, because how could this alley cat be so sweet and upbeat when he had grown up in these conditions for more than a decade?

"Pres?" Luke stepped closer with concern in the knit of his brow.

"Uh… no. They lost the scent." He turned forward and summoned the rats back to him, coaxing them into his pockets so they wouldn't get trampled.

"We can keep looking. They're in here somewhere, right? Plus, then I can get a change of clothes." Luke smiled and nudged Preston's arm for him to follow. "On the way, we can still be productive. Hey, Hilary! Can I talk with you a sec!" he hailed a passing tiger. She looked strong, if a little older, and Preston could smell a hint of magic on her.

Luke didn't hesitate to approach everyone along their path, recruiting for the cause to take back the den. He told each person to keep things quiet from anyone they didn't trust to be on Bash's side, that rumors of a souped-up drug going around were bad news, and why so much buzz was circulating online.

People had heard about the YouTube videos and news coverage of the convenience store. No one at the Shelter was jumping at the chance to try any Moondust. They were worried, even more so when Luke admitted the den had been taken by the McDonoughs. Yet Luke had this disarming way with everyone, this ease and assuredness that kept down their hysteria instead of fueling it, just like Bash had recognized as Luke's most valuable asset.

As awful as the conditions here seemed to Preston, it also appeared homier and with more camaraderie between its denizens than the Rathaway family manor ever had.

"When we call, be ready." Luke shook hands with his latest recruit, the numbers already worthwhile enough that Bash would be pleased.

No one had liked Baraka, and few liked Sean McDonough either.

"Okay." Luke turned to Preston with a long exhale since he'd been doing all the work. "My room is just around the corner—"

"Lance, there you are!" An old man appeared, clamping on to Luke's elbow. He was another alley cat and looked to be in his 70s or 80s, with hard lines etched into his face and the glimmer of whiskers— as in shifter whiskers, not scruff—proving he couldn't hold the various stages anymore, like a young child. "I can't find my reading glasses, and your sisters aren't any help. Have you seen them?"

"Don't worry, Pops." Luke smiled and patted the man's hand. "We'll find 'em. In fact, I think I just saw them." He reached for the man's head, where a pair of reading glasses sat atop slightly unruly white hair. The man didn't seem to notice Luke pluck them from the tangles. "Here we go." He slowly brought them down.

"Bless you." The man shakily placed them back on his face. "I was hoping to read the paper. Find out more about all this Y2K nonsense."

Luke took hold of the man's arm, gently guiding him back the way he had come from. "Let's get you in your chair, then, huh?"

A knot formed in Preston's chest over the frailty of this man and Luke's automatic default to help him. No wonder Bash had wanted this kid to be Councilor, not that Preston had been doubting Luke's abilities much anymore.

Down a narrow hall was a room with mostly other elderly shifters, surrounded by games, magazines, and crossword puzzle books, as well as a newspaper beside a recliner, where Luke led the old man. It likely didn't have anything in it about Y2K, but it might be from a few months, even a few years back, given the state of its pages.

Luke helped the man reclaim the chair and didn't back away until he was settled reading.

"He called you Lance," Preston said once Luke rejoined him.

"Gary forgets sometimes," Luke said. "Smells another alley cat and thinks we're his kids. I don't even know where they are or if he has family still around or alive, but we try to play along, ya know, keep him comfortable and calm."

"He should—" Preston stopped because what could he say? He should be in a home or somewhere with medical care? They couldn't do that for shifters, when dementia went hand in hand with losing control over changing forms. It was too dangerous to let someone like that be amongst humans. Usually, shifters took care of their own elderly, but that wasn't always possible. The Shelter was supposed to be the alternative.

Preston bit his tongue and caught the sorrowful expression that marred what was usually so jovial about Luke.

"He should." Luke shrugged. "But he's here."

Preston watched an older woman, maybe 50s, notice the man's return and kneel next to him. She cast a kind smile at Luke, and he waved before leading Preston out of the room.

"We look out for each other. Kiddos too." Luke paused at another open doorway that led into a nursery. There were kids of all ages, even a few in cribs, with various older shifters caring for them, though several children were playing alone, a little listlessly like they would rather be anywhere else.

Then one of them saw Luke.

"Story time?" he asked in a rush, sprinting toward them.

Several others caught wind of this, recognized Luke, and ran over too, all pawing at him and trying to pull him into the room.

"Aw, not today, Pauly. Sorry, guys." Luke waited for them to dejectedly release him rather than yank himself free. "Got some big ol' Councilor shoes to fill."

"What's a Counc'lor?" a little girl asked.

"Means I get to watch out for everyone, Elly."

"You already do that," Pauly said.

"Sure, but now it's official, from the Alpha himself."

"The new one who's nice?" another girl asked.

"Nice enough." Luke winked. "Way nicer than the old one. I gotta help him with something today, okay?"

"This him?" Pauly asked, tilting his head at Preston.

"Nah, this is my friend. Preston is a rat, and a real powerful witch."

"Not that powerful," Preston said.

"He lies sometimes too," Luke mock-whispered, making the kids laugh. "Soon though, when I sort through things, I'll be back for story time. You guys get a book picked out, got it?"

They all raced over to start looking through a pathetic collection of children's books, some of which were old enough to be missing front covers.

"It's okay," Luke said softly, something it seemed he'd been telling himself for too long. Maybe Preston's expression betrayed that he didn't agree, because Luke said, "Really. It's okay. We're gonna fix things, right?"

"Yeah," Preston said, not having realized how much change was needed in places he hadn't seen. He'd been too focused on changing things for himself to recognize how much everyone else had pits to crawl out of. "We are."

Luke smiled, and some of the knot in Preston's chest unraveled as they moved back to the main hallway toward another collection of rooms.

There were activity rooms for older kids and general ones for adults. The kids' TV room included one of each type of gaming console, several of which Luke admitted to maybe possibly having stolen himself. Anything the people here needed or wanted they had to fight and scrounge for. It was no wonder none of the ones Luke had tried to enlist had said no.

"Ta-da!" Luke swept his arms out when they entered a room with four beds, which was better than most setups, probably because Luke had been here for so long. He went to what must be a communal closet to grab clothes. "Home sweet home. Want anything?"

Seeing the very homemade printed TEAM JACOB shirt Luke pulled on, which Preston hoped was scavenged from the trash and not a conscious fashion statement—and not because Preston was TEAM EDWARD or anything—he shook his head. "I'd say change of underwear, but you don't appear to own any."

"I do too!" Luke laughed. "I just don't always wear 'em. Seriously, anything?"

"Maybe grab a few things to bring with us. There's no telling when we'll be back in the den."

"Will do. I'll grab a bunch in case anyone else needs something." Luke pulled a bag from the depths of the closet and started shoving various articles into it, while still needing to change his bottom half. He eventually set aside a pair of underwear and non-hole-ridden jeans.

"What are we going to do about the Marleys?" Preston asked.

"No one I asked said they'd seen 'em, but people tend to keep their heads down here. We can take a deeper look around and maybe hit the last buyer if we strike out? At least that'd be something."

Preston leaned against the wall beside the door, feeling a gnaw of unease. He didn't like this place. The options shouldn't be between a good home with awful company or a bad home with kind ones. There had to be a middle ground somewhere.

Although Luke's unabashed ease with stripping wasn't completely terrible since he shed his torn pants right there in the middle of the room with the door wide open. Bari and Bash might be more classically GQ attractive, but Luke's litheness, with freckles on his shoulders, ginger hair, and too skinny limbs with the occasional flex of muscle captured Preston's attention far better.

He mourned the lost view when Luke finished covering up again.

"Hey there, stranger," a female voice preceded the blur of someone entering, right past Preston without noticing him against the wall.

Another cat, smelled like. She sure walked with the slink of a feline, too skinny like most people here, but flaunting her long, lean lines in black pleather leggings, a crop top, and more bangles on her wrists than Nell. Her long curled blond hair made Preston picture a heavily painted face in drug store makeup, but he couldn't see for certain with how she focused on Luke.

"Hi, Cookie!" Luke greeted. "What are you doing hanging around the Shelter? I thought you got an apartment with Marney."

"I did. But I had to come calling to ask *you* the same thing. Everyone says you're hanging around still, while word is you got a seat at the circle. Did Bash really ask you in person and whisk you off in that big fancy car of his father's?"

"Yep!" Luke laughed. "It was wild! I'm on circle business right now. Uh—" His eyes darted to Preston as if readying to introduce him, but before he could say anything, Cookie twined her arms around Luke's neck. She plastered herself on him like cling-wrap, and as Luke's eyes went back to her, his arms instinctively went to her hips like they'd been in this position before.

"Busy boy. Guess that means you don't have time for an old friend?" She teased press-on nails along the collar of Luke's shirt, reminding Preston of that rent boy back on Shaw Street. "Maybe when whatever business you're doing is done, I can come see you at the den. Always wanted to see what those rooms look like. Bet you got a real nice one."

"Haven't picked one yet," Luke said, flexing his fingers up her waist. "But sure! I can show you around. It's wicked awesome."

"Like you." Cookie's voice fell softer, and when she lifted onto her toes, Preston's instinct was to seize her with his spirit chains and yank her out of Luke's arms. But then she kissed Luke like had obviously been her intention, and Luke didn't stop her.

The connection was deep, comfortable, and practiced, and Luke smiled when she pulled away with a final flick of her tongue at his lips.

"Don't forget the little people, huh?" She tugged on his shirt collar, snapping it against his chest, and pivoted to make a grand exit. "Oh! I didn't realize we had an audience." She grinned, meeting eyes with Preston the entire way out the door.

Luke's face went from dazed to *shit* in seconds.

"It's not what you think!"

"So, you just kiss everyone like that?"

"It was reflex!"

Oh, Preston wished he had something to snap in half.

"No! I mean…." Luke dug his hands into his hair. "Okay, yeah, we've hooked up, and I'm sorry the kiss was automatic, but there's nothing between us. Nothing real. We're just, ya know… friends with benefits."

"Urg." Preston blinked eyes that suddenly felt hot. "What did I expect? Obviously not restraint or propriety. You are so—"

"What?" Luke finished before Preston could say it. "Disgusting? Forgot for a second. Coz I'm just a low-born Shelter kid, right, who doesn't know any better?"

Preston pursed his lips for a comeback.

"You haven't been able to wipe that sneer off your face the entire time we've been here," Luke said, stalking toward him, "which I thought was sympathy from the little rich boy who didn't realize how bad other people had it, but guess it was just loathing."

"*Hey*," Preston growled, "you're the one who kissed someone in front of me after you've been rambling on about fairy tale nonsense because of a smell."

"It *was* nonsense before you!"

Preston pushed from the wall to leave, only for Luke to grab his arm.

"*She* kissed *me*. And it didn't mean anything. This has been my life, in case you forgot. So, sorry if taking mutual, consenting pleasure in the few people I could trust growing up here was the only way to feel safe and like anything mattered about my existence. I thought I was lucky to be alive most days, and that... maybe someday having a mate was a nice dream to imagine if I lived long enough.

"Then I caught one whiff of a pretty rat...." He trailed off with the glimmer of a smile returning and reached for Preston's face.

Preston leaned away from him, but Luke held firm. When he slid his palm against Preston's stubble, Preston's eyes grew hotter, and he blinked again to banish the impulse to enjoy this.

It's just impulse, Trace, the sort of thing mongrels give in to. You don't truly like that boy the way you think. Impulses trick us into doing dirty, dreadful things, but given time, those urges will fade.

"It wasn't a fairy tale after you," Luke went on with soft, breathy repose. "I just gotta retrain my brain a little, which, be honest... you do too." He smiled wider, sweeter, and seemed to rethink holding Preston in place. He dropped his hands. "Sorry about the kiss, especially since I'd rather—"

Preston wasn't sure which part of his brain surged him forward, but he knew the catalyst was a mix between his parents' voices in his head and Luke's right here in front of him.

The kiss was too harsh, with a clack of teeth putting dents in their inner lips. Preston wasn't sure how to open his mouth the right way to make their tongues connect as wonderfully as they had yesterday, but it was still better than fighting what he wanted.

The heat in his eyes had traveled to his cheeks, and when he pulled back, he swiped a tongue over strawberry-flavored lips.

"Crap," Luke cringed, smacking his lips together. "Lip gloss."

Maybe half of Preston still wanted to storm out.

"Please don't let me being an idiot ruin this!" Luke sputtered.

"Don't call me a little rich boy."

"I won't."

"Or kiss other people."

"I won't! I really am sorry. Maybe we can… try that again?" Luke made a point of scrubbing the remaining lip gloss from his mouth, and Preston didn't deny his renewed descent.

Luke controlled the kiss this time, which was softer, slower, knowing just how to coax Preston's lips apart so that the breach of his tongue happened as naturally as the gasp it evoked. Luke tasted a little like strawberry still, but Preston intended to lick away every trace and replace that taste with his own.

The squeeze of Luke's hands at Preston's hips told him it wasn't practiced with that girl because she meant something, but because Luke had experience with things Preston didn't, and that's where hands were supposed to go when someone held you. Preston reached for Luke's hips too, and the T-shirt, however appalling, was soft, though not as soft as Luke's skin when Preston teased his thumbs up underneath the fabric.

Luke offered one last coil of his tongue. "Maybe I can keep making it up to you by… kissing somewhere else?"

The first divergence was a kiss to Preston's cheek, and then Luke moved with slow, gentler kisses across his jawline and down his neck. Where Preston's stubble faded to smooth skin, Luke's tongue darted out, causing a tingle down the back of Preston's neck that traveled low into the depths of his belly.

His shirt was a button-down, and Luke undid the next two buttons to spread it wider and kiss across his clavicle. Luke unbuttoned the rest, but changed course with his mouth, kissing hot and wet and so slow back up the path he'd descended. It was the barest Preston had been in Luke's presence aside from Isabella's, but this felt more exposed, especially when Luke's hand traveled lower with light fingers dragging over Preston's crotch.

"Whoa!" Luke's hand and mouth flinched away as Bernard and Bianca scurried out of Preston's pockets. He chuckled, turning to watch them climb onto one of the beds. "Probably wanted to get a better view, the pervs." He looked back, and his eyes were alight with mischief. "Should we give 'em something worth watching?"

Preston didn't realize how close he'd returned to the wall until his back hit it. He let his weight sag, having no idea how to respond to Luke reaching to unbutton his slacks.

"W-we don't have time for this!" he said when Luke slowly drew down the zipper and slid his hand inside.

"Ya sure?" Luke's grin was wickeder than the gleam in his eyes.

He dropped to his knees.

Ambient sounds faded, like Preston had been plunged into his own private bubble where the only things that existed were him and Luke's hands reaching up to pull his pants down.

"Um, you not saying stop or no is great and all, but… I kinda need you to say yes." Luke paused with both sets of fingers folded inside the hem of the slacks.

There were only two possible answers, and Luke was blinking up at Preston with mischief fading to affection and so much patience. He wasn't only attractive, he was sweet, caring, and so wonderfully dorky, without ever seeming to feel shame for any of it.

We'll find you a nice, proper rat girl, and you'll forget all about such… fancies.

He was eleven when his father said that, with a crush on a boy at school, not even striding into puberty yet, but he knew. He didn't forget—ever. And there was never a nice or "proper" enough girl, rat or otherwise, to change that. College had been Preston's last chance. If he didn't escape the mandate to find and bring home a mate, his parents would start looking for him.

But the only person who'd even come close to capturing his attention…

Preston breathed in with a deeper sag against the wall.

…smelled like *sage*, attempting to banish all his life's negativity with a bat of blue eyes.

"Y-yes."

The cool air striking him at being pulled free with his pants and underwear dropping was magnified by how hot his skin had become. Luke's first tentative stroke down Preston's shaft made his head snap back with a sharp thud against the wall.

"*Fuck.*"

They were to the side of the door, hidden from view, but with no desire for interruptions, Preston lashed out with an invisible tether of telekinesis to swing the door closed.

There was wetness budding at his tip that Luke boldly swiped a thumb through, coating Preston's head with winding circles. Preston had rarely allowed *himself* to do this. He'd never realized how much another person's touch could amplify—

"Ah!" He bucked into Luke's grip, and it felt like heaven with a wet slide to pave the way through those pearly gates. His hips started an automatic rocking, in and out of the pressure Luke offered.

"Shit, you're pretty. So pretty…," Luke muttered from his prostrate position, blinking upward with Preston's cock so near his face. "Rosy cheeks, stubble, eyes all dark, and panting with your lips falling open like they need something between 'em. I know mine do." He bent closer, and already Preston feared he'd finish in a juvenile burst of oversensation and stain Luke's crooked smile.

The light calluses on Luke's hands made Preston's eyes water from the textured stroking.

"These thighs are like cream I wanna lap up." Luke pressed a kiss to one, and his ginger hair tickled Preston's shaft. "Your pretty cock too…." He breathed hotly upon it. "Bet it's been real neglected."

"A-a cock can't be pretty."

"Eye of the beholder." Luke grinned, and then looked contemplative. "Is that why they call it a beholder in games and D&D? Coz of the eyes?"

Preston stifled a laugh behind both hands that he knew would erupt into a moan that any sharp-eared shifters outside the room would hear. How could Luke be so… *Luke* while rhythmically pumping Preston's cock?

Luke grinned wider at the reaction. "I sure am beholding a whole lot right now." At last, he bent the last bit closer, slowing his pumping hand, and squeezed tighter as he brought Preston's cock to his lips like he was readying to tongue a push-pop.

A mouth was so different from stroking fingers, almost too much, making Preston squirm and pant as his hands fell to his sides with a whimper.

This was practiced too, something familiar to Luke, the way he'd squeeze from Preston's head to his base, following the stroke with his whole mouth swallowing Preston down, and then pull off to do it again. Practiced—because he'd done it before, for others, and the thought of Luke on his knees for anyone else made Preston's chest burn with envy.

Luke wouldn't kiss anyone else, not anywhere on their bodies, ever again. The spike of possessiveness was a promise in Preston's mind, just as Luke had promised in words, and it eased the jealousy that this was his now.

His.

Luke changed patterns with a spread of both hands up Preston's thighs to nudge them apart and frame his balls between thumbs and forefingers, swallowing Preston deeper and bobbing with more frantic rhythm.

Everything was white when Preston squeezed his eyes shut, and when he opened them, the whole world exploded in fireworks. He clawed at the wall, but it wasn't enough purchase, prompting him to reach forward, still trembling, and grab the lone anchor of Luke's fiery hair. It was soft and wavy, and gripping it in both hands and lightly holding Luke's head with a gentle caress down the back of it seemed to spur Luke to suck harder—

Preston's orgasm startled a squeak from his lips, with Stage Two aspects flickering over his form unbidden. He reined them in quickly so his claws wouldn't scratch Luke's head in an unpleasant finale. His cheeks burned from not having warned Luke first, but the impish and very much *purring* alley cat licked his lips and blinked lazily upward like he had enjoyed that just as much as Preston.

"See... it's you," Luke said, lips shiny and reddened. He butted his head against Preston's thigh in a soft nuzzle and even lapped out for an extra taste of Preston's softening cock. "Definitely you."

It took a few steadying beats for Preston to feel capable of rational thought, or movement, or any response to how incredible that had felt. His legs were jelly, and if it hadn't been for the wall, he might have oozed right to the floor.

None of this felt like a maybe anymore.

Luke stood, bringing Preston's pants and underwear up to tuck him away.

"What about you?" Preston asked, feeling something firm and eager digging into his hip.

"We got work to do. You can pay me back later. If you want to," Luke said, and it should have been impossible for someone to look that sexy and soft and roguish all at once.

Preston kissed him, allowing the firmness of Luke's clothed cock to dig harder into his hip. The salty tang of his own taste in Luke's mouth was overshadowed by the smell of sage that evoked its own faint taste, like refreshing herbs in a garden he could have happily lounged in like a contented... cat.

Luke's arms wrapped tighter around him, and even if it was annoying that he, like most people, was taller than Preston, Preston didn't think he minded as much being engulfed by these arms.

"I don't know!" A loud but fading voice moved swiftly past the door, like someone storming by in the middle of an argument.

"Stop! *Jordy*!" a second voice cried.

Luke's head snapped to the door, and Preston leapt from the wall to retrieve Bernard and Bianca and slip them back into his pockets. Without words needing to pass between them, they were out of the room in seconds, following the retreating voices at a stealthy pace.

"Would you stop already!" Jude bellowed, and Preston held Luke back from cresting the corner they had just watched the foxes turn, since they had obviously halted. "What do you mean, you don't know? Where to go through this place? Because at least that I'd understand, since it's a damn maze."

"I am looking for an exit to get out the other side."

"To go where?"

"I can't tell you."

"What are you talking about? Me? You can't tell me? What is it you think I won't understand?"

"It's not that. I can't tell you, because…."

"Because you don't know," Jude answered with a scoff. "What about where you went yesterday? Can you not tell me that either?"

"I'm sorry," Jordana said softer, her voice fading as if she was backing out of her brother's hold. "I need to go. I need to get there."

"To *where*?"

"Please… just go back to the others." The sound of heeled feet came next at a brisk run, but no pursuing feet followed.

Preston squeezed Luke's arm, and together they moved around the corner to find Jude defeatedly slumped against the wall, with Jordana already out of sight.

When he saw them, he sighed but didn't try to flee.

Preston straightened to the tallest height he could manage. "You better start talking."

Chapter 11

"YOU KNEW she left, had no idea where, and still didn't say anything?" Preston barked.

"She's my *sister*," Jude answered. "I wasn't going to rat her out before I knew what was going on, but she won't tell me anything. Keeps saying she can't, doesn't know, isn't trying to hide anything, but then what the hell is she doing?"

Luke had the bag of clothing he'd packed over his shoulder. They were walking as they talked, following Jordana at a safe distance. Once she was out of the Shelter, Bernard and Bianca had been able to pick up her scent again, but Luke and the others had decided to hold back and see where she led them.

He was trying to keep a calmer head, but he was a little disappointed their new friends had been hiding things after all.

"Don't say 'rat her out,'" he said. "It's offensive."

Luke was only half-serious but appreciated that both Preston and Jude cracked smiles.

Jude dug a pack of cigarettes and a lighter out of his pocket, which wasn't easy with one arm sideways across his body.

"*That's* offensive," Preston said when he lit up.

"We're outside, aren't we? Just let me have this." Jude took a slow puff with the cigarette between his teeth while he shoved everything back into his pocket. Even like that he looked cool, dashing in that James Dean kind of way but sexier with his long hair. What would usually be a confident demeanor to match, however, was a far cry away. "Jordy's never kept secrets from me before."

"Then it's gotta be something big," Luke offered, and then spoke on to appease Jude's drooping shoulders, "and it'll be better once we figure things out. She had scratches on her arms. Those were from before the attack on the den, weren't they?"

"Yeah, when she snuck out. I don't know from what."

"What's your real story?" Preston demanded, playing bad cop again with a less tactful tone. "How did you end up at the Glenwood Shelter? There was something you didn't say before about your family."

"That has nothing to do with what's happening now," Jude snapped.

"Humor me. I want to know."

Luke had almost forgotten how he'd put his foot in his mouth, asking how well the foxes had known their parents.

Jude was between them, making them an inverted *V* along the sidewalk. His amber eyes slid to Luke. Given anything could have relevance on the situation, he nodded in encouragement, and Jude let out a long breath, billowing an added puff of smoke.

"We weren't always Shelter kids."

"Accident?" Luke prompted.

"Not exactly. You remember I said we were born in Brookdale? Mom's last name was Marley, but Dad's was Schwarz."

"As in *Benedict* Schwarz?" Preston queried. "Son of Matron June Schwarz?"

"Why do you think both our names have *J*s in them?" Jude smirked grimly.

"Should I know these people?" Luke asked.

"Think of my family here," Preston said, "only foxes and ten times wealthier and more powerful. If Brookdale wasn't so traditional about wolves being in charge, the Schwarzes would be the ones running that circle, Alpha and all."

"Like, a long time ago? Can't be now if Jude and Jordana...." Luke trailed off at the extra pinch in Jude's brow. Rather than put his foot in his mouth again, he clamped his mouth shut to let Jude explain.

"About the time Jordy and I turned nine, dear old Gran discovered that when Mom and Dad got hitched, Mom was already pregnant—from a different fox. It was a whirlwind marriage she now figured was a sham, and her grandchildren weren't really hers.

"You don't humiliate someone as powerful as Matron June. She not only kicked our mom to the curb, she took us away from her and made sure to send us to a different city's Shelter. We never knew how to track Mom down, and she never found us."

"What about your dad?" Luke asked.

"If he looked or cared... he never found us either."

Luke met Preston's eyes, while Jude's were trained ruefully forward. Between them, it really was a who's who of who'd had it worse with parents.

"That sucks, man," Luke said, nudging Jude with a buck of his arm. Sometimes those were the best words, not I'm sorry, and definitely not it'll be okay, but simply....

Wow, that blows.

"Yeah... it really did," Jude said. "But none of that has anything to do with the mess happening now, other than proving Jordy can't be doing anything malicious on purpose. She wouldn't. Not without telling me. We've been all each other has our whole lives. She wouldn't not tell me this."

"Then why hasn't she?" Preston asked.

Before Jude could answer, Preston thrust out an arm to keep them from continuing. With a tilt of his head, he closed his eyes and frowned.

"The rats lose her again?" Luke whispered.

"They got her. It's where she's going that worries me." He opened his eyes and dashed forward into a jog. "Come on!"

They were on the same streets where everything else had happened, sprinting past shifters heading to and from businesses or loitering on sidewalks. This was right in the middle of the most concentrated of shifter populace, back on Shaw Street, where Preston had first seen that rune.

It was that exact alley he led them down now.

A twist in Luke's gut made his steps stutter, last in line as he followed Jude, who followed Preston, neither of whom seemed to realize that fur was beginning to sprout over their skin, claws extending, fangs growing, and even Luke's eyesight had sharpened.

Shit.

"Jordana!" Preston snarled, and it *was* a snarl, for all three of them were beginning to shift, coming upon an entranced Jordana as she pulled something from a hidden notch in the wall.

"Wait!" Luke tried to warn them to stop, back away, leave the alley, but even as he stilled his feet, he couldn't prevent the shift from happening or will himself to turn around and flee.

It *hurt*. Not even the very first time shifting did he remember feeling such pain, like his body was being stretched and snapped into a different shape by foreign hands. Finally, Preston and Jude realized the same was happening to them, staring in a panic and howling with the same pain.

Jordana alone was unaffected as she drew the object closer to her chest. She cradled it, turning toward them with eyes blank, almost pupilless, as if unseeing or a puppet.

"I will gather the flock," she said monotone and held the object outward—a totem, small enough to hold in one hand, depicting each of the five tribes from bottom up: wolf, cat, rat, lizard, and raptor.

A scream was expelled from Luke's throat as his body burst to Stage Three like his skin was tearing, and he clawed at his clothing in a vain attempt to dig past the pain. The bag he'd been carrying dropped, and just when he thought he had never been as monstrous a version of himself, the strain and stress of the forced shift lessened, and he shrank, smaller and smaller, until what little of his clothing remained didn't matter anymore, because he was an average-sized alley cat.

He wanted to check on Preston and Jude, but Jordana was walking toward them, still holding the totem, and the closer it got, the more Luke couldn't do anything but stare at it.

"*We* will gather the flock," she said, and as she moved past them to exit the alley, Luke, Preston, and Jude all followed.

THIS WAS definitely not the same as the Moondust.

Try as Preston might, his feet kept moving forward—all four of them—right on Jordana's heels, amidst Luke in his tabby form and Jude as a white-and-red fox.

What was worse was Preston could *think*. He didn't want to do this. He didn't want to shift at all, yet he and the others were slaves to Jordana's whims—or rather, to the totem's.

"The hell?"

"Who are you?"

"What's—" A flinch ended the final utterance.

It was Joey the rent boy and his fellow streetwalkers, all of whom keeled over in Jordana's wake and began to shift. Others along the street and exiting businesses took note of Jordana too, hardly able to ignore a beautiful unblinking redhead holding a shifter artifact, with a gaggle of animals trailing her.

The screams of those affected were terrible and drew more attention from others, who raced out of buildings and approached, only to suffer the same awful pain, forcing them through the stages to their basest selves. Preston with his rats wasn't the Pied Piper, the totem was, tethered to Jordana, ensnaring every shifter who came close, until a horde of rats, cats, wolves, lizards, and birds all followed her like Noah leading animals to the ark.

Only Preston couldn't begin to guess their destination. It seemed to be go forth and gather, adding to their masses, but eventually they would spill out of shifter territory to areas packed with humans. Everyone would see their neighbors turning into monsters and then animals, following the will of some strange, ethereal woman, and the disaster that would bring if it wasn't stopped was insurmountable.

> *"It begins with an exodus of siblings and charm,*
> *Neither knowing the extent of their greed's lasting harm.*
> *All beasts will howl on and rage, none immune*
> *If the source is not stopped by wane on Harvest Moon."*

Not charm, as in charisma, but an object, a *totem*.

At least now Preston understood the rune and prismatic leftovers from the alley, because Jordana had hidden *item number eleven* in the wall and kept going back for it. If she had been fighting its pull, she was obviously powerless now.

"The hell are you?" a new voice growled.

From Preston's formation nearest Jordana, he could barely see the man but watched him pull a vial and down its contents. The man started to shift, but not like the others.

One of McDonough's men, maybe on the streets looking for Preston and the circle, was pitting fire against fire. He charged as soon as he became a towering werewolf, swiping aside animals like swatting flies and opening his great maw to snap at Jordana with a lunge—before he was swarmed, and *swarmed*, because as strong as he may be, he was no match for the sheer numbers at Jordana's command.

The werewolf was overcome in moments, bitten, clawed at, and piled on to bring him down. As soon as Jordana moved past him, even Moondust wasn't a match for the totem, for the werewolf shrank. By the time Preston and the others had gone by, he was a simple wolf, who limped to his feet to follow in line.

A fireball exploded in a cluster of their multitude. All Preston's instincts urged him to flee, but the totem's thrall forced him to stay. Word must be spreading, because a line of magic users could be seen in the distance, trying to prevent them from leaving the safety of these streets.

Another fireball struck, hitting between them as a warning, but none of the animals could heed the threat.

Someone at the center must have very strong magic, for she formed a ball of lightning larger than any Preston could fashion and released it in an ever-expanding wave. It struck with enough force that Preston was knocked prone and almost flipped completely, too light in rat form to hold his ground.

Jordana didn't slow. The magic hardly seemed to touch her, and even the wave of lightning barely disturbed the gentle billowing of her long ginger hair.

Some of the magic users charged, and all Preston could do was mourn their folly, for nothing he asked of his limbs was answered. He was back in line, between Jude and Luke, with no idea how to sway this in their favor. Anyone who got too close was added to their numbers, and anything thrown at them from farther away couldn't do enough.

Then Preston saw Siobhan join the witches that must be her agents.

Deanna was there too.

No. They needed to get away. They didn't understand. Just as pure firepower wasn't enough to take down Moondust users, it wouldn't be enough against this many animals, even when some were small. Preston knew firsthand how much more effective numbers were than strength. He counted on it every time he summoned his rats.

His rats!

Bernard and Bianca!

Maybe he couldn't deviate from where Jordana led him, but Bernard and Bianca could, and they were still nearby. They were normal rats, not shifters, and as Preston reached out to summon them, he realized he could, and willed them to race toward Siobhan and Deanna.

The horde moved slowly, but Bernard and Bianca zipped through their ranks, urged by Preston's pleading for them to hurry—*hurry, don't be afraid, just get to them and make them understand.*

More of Siobhan's agents and passersby were succumbing to forced shifts, unable to slow the momentum of the masses descending on them and still not understanding that they were throwing themselves into the fire.

Then Bernard and Bianca reached their targets.

Preston feared Siobhan and Deanna might fling them from their shoulders, clearly wary to suddenly have rats climbing up their bodies when so many shifters were proving to be enemies. But these women, who Preston knew so little of after only days in the circle together, were exceptional, like everyone else Bash had tapped.

He saw the moment they recognized the smell of these rats as not shifters, but creatures they knew, nuzzling them frantically instead of attacking.

Both women's eyes darted back to the horde, and Preston knew they understood. The shifters couldn't control themselves and Preston himself was among them.

"Stop!" Siobhan cried.

"Get back!" Deanna joined her. "We need to—"

"Freeze! We—we…." The at first commanding shout trailed off as two police officers rounded a corner from the next street down.

Shit. Someone must have fetched them, or maybe they'd heard the commotion of screams and fighting and came on their own, but they had to be human, given the way their aimed guns dropped at the sight of a zoo headed toward them.

There wasn't time, and with the failure of magic and the inability to get closer to Jordana amidst the throng of beasts she commanded, Preston had to admit, what Deanna chose to do next was the only course of action.

She snatched one of the officers' guns and fired.

Chapter 12

DEANNA HIT Jordana in the shoulder, merciful but still thankfully enough to send her reeling.

Preston regained control of his limbs like a whiplash, a taut cord pulled tight enough to snap. Not knowing how long the reprieve might last, he howled as he shifted human, lashing out with his spirit chains to wrap around the totem loosened in Jordana's grasp.

"No!" she shrieked as it was ripped from her fingers, and batted after it, causing it to tumble free and spin end over end through the air.

Luke, human again too, leapt up to catch it, grinning in triumph when he landed on the pavement. The longer he held it, however, the more his smile molded into a grimace, and Preston could feel that same lurch in his gut as when the forced shift first happened.

"Drop it!" Jude cried, also human, but when Luke merely stood there, Jude wrenched the totem from his hands and snapped it in two before the chaos could start again.

Luke gasped, blinking rapidly, as the sensations that had been returning in Preston vanished.

Jordana blinked too, shaking her head as if waking from a deep sleep, and more around them began to turn human, creating a mass of naked bodies in the street that the human officers gaped at.

Jordana collapsed.

"Jordy!" Jude's knees hit the ground beside her, and he dropped the remaining pieces of the totem, which Preston hastily gathered. It might be powerless now, but they needed to figure out what it was and where it came from.

Meeting eyes with Luke, who stood amidst a backdrop of bare skin, Preston figured this incident would probably rid him of ever being bashful around naked bodies again.

Deanna and Siobhan took charge, sending out agents to aid everyone and help clear the scraps of torn clothing from the street. Must have been a gas leak or something, had everyone seeing things, fights breaking out, and a little too much friskiness going on, they could be heard explaining to the officers, who seemed only too happy to believe something that fit their worldviews over *Animorphs* existing.

The one whose gun had been taken didn't even seem to care as it was passed back to him, and the explanations allowed everyone to disperse for any needed medical attention and to find new clothes—aside from the wolf who'd taken the Moondust and was now extra fatigued, as it seemed the totem had counteracted any lingering effects.

Preston offered his fellow circle members grateful salutes, summoned Bernard and Bianca back to him, seized the wolf before his strength returned enough to protest, and once he was certain the cops weren't looking, he ported them and Luke and the Marleys back to his dorm room.

LUKE WASN'T sure he liked that *Dimension Door* thing after a second experience, though maybe the reason his stomach roiled was because of the forced shifting.

Since he'd once again lost his clothing, he had Preston port the two of them back to the alley to collect the bag with extra outfits, allowing him to then pass around something to wear for him, Preston, Jude, and the wolf who Preston had nabbed.

Dash and Dari were there, and rightfully concerned at the state of the people who'd popped in unannounced. After settling a passed-out Jordana on the bed to treat her wound, they could finally get some answers.

"I don't know shit!" the brutish wolf spat, but Luke recognized a liar when he saw one.

Or he'd always thought he did. Jordana was an outlier he hoped would have a good explanation when she woke.

"It would be in your best interest to know something," Bash warned, "or you might run out of usefulness."

The wolf squirmed in the desk chair they'd bound him to using fragments of old clothing. "Question *her*." He jutted his chin at Jordana. "She's the one who caused that madness."

"I plan to," Bash said, "but right now I'm questioning you." He thrust the chair backward and slammed his hands atop the desk on either side of the wolf, bringing them threateningly close. "Even if Sean didn't know about that totem, he knows something. *Someone knows something.* So, you are going to tell me, along with who besides you is out on the streets, who is at the den, and how far along they are with making more Moondust."

The wolf had to be twice Bash's size, but even if Bash hadn't been hovering, his presence would have made him seem larger. It was the type of authority someone had to be born with and was always true of Alphas.

"Sean didn't know about… whatever that thing was," the wolf said. "No one did. The first artifacts we ground up didn't do nothing like that."

"Ground up?" Bari said, like that was the most horrifying revelation.

"How else were we gonna get enough? The plan was to find a synthetic way to make more, but we needed another stash of the real thing. Some cursed charm wasn't part of the plan. What that fucking thing did was insane."

"Yeah, well, so was the carnage left behind by one of your partners in crime," Preston snapped. "That mess left at Conrad's club was worse than what we just went through, and all because of that drug."

"No!" the wolf roared, and then furrowed his brow with an added snarl. "I mean… fine, Harry was taking the drug, but it doesn't make you crazy. Something else must have happened to cause him to tear through people like that and bust up a convenience store."

"*What?*" Bash demanded.

"I don't know. Never seen anything like what that totem thing caused while we were testing the drug, okay? All I know is the base for it is ancient bone dust from shifter artifacts."

"We know that," Preston said. "We also know that's why your boss and others were going after more. What we don't know is who gave those foxes over there the original lead that the items stored with the totem were the next best take."

"How should I know?" the wolf said with what Luke had to admit seemed like honest confusion. "I don't even think Sean or Connie do. They just wanted the goods. But I ain't telling you shit about anything else!"

He put on a good poker face, but Luke almost laughed, because he could easily read when Bash leaned closer into the wolf's space that he would cave.

"I think you'll tell me everything."

By the time Jordana roused—the bullet in her shoulder thankfully having gone straight through—Siobhan and Deanna were back from damage control, and the wolf had spilled his guts and then some. So long as he didn't try to escape, he'd be allowed asylum for his assistance after they retook the den, when everyone else with the McDonoughs would be banished.

Whether the same would prove true for Jordana, Bash still seemed to be deciding.

"I swear… I couldn't control what I was doing," she said, sitting up but leaned against the wall the bed rested against, sporting a matching wrapped shoulder to her brother's. "I couldn't even say anything about it. I tried. Jude…." She looked to him with moisture pooling in her eyes. "I tried so many times to tell you, but I couldn't. Some force took the words from my tongue. Half the time, I didn't even remember what happened."

"But you remember now," Bash said.

"It was after we got here and were holed up where we had the items stashed. I was cataloging everything, and… when I got to the totem, I couldn't stop looking at it. We were lying low for a few days before meeting with the buyers to make sure any immediate heat from the theft had died down. I went out a few times and didn't even realize I had the totem in my pocket."

"Which was when the original forced shifts happened that got recorded," Bash surmised.

"Yes?" she answered like she wasn't certain herself. "The pull from it, what it could do, wasn't as strong at first. I'd snap out of it, realize what happened, and try to get rid of the damn thing, but… it always ended up back in my pocket."

"Then we had our first meeting, when Isabella tried to renege on our deal, and we ran. Jude and I got separated, and I was afraid, so afraid, that if Isabella or her people found me, they'd take the totem. I knew I couldn't let that happen, so I hid it. Then I circled around to make sure no one saw."

"Which was when you ran past us," Luke said.

"I didn't mean to keep anything from you. I couldn't remember, couldn't think, couldn't say anything to anyone." She started to cry more openly, and Jude went to her to hug her to his side.

Bash looked like he might protest, but a pleading look from Bari beat Luke to the act of doing the same.

After a few moments of letting Jordana collect herself, Bash questioned her again.

"What happened next, when you snuck out of the den?"

"I never stopped thinking about it after tucking it away." She sniffled, staying in the hold of her brother. "It was like a siren song in the back of my head, like an actual voice, calling me to return to it. You trusted us more, and Jude was sleeping, and no one else was watching me, so I... left. I took the totem from its hiding spot, and the voice told me where to go."

"The speakeasy?" Preston asked.

"It wasn't specifically there, more like... anywhere I knew there would be a lot of shifters. There weren't many on the streets, and my feet just took me there. I saw your agents." She glanced at Siobhan. "They were hanging around the entrance. Before I reached them, the door opened, and this big wolf shoved the lizard woman outside. I remembered her. She was screaming for asylum. I... I think she'd known about Moondust before, and it was just coincidence that I'd caused her to shift.

"She thought it was connected and wanted protection from it all, but the wolves wouldn't listen. The agents intervened, tried to calm things down, but the wolf who'd shoved her outside took some Moondust to warn them away. Then I entered the alley... but they didn't see me at first.

"The others all started shifting, but it was slower with the wolf who'd taken the drug, and he... panicked, I think, believing what he felt was because of them, so he... started tearing them apart to make it stop. By the time he realized it was me, they were dead, and everyone else from the club was screaming and running past me, not staying long enough for the totem to affect them. That's when he ran too, before the change finished and he turned into an animal.

"The totem told me to follow. I think that's why he went into the convenience store and was crazed, because he could feel its pull just out of reach but didn't know how to escape.

"Maybe the totem wasn't as powerful yet, because seeing Siobhan and others snapped me to my senses, and I remembered seeing the bodies, and... I just wanted it all to go away. I stored the totem back in the alley and returned to the den before anyone noticed I was gone. You were all busy cleaning up my mess, so... it wasn't difficult. Jude was the only one who realized I'd left because he woke up while I was out, and then I couldn't tell him where I'd gone.

"I'm sorry," Jordana said again, hopefully feeling some comfort in how her brother tightened his hold—or as best he could with them both one-armed.

"Bash…," Luke appealed, pleased that almost everyone looked sympathetic, but Bash was impossible to read with his stony expression. "I believe her. None of this was her fault."

"Even though my agents died for it," Siobhan said, "I believe her too. She doesn't deserve to take the fall for this."

Bash looked at them, his circle and brother, standing in an arc around the bed with him at the center. "Being you're my advisors, and I think I agree with you… I'll heed your advice." He returned to Jordana, who sniffled harder like she wasn't sure she wanted to be forgiven. "You weren't in control of your actions. You aren't to blame. And we have one less disaster looming. Assuming there's no more threat associated with that thing?" He glanced at Preston, who held the totem's pieces.

Luke wasn't sure he could explain what he'd felt those few seconds while he held it. It was a haze clouding his mind, like the memory of a dream after waking, but he thought he remembered a voice too.

He never wanted to feel that or a forced shift again.

"We should finish this privately," Preston said, and Bash didn't hesitate to agree.

They left Bari to keep an eye on the wolf and foxes, as the five present circle members gathered in the corner.

"Why am I not thrilled with what you're going to tell us?" Deanna said.

Preston snorted, holding the pieces of the totem out in one hand. It was honestly sort of cool-looking, and strange to think that something so small had been such a menace. "It's dormant. What troubles me are the details we still don't know. There was some sort of curse on this thing, but it shouldn't have been able to do what it did unless it was activated. If it was active when they stole it, they both would have been affected during the trip from Glenwood to Centrus."

"Maybe Jordana activated it on accident somehow," Luke said.

"Maybe. Or maybe someone was controlling Jordana through it. There's no way to know, even if whoever donated everything planned this. But why? Why would anyone want this to happen?"

"We can't find out who did the donating?" Siobhan asked.

Preston pocketed the totem fragments and pulled out the donation slip and list of artifacts. "We could try digging deeper with the people at the museum, but they might not listen to a bunch of kids from another city, even if they're shifters and heard about Bash becoming Alpha."

"Maybe in a few years," Deanna joked.

"Then all that matters is one disaster was averted," Bash said. "Now we need to fix the other one."

"Wait," Luke interjected, letting his voice carry to attract Jude and Jordana's attention. "What do you two know about the person who sent you on this path, to go after those specific artifacts?"

"It was just a tip," Jude said, "passed through the usual channels. We never met the originator, only knew we had buyers lined up."

"Anonymous tip?" Siobhan grumbled. "And an anonymous donation... great."

Luke didn't have suggestions for how to find out more; he just couldn't shake that they were still missing something. After all, Preston believed someone might have been using the totem to control Jordana through it, which was very different from a spell gone wrong or a curse.

It didn't assuage him that Preston had gone quiet and was staring with wide, haunted eyes at the lists in his hands like he'd discovered something else worth panicking over.

"What?" Luke prompted.

"*Fuck.*" Preston glared at the papers—at the buyers' list specifically. "Fuck!"

"What?" Bash asked more sternly.

"I know who the third buyer is."

"Seriously?" Luke squawked. "The weird-named guy, after all this time?"

"It's not a weird name." Preston dropped the papers with a snarl. "Payara Northwest is an anagram. Change the letters around and you get.... Preston Rathaway."

Everyone blinked at him—Luke and the tied-up traitor wolf included.

"Preston Rathaway the *second*, in this case. My father."

Chapter 13

DAY 5

HE SHOULD have seen it. He should have known.

Preston was almost certain he *had* seen the name Payara Northwest before, which was why it had seemed familiar at first glance, the address for that buyer too—because it was one of his father's shell companies—but he hadn't put the pieces together. He'd been distracted, careless, and so concerned with helping prevent Bash's prophecy that he'd missed one of the biggest clues to do just that.

His father was involved.

So much for not seeing his parents until they solved this.

The Rathaway family manor had a garishly large plot of land for still being within city limits, but then everyone on their block—if how far each enormous house was spread out from one another could still count as a block—was similarly gaudy. The main house was massive, even larger than the circle's den that was meant to house dozens of people if every circle member had a mate and children, with still enough room for guests. There was also a pool house on the family property, as well as a guest house nearest to the gate.

Preston stood at the gate now, having portalled directly there. It was early the next morning, with their clock ticking down faster than ever to the Harvest Moon. A power-hungry former Second in control of a dangerous drug was just as likely to cause Bash's prophecy as that totem.

Having mimicked Jordana's recent behavior, Preston snuck out before the others woke. They knew he planned to see his parents alone, they wouldn't cry, well, *wolf* with him being missing, but Luke had been adamant until the moment they passed out last night that he wanted to come along.

No way could Preston allow that, especially since this would be awkward enough when he didn't have his own clothes and was wearing a magenta T-shirt with the word *Chillax* emblazoned across the chest. None of the other options had been better.

Knowing the code for the gate by heart, Preston headed inside for the long walk through the grounds to the main house. He could have portalled closer, but he needed the trek to calm his nerves, passing perfectly trimmed hedges along both the driveway and the walking path beside it, with flowers planted along the edges, wilted from the heat, that would soon be in hibernation when the temperatures dropped.

Preston didn't bother knocking once he reached the front door, but their butler was waiting for him with a stern frown, alerted by the gate opening.

"Hello, Myerson," Preston said. "It's just me."

"Master Trace." The butler frowned deeper. "You didn't announce a visit today."

"It's an emergency. Are my parents both here?"

"Enjoying breakfast in the second dining hall. Would you...." He gave an abortive step forward when Preston made to move around him in the direction indicated and cleared his throat with a none-too-subtle scan down Preston's body. "Would you prefer a jacket or other change of attire, sir?"

"No," Preston said shortly, filled with the sudden desire to not change anything at all about his person. "Thank you."

The second dining hall was small, meant for breakfast or tea or intimate gatherings. Preston supposed some people might consider it quaint and sweet that his parents—and him when he'd lived here— always dined together, but when conversation was a mix of silence and stale topics, it was hard to think the same.

"Goodness!" Preston's mother exclaimed the moment he entered the room.

There was a six-person table with Preston's father at the end and his mother beside him to the left. The food and various types of drink littering the table was more than either would consume, and much of it would go to waste if not nicked by the servants.

And there was more than just the butler, all meant to be seen and not heard, and not seen either wherever possible.

"Trace." His father looked him over with as much scrutiny as Myerson, given he was in a suit. He always wore a suit. "Your hair's as unkempt as some stray. And what are you wearing?"

Preston looked like his mother—*pretty*, with the same dark hair and eyes—but her hair was up in a perfect bun, and she wore a sleeveless pantsuit in seafoam green. She was half Japanese, half Korean, and his father Thai. The surname Rathaway had originally been Rathawaha, but they'd changed it to fit in with American industry generations ago.

Of course, none of the more human politics or borders mattered to shifters, but their own prejudices made up for it.

"I'm afraid your thieves won't be coming," Preston said, flinging the list of buyers onto the table, which fluttered to land atop a stacked pile of croissants.

His father's neat stubble was the only similarity between them, and even with that, Preston saw both parents as alien now, after only a few days in the trenches with people who, until recently, would have been alien to him too.

His mother shifted her gaze between them, as Preston's father grabbed the list with more stoicism, and then crushed it in his fist.

"Drugs?" Preston spat at him. "I realize our family's dealings are far from legal to keep up this lifestyle of yours, but you have literally put the entire pack in jeopardy."

"Trace!" His mother leapt to her feet, tossing her napkin on the table like a glove thrown for a duel—though Preston had done it first. "How dare you barge in here without announcing yourself in that… getup, and hurl accusations at your father—"

"*Ari.*" The slice of his father's words made Preston's insides spasm, and he fought to not visibly flinch at the tone.

His father's eyes were lighter than his mother's, a contrastingly warm brown for a cold man.

"I don't know where you got that list—"

"I know what you've been doing," Preston cut him off, and his stomach heaved again, but he clenched his fists to keep steady, "so save me your bullshit and tell me if you had anything to do with giving the lead to the thieves, because whatever we don't know now, we are going to find out."

"We?" His father sneered as he stood to join his confused mother. "Just whose behalf are you speaking on?"

"Does it matter? Which authorities should I go to, hm? Maybe humans just to make things difficult for you, or how about straight to the Alpha?"

"Bashir?" his father scoffed. "Please. Baraka's whelp is not fit to defecate in his father's shoes."

"Dear—"

His father held up a hand, and as was typical in this house, his mother silenced. "You do not understand what you have involved yourself with. No, I did not contact those thieves, I invested in the operation. This drug will be monumental in the next phase of shifter evolution, and in the ascension of more worthy tribes to leadership. Baraka began the research—"

"But Sean McDonough and his brother continued it—I know," Preston said evenly, keeping his fists clenched to maintain his resolve.

"Then you must know what's become of it all, something I expect you to share. Do you understand what this could mean for tribes without as much physical power?"

Preston gawked at his father's naivety. "Everyone on Moondust I've encountered—and yes, I've encountered plenty—have been wolves or large cats. You think this drug can help our tribe grab more power? You're being used and more delusional than I thought."

"Enough!" his father barked, and again, the inclination to flinch and submit was hard to shake. "Our tribe must play the long game to find a foothold, you know that. Do you think it better to sit on the sidelines and allow this coup from a wolf barely older than you? Bashir is going to run this pack into the ground. We have heard rumors he's even let cats and a lizard into his circle. He is hardly fit to lead."

"Right...." Preston gave a bitter laugh. "But a dangerous drug, and someone like McDonough, who's willing to completely go against tradition, is okay so long as it fits what's best for you."

"Darling...," his mother tried to interject more softly, but Preston knew it was more to appease his father than him, "the family comes first, always. That should hardly be a surprise to you."

Meaning if she had known about this before now, she didn't care.

"Does it?" Preston asked. "In the ways that matter? Although, you know... maybe family shouldn't always come first. Not blood anyway. Maybe there are more important things than the next piece of jewelry you get at a fucking bullshit charity auction."

"Trace!" his father roared, and oh, the desire to flinch was strong, but Preston wouldn't—he *wouldn't*.

Then yelling from outside the room jerked all three of their heads to the door.

There was arguing between a more frantic voice and Myerson trying to keep his decorum, while insisting that whoever had burst into the house needed to leave.

Preston knew the more frantic voice.

Shit.

"Sir, do not force me to call the authorities—"

"Oh, can it, man, I'm friends with—Pres." Luke startled with a relieved smile upon appearing in the doorway—wearing a worse T-shirt than Preston, since it said "I'm with Stupid" with an arrow pointing down, and what did that even—urg!

Preston was going to skin that cat alive when they were alone, and he saw the exact moment when Luke recognized his fate.

Good.

"*What* are you doing here?"

"I… I thought—"

"Young man, you are going to listen to me very carefully," Preston's father spoke over them like a viper dripping venom, and Preston looked back to find him beet-red with anger hotter than his own. "You are going to get that *riffraff* out of my house, change out of that ridiculous shirt, stow your opinions about things you do not understand, and explain to me exactly why you are not at school right now where you belong."

Everything about the order made Preston want to bow his head, avert his eyes, *obey*, like he had countless times in the past. He might still be young, but he was a grown man who didn't need to heed every word his parents told him. He shouldn't. Especially when those things went against every instinct he had.

"Remove that *cat* from our sight," his father directed Myerson when Preston didn't respond. "Now."

"Don't you fucking touch him!" Preston growled, summoning a crackle of lightning up his arm.

"Trace!" his father warned, while his mother gasped.

"No. You may have treated me like some extension of you to fit your ideals my entire life, but I will not let you call him riffraff, or mongrel, or anything else you think is somehow true about everyone but yourself, even if I didn't want him to be here.

"You are such a hypocrite. The long game? Sure, the long game can excuse anything, even groveling to evil men with evil intentions just to get one claw's worth of extra power. Like me, right? That's all I ever was—a witch and a Rat King with power you never had. But that's not how it should be. That's not how it's going to be with Bash ruling, and you won't belittle Luke either, not because he's a cat and sullying your pretentious-as-hell house that two people do not need. Turns out I like cats. A lot. Because I'm taking one as my fucking mate."

The gasp came from Luke this time, and Preston pictured him beaming behind him, but he kept his firm glare on his parents, arm still crackling to remind them of his power that they did not share.

"Is that some sort of joke?" his father snarled.

"I don't know if I believe in fated mates," Preston said, "but I know how I feel, who I want, and it is not a rat."

"No son of mine is bedding some bitch feline!" his mother shrieked. "You are to carry on the family line!"

That she could be so dense made Preston laugh. "Don't worry, Mother, Father, that's fairly impossible anyway, but thankfully, I don't care, since *he* gives really good head."

Preston seized Luke by the arm and stormed out before either of his parents could respond.

Half-formed syllables sputtered after them from his mother, his father screaming for him to come back, ordering him like always, but the adrenaline inside Preston was so boiling hot with a clang like gongs in his ears, he couldn't flinch or stop or hardly breathe. He just kept moving.

"Trace!" His father was on their heels as they neared the front door. "Trace Rathaway, if you walk out that door—"

Preston laughed, because really—really? But with the exit in front of him and Luke never once having fought their harried retreat, Preston spun back around.

His father was halted an arm's length away, and his mother could be seen several paces back, clutching her chest like proverbial pearls.

"I'll be sure to slam the door on my way out, because believe me, I am never coming back through it. Oh, and by the way," he added with a manic grin, further fueled by the buzzing in his head, "I'm the new Magister. Don't expect any favors when we win back our den."

The sound of the name he'd always hated followed him in harmonized cries from his parents as he marched the rest of the way out, Luke in tow, as fast as he could.

Until the long walk from the manor home to the gate was suddenly far less appealing than the walk there, allowing his adrenaline to cool and the weight of what he'd done to sink so low it hit his feet and made them feel like lead. Preston trudged the last few paces, distantly hearing Luke asking if he was okay, if he needed anything, if he wanted anything, but Preston's ability to breathe was dwindling fast as they neared the gate.

"Oh wow… I think you might be having a panic attack, so umm… come here."

Even those words seemed far away, like the tunneling of Preston's vision, and he barely felt when him leading Luke became the other way around, and they were somehow inside the guest house, with Luke leaning him back against the wall beside the door.

"Breathe. Just breathe, okay?"

"What did I do? What did I *do*?"

"You were incredible." Luke's brilliant smile hovered in front of Preston's darkening vision.

Preston laughed, a little more deliriously than before, but did his best to breathe in and out slowly to calm the racket of his heart in his eardrums.

He let the laugh dwindle as the worst of it passed and remembered that he was supposed to be angry with this meddling cat.

"I'm still mad at you."

"What? You ditched me!"

"It's *my* family, and it was my choice whether or not to involve you."

"Well… ya kinda gotta involve your *mate* with your family, doncha?" That perfect, crooked grin returned.

"You are so—" Preston pushed from the wall, not realizing how close he was to an end table beside the door, which he knocked into with some priceless-looking vase on it that crashed to the floor.

He froze in a panic—his parents would be so angry—but that instant reaction was replaced by the corners of his mouth twitching up.

"That… felt kind of good."

"Yeah?" Luke stepped toward the end table on the other side with its matching vase, his grin looking a lot more devious, and reached out with a very light but purposeful tap.

"Luke!"

The second vase shattered like the first.

Luke dashed into the guest house with a spin on his heels. "Better stop me before I trash the whole place!"

"Wait!" Preston rushed after him. The house was large by normal standards, and while it wasn't as densely packed with antiques as Baraka's version of the den, what it did hold was three times as expensive.

Luke raced into the dining room, snatched a table clock along the way, and tossed it over his head.

Miraculously, Preston caught it, but when he looked up at his continued momentum, Luke had leapt out of the way, and Preston was barreling toward a china cabinet.

He threw his weight backward to keep from plowing into it, and instinctively chucked the clock forward—where it smashed through the glass, destroying most of the dishes inside.

Oh God....

"Wanton destruction makes for a great first date!" Luke jogged in place at another exit, before dashing away again. "And technically we haven't had one yet!"

"Luke!" Preston gave chase, but he couldn't deny how much laughter remained in his reprimand. "What are we doing?"

"Having fun!"

"We're destroying my parents' guest house!"

"Less fun for them, then!"

On Preston's next dash after Luke, he was tripped up by the appearance of a grand piano in the music room. Before he could crash into it, he hurled a ball of lightning, and the piano burst apart into chunks with an eerie twang of broken notes.

"Destruction can be therapeutic!" Luke called.

"That claim has been wildly contradicted!"

"Annnnnnd yet." Luke winked and escaped into the hall.

The house didn't have enough clear pathways for a fight, let alone a playful chase, and around the next corner, Preston did crash into something—a table covered in porcelain figurines.

Before he realized what he was doing, he picked one up, continued after Luke, and flung the figure into a case of fancy decanters.

It shattered like the china cabinet, and liquid oozed onto the floor.

"That's the spirit! Catch me if you can!" Luke bounded up the stairs.

More vases and figures and glass wastes of space and money fell to pieces around each corner and new room entered. Preston found himself purposely staying one step behind Luke, relishing every opportunity to ruin more of his parents' guest house.

Luke never stopped talking, never stopped urging him on to finally burst out of the shell he'd been encased in that never allowed for a single mistake or crack in his perfect façade.

He'd done a hell of a lot more than make cracks today.

Finally, when Preston nearly tripped over his own feet from how much he was laughing, he held up a hand for them to stop.

"Enough! Enough, I'm good, *shit*...." He hunched over, leaning on his thighs, with Luke huffing and grinning in equal measure ahead of him.

They'd ended up in one of the bedrooms. There was no other exit, and Preston waited until Luke's guard was down to propel himself forward and catch himself a cat, pinning Luke to the wall.

"Aw, gonna punish me now?" Luke husked.

His face was sheened with sweat from the chase, and this close, Preston could see the varied shades of sapphire in his eyes, looking all sorts of amused and content.

"Or...," Luke prompted.

"Or...?" Preston's heart was racing, differently than before, filled with the happy side of adrenaline that made him want to surge forward in the aftermath.

The rumble in his gut, anxious but not unpleasant, as he crowded Luke, was a telling sign of what he wanted. He'd admitted as much to his parents—*fuck*, he'd come out to his parents and finally stood up to them, and he might not have done either if not for Luke.

"There are other ways to let off steam," Luke said, softer, with their surroundings strangely quiet now after all that turmoil.

Preston was aware of the heat from Luke's body as he let himself sink into him, the full lines of their bodies pressing tight.

In a bedroom begging to be christened by something better than pretension, right there in his parents' ruined guest house, Preston kissed his *mate* and let the smell of sage engulf him.

Chapter 14

HIS MATE. He'd said it out loud.

Preston called Luke his *mate*.

Luke had never been so happy. Even trashing the house—and who had a second house on the same property anyway—fun as it had been, was a pale comparison to the utter joy of hearing those words and having Preston in Luke's arms now.

He knew he shouldn't have followed Preston, but he hadn't been able to stop himself. The little he knew of Preston's parents made it impossible to imagine leaving him to their mercies alone. Seeing the house where Preston grew up hadn't changed his mind.

Sure, the place was like… holy shit fancy and huge and a butler—really, a *butler*? But all that luxury, all those things, all the food on that breakfast table and Preston's parents dressed to the nines, only made Luke think of the sludge coating it all.

Dirt could be washed away. Inexpensive items could be adored, no matter the price tag. But black hearts stayed shriveled if they weren't willing to change.

Okay, so maybe Luke had learned most of his morals from comics, cartoons, and video games, but at least his intentions were pure.

Though maybe *pure* wasn't the best word for his intentions right now.

Preston felt searing, even compared to the fever in Luke's body from their chase and lead-up to another much overdue kiss. If this was how Preston intended to punish him, Luke was all on board.

He wrapped his hands around Preston's waist to pull him closer, their near-matching heights meaning their hips aligned just right, and the barest buck forward stirred Luke to life with a strain in his jeans.

Preston pulled back so suddenly that Luke groped after him. He worried Preston was still mad at him, until he saw the wily glint in Preston's eyes, teasing him on purpose.

"*Pres*…." Luke draped himself back against the wall for whatever he was in for.

"You seem pretty eager." Preston was back in his space faster than Luke's slow blinking could catch. Even if Luke was overheated, Preston's added warmth was welcome, and as soon as he felt those lips on him again and that tongue, Luke lunged for it.

The contrast of cool air and warm skin as Preston undid the button of Luke's jeans made him shiver. Preston splayed his palm, able to feel the beginnings of hair there, so indecently low on Luke's belly.

"I never paid you back, did I?" Preston spoke against Luke's lips, making him ache for more and displaying a dominant, confident side that Luke had so known was in him. Then Preston drew down the zipper. All he had to do was reach in. "Do you want me to touch you, Luke?"

It dawned on Luke that, other than Preston screaming his name throughout the guest house, he hadn't really heard it on Preston's lips much, and to hear it like that... *yes, please.* "Please," he whimpered aloud, head leaned heavily against the wall, body sagging and drained from running but tingly where Preston was touching him.

"Do you want me to touch your cock? Get you off?"

"*Fuck....*" That Preston hadn't touched him yet was torture, but then his hand curved, fingers tilting downward instead of up, and he delved into Luke's undone jeans, taking hold of his already hardening length.

"I want you to touch me too." Preston leaned his forehead on Luke's, shaking fingers betraying that his confidence was more in words than actions, but he was trying, exploring, and fluttered his fingers across Luke's leaking slit. "Then I want to ruin that bed the way we ruined every other room in this house." The skin of their lips nearly touched with each new word but didn't yet meet as Preston palmed him, and stroked, and God—*oh fuck, oh yes.*

Luke's own hand shook as he reached forward, fingers pressing to the softness of Preston's shirt—which he seriously looked amazing in, clothed in magenta, but he probably hated the *Chillax* part—and slid down to find the hem.

It was difficult, working open a pair of jeans with one hand, but the attentions being given to Luke made it impossible for his brain to control more than one at a time. He hummed, arching his neck and gently rocking his hips in time to Preston's strokes—so warm, so good, and better with each steadying and more confident pump of Preston's fist.

Returning the favor wasn't made much easier. Luke was caught up in Preston actually touching him—for the first time directly touching him, *shit*—hand inside his underwear, and saying such wonderfully filthy things.

Finally Luke managed to part Preston's jeans, push up that soft magenta shirt, and dig his hand in to feel the hot flesh awaiting him.

Breath puffed on Luke's lips as Preston shuddered and increased the speed of his thumb passing through the wetness building, easing his strokes.

A growl built within Luke, always so much more like a purr or actual cat's prrp, as the fire in his belly urged his body to give over to his animal side. This type of near involuntary shifting was pleasant, surrendering to their true nature, and Luke let his mouth drop open to show fangs so Preston would know just what he was doing to him.

Preston's own fangs grew, and his eyes flashed so black behind his glasses, they hardly had pupils.

"I'm glad you came," he said, and a rat's voice was so different from other shifters at Stage Two, not growly but almost two-toned, high-low melding together, "but next time, you ask first."

"To come?"

"I'm serious—"

"I will, I will!" Luke laughed, thankful Preston's frustration still had some adoring in it. "I promise, just… *please*." He rolled his hips.

"Please… what?" Preston's strokes grew harder, faster, but he kissed Luke softly, and that too was warm and so, so good.

"Please… let's make a mess of that bed."

Preston pulled away as abruptly as the first time, fumbling to remove his jeans. After that it was a whirl of kicked-off shoes and clothes flying. Preston's glasses landed somewhere amidst it all, their hands groping for each other along the way, until Preston dropped back on the bed, and Luke atop him.

"Not sure I like being on the bottom right now," Preston mused.

The one item of clothing remaining was Luke's "I'm with Stupid" shirt, which currently pointed at Preston.

Luke threw his head back in another laugh.

Their erections brushed for the first time, and *wow*, yes, Luke could set up camp right there on Preston's hips. Grabbing the hem of his T-shirt, Luke sat up to lift it over his head and swung it back behind him.

Preston's confidence showed a visible waver, much as he looked hungry for all he saw, so Luke moved very slowly, dropping down, hands sliding up that lean, pale stomach and chest until he found a natural hold around Preston's shoulders. Luke kissed him, rocking his hips just as slowly as his descent, and Preston shivered with a tight clutch at Luke's waist.

Luke could do just this and be content, letting his cock glide along Preston's with a scorching slickness, their tongues tangling, mouths suctioned snugly. But he figured Preston had done next to nothing before. Definitely nothing with another person, and it made him wonder if he'd ever dared play along the puckered skin of his entrance or press inside.

The likelihood of needed supplies in this place was a zero, but Luke didn't require more than spit and precum for what he had in mind.

Shifting his weight, he unwrapped his legs from Preston's waist to settle between his legs, nudging Preston's thighs apart and rocking his hips back. Their cocks barely had to be out of alignment to accomplish that, and once Preston hooked his ankles around Luke's lower back, reaching down between them to get beneath Preston was easy.

A gasp tore Preston's lips from Luke's at the first faint brush of a finger against his hole. They were both partially changed, but Luke's claws were easily dismissed while keeping fangs in his smile.

That was a good gasp, a "*fuck yes* that felt amazing" gasp, and the rosiness in Preston's cheeks darkened.

Luke did it again.

"*Shit*, that… that's…."

"Good, yeah?"

"Yeah. You too? I-I mean… you like someone doing that for you?"

"Oh yeah."

It wasn't only curiosity asking.

"*Fuck*." Preston's claws grazed Luke's hole before he retracted them and rubbed with the pad of his finger, mimicking what Luke was doing in turn.

The need to nip and lick and get that much closer surged through Luke, and he nuzzled Preston's neck with gentle bites in a slow dragging of his fangs along the skin. Preston returned that gesture too, his shifted teeth larger but less sharp, different from any Luke had ever felt on him, but then… he'd never had someone do *this* before. Fangs had nipped at Luke's thighs but never his neck, so much more intimate for their kind, the act of marking like a claim.

Luke licked a finger he hadn't yet used on Preston, gathered more wetness from between their leaking cocks, and reached back down to Preston's hole. The questioning in Preston's gaze, and then fluttering of *his* eyes at the push of a fingertip was like reliving Luke's first time, only this was better. He'd never felt this all-encompassing connection to someone before, where he wanted so much more than a partner to feel good with for a few minutes, but a partner forever.

Wow.

Forever.

Preston's eyes opened with an added heaviness and drop of his mouth open to pant. He held Luke's gaze as he pulled his own hand free between them and mirrored Luke once more, licking a finger, reaching down to pump their colliding cocks and steal some wetness, and then returning around behind Luke to push—

"Ah!" Luke bucked down, and the upswing drove Preston's finger deep, while the thrust pushed his own finger farther inside Preston.

"Yeah… oh yeah…." Preston rocked with him, hips rolled back even more and cocks squished and grinding, with Luke's hand wedged beneath Preston and Preston's arm wrapped around Luke in a half hug to keep him close. They found the best seesaw rhythm ever embarked on, with a hot slide inside and against each other.

"Like that…." Luke nodded. "Just like that… *fuck* yeah…."

"Fuck… *fuck*…." Preston echoed, head lolling as he gave in to properly soiling one last goddamned room in this house.

He seemed to read that wicked thought from Luke's mind, or maybe saw the hints of Luke's smirk, because he matched Luke's stare and seized him by the back of the neck, crashing their lips together.

Their rhythm barely stuttered, even when Preston's hand shoved between them again to aid their cocks. There was no tremble in his fingers now, no hesitation, and though he fumbled, unpracticed at taking two cocks in hand, his grip was sure, and fast, and *tight*.

Preston thrust his tongue deeper and hips harder, spilling first, with a cry cracking from his throat and head lolling back again with the sweetest ending mewl.

Despite his blissed expression, Preston still managed to stroke Luke and thrust his finger in deeper, while Luke lazily withdrew so he could grip Preston's hip for better leverage.

"Come on… come *on*…." Preston huffed, and a bite at his lower lip completed Luke's tip over the edge like that last teasing nudge to shatter the vase.

Luke nearly collapsed from the release but figured the weight and worsened mess between them wouldn't be appreciated.

He still joked, "Now… a gentleman… would use those nifty powers of yours to, um… prestidigitation and clean us up."

"That is not what that word means." Preston snickered.

"Close enough."

Luke grinned through the aftershocks of finally having a naked Preston in his arms without a fight having occurred or an audience in tow and bent just enough to claim a kiss.

Not-prestidigitation did clean up most of the mess, and they lay out side by side. Luke breathed deep, and even though this place—whether the guest house or that big one down the driveway—was never a home for Preston, being here with him still smelled like one.

Which made Luke wonder.

"Hey. What do I smell like to you? I never asked."

Preston paused a beat or two before saying, "Sage."

"Yeah?" Luke grinned, seeing Preston's eyes still dark and shimmering at a lingering Stage One. "Coz I'm down-to-earth and refreshing?"

"Something like that," Preston snorted. "What about me?"

Luke rolled closer to nuzzle his nose into Preston's neck. Breathing in with as over-the-top of a sniff as he could, he said, "Like the best damn pie in the world. Like Christmas, with cinnamon and apples—"

"*Pie?*" Preston lurched away. "I smell like pie to you?"

"What's wrong with pie?"

"It's a dessert!"

"Well, you are a *treat*." Luke giggled, dragging Preston back to him and forcing him into a snuggle against halfhearted struggling, because Preston was laughing too. "A treat… and my one true…." He purposely trailed off, waiting for Preston to stop him, even though he'd said the word himself now, and to his parents, no less. "Mate."

The shimmer in Preston's eyes turned damp, his laughter fading to honest contemplation. "Why…," he began with hesitancy, "why would the universe want a rat and a cat to be together, especially when we're both…."

"Guys?" Luke finished, knowing it wasn't truly doubt Preston meant by these words but the need to say them, because he hadn't been allowed to think otherwise for so long. "Because neither of those things matter."

"I know, but… we're still from very different worlds."

"And the same too. Both being nerds and all." Luke bumped Preston's nose, eliciting a sniffle of a laugh and a brief dart of Preston's eyes. "What matters is how we connect, how we make each other feel. Maybe the universe brought us together because… I don't have a family, and yours kinda sucks, and both our younger lives were crappy, but we can be each other's family now, with our friends, who never had it better somewhere else either.

"Maybe… it's you because I want it to be you," Luke finished in a whisper, sniffling back his own unbidden tears. This was different; he knew that much. This was special. And even if they were total opposites in many ways, it felt right. It felt comfortable.

It felt like….

Home.

"After that, well, all that matters is if you want it to be me."

Preston dipped forward to bump their noses in echo. "Yeah… I think I do."

A ringing from the floor made them both snap back, mostly because, to Luke, he feared an alarm had finally gone off and they'd been caught, but the sound proved to be Preston's cellphone.

"I cannot believe them," he snarled, staring at the retrieved phone with the caller name blinking *Father*.

"Maybe they want to apologize," Luke said, scooting beside Preston to sit with him on the end of the bed.

"If that was true, it wouldn't have taken this long. They just finally figured out what bullshit to spew to keep in my good graces enough to benefit from an in with the new circle. Or they think I'll make a bad name for them if the raid on the den goes sour."

"You didn't technically tell them about that."

"They'll assume it. McDonough should too. I almost hope my father tries warning him somehow, just so Bash has enough excuse to banish my parents from the city."

"You know, he might anyway if you ask him to," Luke said, "especially given involvement with the drug."

"I know." Preston sighed and finally hit *DECLINE*. "But I'm probably going to ask him not to."

"Really?" Luke didn't expect the fresh smile that crept into Preston's expression.

"I want my parents here," he said, taking hold of Luke's hand, "to watch us make this pack better and completely unrecognizable to what they'd want."

Yep, this rat was definitely Luke's mate. "Sounds like a goal," he said and leaned in for a kiss.

Since they hadn't been discovered, they cleaned up further in the bathroom, dressed, and took their time heading out. They planned to port, but Preston wanted to walk back through everything to enjoy the view.

He still looked a little like half his brain wanted to panic, but the other half was experiencing some much overdue....

"What's that word that means relief or... release? But sounds like catheter?"

"*What*?" Preston sputtered. "You mean catharsis?"

"That."

Even without hearing Luke's inner monologue, Preston seemed to understand. Any remaining panic flittered away.

"Too bad we didn't learn anything new. Or did we?" Luke asked.

"We know McDonough didn't have enough Moondust to make a brute out of too many shifters, and he has all of it that we didn't confiscate from Isabella, since my father never got any. Nell must be stalling well, since they haven't made any larger moves. With the backup we have so far, I think we can take them." Preston looked more confident than ever, holding Luke's hand again in the middle of some very earned carnage before portalling them to the dorm room. "I have a plan."

Chapter 15

"YOU RECALL when I said that waiting until day *six*, giving us only one day before the Harvest Moon, was my absolutely last choice for when we ended this?"

Preston did recall Bash saying that. Waiting until tomorrow to storm the den wasn't his ideal either, but the time it would take to gather everyone who'd agreed to help, explain the plan, the layout of the den, and assure everyone that yes, porting groups into various locations on the property was an entirely safe—if taxing for Preston—idea, it would be late into the night. Executing a plan was best done when everyone was well-rested.

And Preston was going to need practice.

"You mean we could have ported back into the den right away?" Deanna barked. "We could have saved Nell that first night!"

"No," Preston countered calmly, "because anywhere in the den could be teeming with those roided-out wolves, and the only potentially safe entry point would have been Nell's workshop, which I hadn't been to frequently enough to visualize."

"What's changed?" Bash asked.

Preston didn't try to prevent his glance at Luke. "I feel more confident. I know I can do this, with one other person. Luke and I scout, we find Nell, get her out of there if necessary, and then everyone else just needs to be ready."

Once again, Bari would be watching the foxes, who were deemed too injured to fight, despite Jude almost having healed enough to be out of his sling and bandages and both Marleys' best protests. Someone needed to stay behind to ensure their captured wolf didn't do anything stupid, and they couldn't risk anyone slowing them down.

The rest of them and the many people called in for support were on standby the moment the sun rose on the sixth day of their seven-day countdown. Preston grasped Luke's hand to make the trip, an easy enough gesture now, even if the hour ahead held the fate of their entire future in its minutes.

It probably would have been a more dramatic moment if Preston wasn't wearing a vintage T-shirt with a giant smiley face on it.

DAY 6

LUKE WAVERED as his feet settled on new ground, clinging to Preston to keep them both steady. He'd only ever been in Nell's workshop once before, and never in the back corner where Preston had brought them.

The runes on various surfaces and potion bottles like a wizard's lair were similar to Nell's family magic shop downtown. It was dark, no windows down here, since it was a basement, and though Luke could see fine with his shifter sight, the ambiance of mysticism added to his nerves.

He was excited more than worried, because as skeptical as he'd been when Bash first asked him to be part of the new circle, he wasn't about to give up a chance for a real home, or to make a better one for others.

A finger snapped to Preston's lips, and he strained his ears to hear around their hidden corner.

Luke could hear it too, not voices, but there was someone shuffling closer while trying to keep their steps soft.

Sparks crackled up Preston's arm, and Luke released his claws, readying to defend against their ambusher, who—*shit*, smelled human!

"Wait!" Luke hissed, leaping in front of Preston and holding up his hands to guard against Nell. A menacingly glowing rune hovered in front of her snarling face after she sprang around the corner. "It's us!"

The rune burst in a shower of sunset sparkles, Nell's expression fading to weary relief. She looked awful. She was always pretty, clean-faced as the more au naturel type, but she wore no added adornments, like her usual bangles or rings, her dress was wrinkled, long hair tangled, and the bags under her eyes said she hadn't slept much.

"Luke, Preston… thank goodness. I was afraid one of the guards was in here spying and might…." Nell darted her eyes around, as though fearful that might still be true, before finishing, "See what I'm really up to." She gestured for them to follow and led them out of the corner.

The modern aspects of the workshop were almost like a CSI lab, with various pieces of equipment complementing the more mystical items. There was a large table in the center cluttered with a combination of both, including vials of Moondust, but she breezed past that to another corner, where a smaller worktable was hidden, with a similar setup.

"I've been making a counteragent to the drug. It's finally finished."

The fruits of her labor had been gathered in a large Ziplock bag, a white powder nearly identical to the Moondust itself—and several recreational options, Luke thought with a snort.

This would totally look like a meth lab if they got raided.

"Counteragent?" Preston asked. "They'd lose all that size and strength?"

"Yep." Nell nodded.

"You've totally been Iron Man-ing them!" Luke laughed and nudged Preston's arm, knowing he'd get the reference since he had that Iron Man action figure in his room.

Nell, however, didn't seem to follow.

"Stalling to give yourself time to make the exact opposite of what they wanted from you," Preston said, "and making sure they didn't notice."

"Exactly!"

Just like everyone else in the circle Bash had formed, Nell was a badass.

"If we can depower McDonough's people, given the rest of our plan," Preston said with even more confidence, "they don't stand a chance."

"Whatever you have planned, we better hurry." Nell glanced around again. "Sean said this was my last day or he'd 'do it without me,' which I'm pretty sure didn't mean he planned to let me go, and tomorrow is—"

"We know. Last day," Preston finished. "How many guards are outside your door?"

"Just one. Even knowing I'm a witch, they weren't taking a *lone human* all that seriously." She stopped Preston when he reached for the bag. "But how are we going to handle delivery? Best if they inhale it for it to work quick enough."

"Any side effects if *we* inhale or touch it?" Luke asked.

"No, it should only react to someone with the original drug in their system."

Oh, Luke was going to have fun with this. "I got it." He claimed the bag before Preston could and headed for the door. "Makes our original plan even easier."

"Wait, what are you doing?" Preston followed.

"Trust me." Grabbing hold of the handle, Luke yanked the door open to the sight of one very large henchman and cried, "Hey, buddy!"

The man spun, and Luke blew a handful of powder right into his face.

"Pocket sand!"

The large wolf sputtered and coughed, instantly willing himself to the overlarge Stage Three that taking the drug allowed him and stalked angrily forward with a menacing snarl.

Shit. Luke backpedaled into Preston, worried the counteragent might not work.

Then, as quickly as the wolf had shifted, his footing stumbled, and he swayed with a pained, cut-off howl as the shift reverted. Like Superman affected by Red Kryptonite, the wolf returned to human, winded and surprised-looking, in stretched-out clothing.

A whip flew past Luke in translucent blue as Preston unfurled his spirit chains to lasso the man closer and then reared back a lightning-powered punch that he unleashed across the man's jaw.

He dropped.

"Fuck!" Preston shook out his hand. "And here I thought that would look cool...."

"It totally did." Luke laughed and leaned over to kiss Preston's cheek.

Nell giggled behind them, and Preston flushed.

"Ahem." He turned to her. "I can send you back to where we've been staying. Let you rest."

"No way! I'm tired, but I can still help. I'm not going anywhere."

"Okay." Preston glanced down at their first felled opponent. "Then time to start bringing in reinforcements."

Nell's door led to a staircase up, where another door exited into the yard. From the top, peering out that second door, they could see the nearby back gate, where one guard was on the inside facing in and another outside facing out. Both were slightly turned toward each other, chatting—which meant neither was looking when Luke followed Preston outside, with Nell trailing them.

Luke had never witnessed Preston port someone from one location to another, only experienced it happening to him. He watched Preston make a scooping motion ending in a fist, and bam, Siobhan and her team of agents appeared after a contraction of darkness over the grass like a *Looney Tunes* hole to nowhere.

Preston snapped a finger to his lips like earlier, motioning to the guards at the gate. Siobhan's team was meant to clear the perimeter.

She nodded, but before she dashed away, Luke held out the bag of powder, mimed blowing it from his hand, and pointed at the guards. Siobhan and a couple agents grabbed handfuls and then jogged stealthily after their first quarry.

No sounds came from the ensuing conflict as Luke and Nell followed Preston along the side of the den. They stayed plastered to the wall to sneak a peek through the sliding glass doors into the kitchen. Two more werewolves could be seen, idly talking with cups of coffee between them at the small kitchen table.

Warmth flowed through Luke at a sudden touch on his shoulder from Nell. She reached past him to do the same to Preston, and Luke saw the way a blue rune glowed and then faded as if seeping into Preston's body. The design was like two pitchforks overlapping facing up and down with a diamond between them.

"For protection," she whispered. "I'll help and heal when I can."

Preston looked to Luke. "You ready? Because as soon as I bring in the next group...."

"I'm ready. What we practiced only meant a couple potshots from my claws. Now I'm better armed." Luke held up the powder.

With a nod, Preston turned to the kitchen. Doing the same scooping into a fist motion, he reached back with his other hand to touch Luke.

Deanna, several old enforcers, and people from the Shelter appeared inside the kitchen. Then Luke felt his stomach drop like the plummet from the top of a roller coaster, and he was in the kitchen too, closer to the men at the table, whose attention was too much on the first arrivals to notice a second ambush.

Luke blew counteragent into both wolves' faces, disorienting them enough to give Deanna's team an opening before the wolves had even leapt up from the table.

The sliding doors flew open as Preston and Nell rushed inside, and Luke joined them with a dash across the kitchen. Several thwacks and sounds of fighting followed, but as Luke and the others reached the opening out of the kitchen, an angry howl broke the quiet.

"They're here!"

Two wolves in the hall past the dining room snapped their heads in the direction of the yell and spotted them.

"Go!" Preston cried.

Another drop in Luke's stomach, and he was across the dining room just as the wolves came roaring through it, giving him clear targets to hit with the counteragent.

"No Hulk Smash for you!" he taunted and ducked free of wild swipes that chased him.

The next group of backups popped into existence across the dining room as Luke hurled himself that direction—and *wow*, he didn't know these people, but they were super… colorful.

Dressed to kill, pun intended, the group of three sprinted around Luke to intercept the angered wolves, one of which, who Luke didn't feel appropriate assuming the gender of, was *built* and very fashionable in heels.

What should have been the worst possible choice in footwear proved quite handy when the person threw one at a wolf's face and followed up with two swift claw swipes. That wolf and the other were downed in moments.

"Bari's friends?" Luke asked.

"Such a dear," Heels-as-Weapons said. "But where Bari doesn't have the stomach for fighting, we make up for it." They winked, readying the other shoe, and just in time, because three more wolves came barreling in from the hallway.

Preston and Nell appeared at Luke's side, forced into the dining room by Deanna's fight spilling toward them too, as several more wolves seemed to have shown up. They must have arrived from outside, not fully taken out by Siobhan's team.

"Keep going!" one of Bari's friends directed, and when the fighting caused the large dining table to topple, Luke, Preston, and Nell bolted.

This next cross-section led to several areas of the house, and Luke stuttered to a stop, somehow having ended up in front and unsure where to go.

"Luke!" Preston alerted him to a charging wolf from one of the other halls, this one fully shifted to mammoth size, which would so not fit indoors if these ceilings weren't vaulted.

Luke readied to leap out of the way, when Preston swept his arms at Luke like a bull fighter swooping his red cape, and Luke found himself *behind* the attacker, just as Preston burst out a ball of lightning to knock the wolf backward.

Luke leapt away himself to avoid being crushed, and as soon as the wolf crashed to the floor, he powdered him like the others.

Connie, the wolf proved to be when his face turned human, Sean McDonough's brother.

Nell ran up and kicked Conrad so hard in the face, Luke heard his nose snap, and a groan ended in his body going limp.

Nell shrugged when Luke and Preston gaped at her.

Never underestimate a human.

After hurrying down one of the halls, with Preston leading again, they finally came to the living room, where Sean could be seen with several other shifters guarding him—much more than the numbers he'd had when they took the den. Pocket Sand-ing them all might not be feasible, but they had to try.

"We got this," Luke said, gripping Preston's arm.

Bash emerged from the final portal with old circle members and everyone else who had yet to be summoned. It didn't feel like enough, especially when Sean's guards started shifting. Then *everyone* started shifting, and the din grew so great, here and bleeding in from the rest of the house where the fighting was escalating, that Luke brought himself to Stage Two to stay focused.

No bigger. He had to stay fast.

"Do it!" he cried.

One stomach dip was immediately followed by another, and another, as Preston ported Luke from enemy to enemy. He'd blow powder into a wolf's face and almost instantly be staring down a new one. The bag was growing lighter, and each grab for more made Luke wonder when he'd run out.

Preston had to be tiring too. How many wolves were left? Luke couldn't tell with the disorientation of being thrown around the room, and he didn't even know if this was helping or only delaying the inevitable. But until Preston summoned him back, he had to—

A hand seized Luke by the throat, wrenching everything to a halt, and his next stomach dip wasn't nearly as thrilling when it ended with him slammed against a wall. Claws slashed with such force at Luke's neck below the viselike grip that he knew he was dead, mincemeat, done for.

Only he didn't feel any pain....

Because they hadn't gotten past Nell's rune!

"Fucking *kids*!" Sean screamed in Luke's face, not beyond Stage Two, like him, but seething.

"Fuck you right back, old man," Luke rasped.

"The hell?" Sean let go with a stagger. "What the *hell*?"

Luke dropped to his feet, feeling at his neck to be certain he wasn't dead.

Not a scratch, but it wasn't his miraculous survival that had Sean reeling.

"Get them off me!"

More rats than Luke had ever seen in one place were swarming the former Second, including when Preston had summoned them into the alleys that time.

Luke had nearly forgotten the real final reinforcements.

As the rats continued to cover Sean, biting and clawing until only tiny writhing bodies could be seen and no part of the werewolf himself, he toppled onto the floor for even more rats to swarm him.

The rest of the fight dwindled too. Luke could finally take it in, as the roars and growls and sounds of claws slicing the air finally stopped. He'd dropped the bag of powder, but there was hardly another handful left.

Not that it was needed. They'd done it.

They'd won.

"Call them off," Bash said, stalking toward the mound of rats.

With a glance from Preston, they dispersed from Sean's body. It wasn't like a cartoon where he was reduced to bones. He was conscious, just very clawed and bitten up, bleeding, and not looking too happy about it.

The rest of the room went still as Preston raced to Luke's side, leaving an equally exhausted-looking Nell to drop into the lone chair that hadn't been turned over. Luke had to laugh that almost everyone was naked again, just not him, Nell, or Preston, the latter Luke almost lamented when Preston clobbered him, but they'd have time for private nakedness later.

He just enjoyed the smell of *pie*.

"Kill me, then," Sean's croak broke the silence that had fallen. "At least I had vision. You're no different than your father."

Preston let go, and they both turned to look.

Bash's eyes held a brutal, merciless glint as he towered over Sean, maintaining a Stage Two prominence with silver fur along the edges of his body, claws flexing, and teeth out in a snarl.

"I am much nicer, believe me," Bash said. "My father would have sliced off a thumb or a few toes by now and kept going piece by piece. But just because I'm nice doesn't mean I can be pushed around. This is about the entire pack, which you are no longer part of." He turned to the room, addressing those defeated. "Sean and whoever else is still breathing will be escorted outside our borders, and if any of you ever darken my city again, I won't be so nice anymore.

"Unless, of course, you'd prefer the alterative?" he asked Sean.

When Sean said nothing, the roar that burst from Bash was thunderous, and as though he had taken Moondust himself, he shifted larger to a full Stage Three, swift and threatening, and roared louder.

It was the first time Luke had heard Bash roar as an Alpha, in all his werewolf glory, and it made Luke and everyone else in the room instantly bow their heads—not in fear or servitude, but out of reverence for their leader.

With a team—a circle—who was going to change things.

"Submit," Bash demanded in a nearly unintelligible rumble, "or shall I have your head?"

"I-I… submit." Sean quaked.

Now they had won, and screw anyone who ever tried to take this from them again.

Preston didn't leave Luke's side. There was much to be done, but as those who had volunteered to help aided in the removal of Sean and his traitors, the circle had the opportunity to gather—those who'd lost their clothing having managed to re-dress.

"Even won a day early." Deanna smacked Bash on the back.

His previously mighty countenance changed from Alpha to amused friend in a beat. "Not too bad for a first week. You all proved I chose the exact right advisors, not that I had any doubts."

"Otherwise, Sean might have gotten away with it," Nell said.

Luke had to laugh, slipping his hand into Preston's, who smiled and squeezed back. "If it hadn't been for us meddling kids."

Chapter 16

"AND FINALLY, in that faraway land, with a faraway people very different and yet not so different from our own, the runaway puppy returned home."

The gathered children of the Shelter stared with shimmering eyes of wonderment, on the floor in front of Luke, who sat amongst them with crisscrossed legs in kind.

"The end," he announced and closed the pages of *The Runaway Puppy*.

"Again!"

"Another!"

"Please, Luke!"

The chorus of eager voices make him chuckle. "Nice try, kiddos, but I gotta get going. It's moving day, remember?"

Several of the excitable faces fell sour.

"Hey, don't look like that. It's a good thing for me."

"But we aren't gonna see you anymore," Pauly said.

"Of course you are. I'll be here all the time. I'm Councilor, remember? That means the whole pack is my responsibility, but especially everyone here. I just won't be sleeping at the Shelter anymore. You'll see me just as often, I promise."

The kids only seemed mildly assuaged, but Luke knew they'd get used to it over time and hardly even notice the difference. For him, it would be a whole new world, having a home with a room and bed to himself.

Well, not entirely to himself.

It had been a challenging few days since the Harvest Moon came and went. Shifter society hadn't collapsed on itself and revealed them to the world via Pied Piper insanity, but they'd still needed to clean up Sean McDonough's mess, banish a whole crapload of conspirators, and assure the pack that all was well.

It *was* well. Very well. Talk of the videos that had originally leaked and incidents of humans witnessing shifters among them had dwindled, the public certain it had all been faked. With those days behind them, Luke finally had the time and conviction to move the last of his things into the den.

"I'll see you tomorrow," Luke said as he stood to replace *The Runaway Puppy* on the shelf of children's books.

"More story time then?" Elly asked.

"Kind of. I'm going to introduce you to a very nice woman who's going to become your teacher. Since you can't go to regular school with humans till you're a few years older, we gotta make sure you're learning, so I hired someone to help. She'll be doing story time tomorrow."

"We gotta learn like… school every day?" Pauly snarled.

"It's a good thing," Luke said.

"You didn't go to school."

"Nope, had to learn things all by my lonesome, and believe me, I wish I'd had a team to learn with instead. You kids are gonna have it better than I did. That's a promise too."

He didn't think they fully understood, but having a real school for the young ones was just the first of many changes Luke had planned for the Shelter. Maybe they'd even thank him for it someday, but the only reward he needed was knowing they really would have it better than he had.

He tried to not get stopped by too many people on his way to his room to collect the very last of his things. He'd already moved most of it, and really, all that remained were odds and ends and shirts he loved, crammed into a bag. A few people still stopped him with questions or requests or just to say hi. It was both the way things had always been and entirely new, because he had authority now, which was super weird and intimidating, but he also kind of loved it.

It was silly maybe, how he paused leaving the Shelter to look back, as if putting a cap on this chapter of his life, which had been his entire childhood. He was an adult now, newly eighteen, yet way older if weighed by experience. He'd be back here tomorrow like he told the kids, but it felt different this time, not having roots here anymore but replanted somewhere new.

Luke smiled. It was a good thing, a happy thing, and he wasn't ever going to take it for granted.

It seemed fitting that he entered the den to the sounds of Preston grumbling.

"What *is* this? Did the former accountant not even know addition and subtraction? These books are atrocious!"

"Are you talking to yourself or the ledgers?" Luke chuckled, dropping his bag beside the sofa upon finding Preston doing his grumbling to an empty living room.

The fierce expression on Preston's face softened. He was mad at the books, not Luke. "I'm trying to focus on the upside, but these are a literal disaster. And technically, I was talking to *them*."

Beside the books on the coffee table were Bernard and Bianca, sitting up on their hind feet as if enraptured by Preston's moaning.

Luke flopped down beside him and reached over to pet both rats on the nose. "Hey, you two, stop encouraging him. There's an upside, though?"

"There are tons of funds we can allocate to better use, even with some of the practices we're going to cease, so your plans for the Shelter should be no trouble. But we definitely need more regular income."

"Like, business income or… 'business' income?"

"Both," Preston said after a pause. "Selling off antiques has helped, but we need more, a business we can operate under the radar, that's something whoever runs it most days is actually good at, where we can also launder funds." As the idea percolated, he jotted down notes in the ledgers.

A Magister wasn't always the circle's accountant, but there was none among them better than Preston. It was what he'd gone to school for, and it was brilliant to watch him crunch numbers.

After retaking the den, he'd slept even longer than after the fight with Lui, totally wiped from all that constant portal magic. Luke had snuggled up next to him for part of it, though this time with permission.

Only a few days had passed since then, and already they'd accomplished much. They'd even better fortified the den against future attempts at takeovers. The codes on the gate and doors had been reset—the previous ones having been known to Sean and the old circle, which Bash admitted he should have changed sooner but he'd been understandably preoccupied. They'd also added warding throughout the den to prevent anyone other than Preston from portalling inside.

"What do you think our business should be?" Preston disrupted Luke's musing. "And don't say restaurant or dry cleaning. Too obvious."

"Uhh… maybe poll the others? You know, see what everyone's good at."

"No dreams to pull from of what you wanted to be as a kid?" Preston asked.

"Not really. I only ever wanted to be, well… what I am now. But like a real councilor. Someone who helps people."

"That is what you are," Preston said, and *wow*, he really was prettiest with a soft smile.

"Guess I am."

"Oops!" a new voice interrupted their lean in toward each other. "Not the exit…."

It was *Joey*, looking rumpled and like he'd missed a shirt button or two, carrying fishnets he must have been wearing earlier, and—whoa, it took Luke's brain way too long to realize that meant he'd slept here.

"Other direction." Bash came in behind him, steering Joey by the shoulders. He was more normally put together, but with an added tousle to his hair.

"Bye!" Joey waved before bolting.

"You have got to be kidding me." Preston sneered.

"What?" Bash said. "An entirely voluntary interaction, I assure you."

Deanna came in next, looking equally tousled.

"Aren't you supposed to prevent him from doing stupid things?"

"You mean Joey? He ain't stupid. He knew exactly what he wanted when he joined us at the bar last night. I was happy to introduce 'em." She patted Bash on the back. "The boss needs to relax once in a while."

"*You* had the idea?" If Preston had a free hand, Luke imagined he would have facepalmed. "As if I needed a reminder that we are literally children…. Could you please be more careful with who you have sex with in this house? We don't need an immediate scandal after the last disaster was averted days ago."

"What scandal?" Bash came up beside the sofa. "I was legitimately questioning Joey about anyone he had dirt on who has real clout in this city, which ended up including a few city council members. Good intel to have. Not any on the mayor, sadly. He's human. It would be nice to get someone into office someday we can utilize… but one problem at a time."

"And questioning turned into…."

"A pleasant evening for all." Bash smirked.

Deanna laughed, coming around the other side of the sofa to reach for Bernard and Bianca. They scurried across the ledgers to the other end of the coffee table. "Hey!" she protested. "I thought we were friends!"

"That was when they were answering my summons." Preston coaxed them to him, and they climbed up onto his shoulders. "They don't like anyone but me."

Luke froze mid-pet of Bianca when Deanna gestured exaggeratingly.

"Don't take it personally." Luke shrugged. "Rats just have very, um… hey, Pres, what's that word that sounds like concerning but starts with a *D*?"

"Discerning?" He snorted.

"*Very* discerning taste."

That turned Preston's face sweet again.

"All right, folks, time to say goodbyes," Siobhan announced as she, Nell, and the foxes came in right on schedule.

Luke had returned from the Shelter, having known their friends were leaving.

"Clean bills of health all around," Nell said.

Shifters healed quickly, and all that remained of the bandages and slings that had been between the pair was down to a barely visible patch over Jordana's shoulder where she'd been shot.

"Better not start those goodbyes without me!" Bari appeared.

It been a full house lately, since Bari's friends had stayed so they could all leave together when he was ready to head home.

Heels-as-Weapons was wearing sparkly ones today.

Luke was a little dejected to see them all go. He liked crowds, thrived on them, but they had their own lives to get back to.

He and Preston stood from the sofa as the flurry of farewells began. Bari hugged both foxes with unabashed enthusiasm, and although done sneakily, Luke would swear Bari's hand reached a little low while hugging Jude.

If nothing else, the Bains had similar libidos.

When it was their turn, Luke and Preston said their goodbyes together, and Luke couldn't help wishing they'd had more time to get to know Jude and Jordana.

"Nervous about seeing Glenwood's Alpha when you get back?" Luke asked.

"No," Jordana soothed. "Seems he thinks he might have use for some talented thieves."

"Careful," Preston said, "might end up recruited into a circle yourselves."

"I could never imagine that!" Jordana laughed.

"Seconded," said Jude, "but I guess the future might surprise us. Keep in touch, huh? Kitten. Fievel." His grin, that had faded over the days of unknowables and fierce battles, was back in full force. He shook both Luke and Preston's hands, but Jordana glomped on to them both, which Luke adored but Preston only seemed to tolerate.

"Pity we never discovered who set all this in motion," Bash said, keeping his distance to allow the more heartfelt goodbyes. "I suppose my father's efforts with the drug would have gone somewhere anyway, even without the extra artifacts, but your theft… that totem…." He trailed off since there was nothing more to say.

"What happened to the donation slip?" Siobhan asked.

"I have it." Jude pulled it from his pocket. "Who knows, maybe someday we'll figure out who wrote it."

Preston had portalled the remains of the totem deep into the earth to be safe. The rest of the artifacts would be divvied between the cities and carefully hidden. It wasn't safe for shifter culture to be displayed openly among human artifacts. It would also be banned to ever use such artifacts to make anything like Moondust again, and with Nell's counteragent in existence, anyone who tried would be easily thwarted.

"Guess we're never getting our cut of the haul," Jude said to Bash.

"Not when it's shifter relics, I'm afraid," Bash answered. "But I think everything turned out exactly as it needed to."

Luke couldn't agree more.

The whirlwind of goodbyes continued, refocusing on Bari after the foxes left.

"You sure we can't convince you to stick around?" Deanna hugged him so tight, he feigned not being able to breathe. "Kinda nice having my other baby brother around."

"Wish I could, darling, but I have my own responsibilities to get back to."

Luke didn't think Bari really meant he wished he could stay. There were too many demons for Bari here, even if the worst of them was dead now.

When Bari hugged Bash, for once he didn't have any words.

Bash seemed fine with that.

"Be good, okay?" Luke said.

"What a thing to say. I prefer to be wicked." Bari winked and threw his arms around Luke and Preston together. "Give 'em hell, kids. I think you're going to handle things here just fine."

"Well, we are *fine*," Preston amazed Luke by bantering with his own flirty tone. "Even if some of us can't pull off those painted-on jeans as well as you."

"*Naughty.*" Bari lurched away in delighted surprise. "Good for you."

Eventually he and his friends left, and everyone else dispersed, aside from Preston, who returned to his bookkeeping, and Luke—who noticed something he hadn't before on the other side of the sofa.

"Are those decorations?" He moved to the box. "It's your Halloween ones."

"I… thought I might put some up later."

"It's the middle of September!" Luke laughed.

Preston hunched.

"And never too soon to celebrate," Luke remedied quickly, "since after November first, it's basically Christmas anyway. How 'bout I help? We can surprise everyone with our kitschy awesomeness." He lifted the box onto the coffee table and sat on Preston's other side. "Plus, I was already thinking of who we can be for Halloween. Betcha can guess."

It was totally Kyo the cat and Yuki the rat from *Fruits Basket*.

Preston looked at him, his expression betraying more emotion than after any of the farewells or disasters they'd experienced and suddenly kissed him.

"What was that for?"

"I just wanted to say, I'm… glad… you loosened me up."

Luke snickered.

"Not…! I did *not* mean…. You know what I mean!"

"I do." Luke snickered again but continued, "And I'm glad you pushed me to let a little structure into my life. Ha!" He couldn't help laughing harder as he looked around the room, since a new *structure* was literally part of his life.

Preston groaned.

"Guess that means we balance each other out pretty well, huh?" Luke said. "Even if I am a *kid*."

"You are definitely not that." Preston smiled softer. "But I guess you are my mate."

"That I am." Luke kissed Preston and let it linger this time with a slow sink. "Now, let's make this place look like a Party City exploded."

PRESENT DAY

A SMILE followed Preston out of dreaming, still with his eyes closed but unable to deny the potent and very welcome smell of….

Sage.

He startled the rest of the way awake, turning carefully to avoid rolling onto the mouse he knew was snuggled on his pillow.

"Hey," Luke whispered, sitting on the edge of the bed beside him.

"Hey…," Preston answered. "You're naked."

Luke snorted. "I was fun-sized until a minute ago! And aren't you used to me being naked by now?" The grin that spread across his face was as disarming as ever, still so youthful, even ten years after Preston first fell in love with its crookedness.

They both began speaking when the silence grew too heavy and ended in quiet laughs.

"Me first?" Luke asked. "I am really sorry I keep saying and doing all the wrong things. It makes me think of when we met, ya know, not really understanding each other or where we came from or how to interact. But I guess we're past the point of a movie moment, where a huge fight erupts in awesome hot makeup sex, huh?"

Preston laughed again, but it was choked with emotion. "I'm sorry too. You know I never think of you as lesser for how you grew up. I don't know why it keeps coming out that way."

"And you are nothing like your dad." Luke found Preston's hands under the covers and squeezed tightly. "I never should have said that. A little structure is good. I wish I'd had more at the Shelter. That's why I made some for the other kids, remember?"

"A little freedom isn't bad either," Preston said.

Lifting their hands out from under the covers flopped the sheets off Preston's bare chest. Unlike Luke, he had underwear on beneath, but he didn't mind Luke being naked. He never minded that anymore, though he still preferred seeing only Luke's nude body to anyone else's.

"I forgot my first job," Luke said. "Well, my first and second jobs. Because I'm your mate first, but the second part is being a good Councilor, and I failed at that too. I wasn't thinking about how this was affecting you. It was easier a decade ago when it was just us against the world, but now we're responsible for a whole other person, and both our experiences with how we grew up sucked so hard."

Preston laughed yet again. Luke had never lost his special way with words.

"We're both afraid of doing wrong by Jess," Luke went on, his own quirk of a smile staying somber. "She needs freedom *and* structure and… just us wanting to care for her and love her. Like we love each other."

The catch in his voice was too unlike him, urging Preston to say, "I love you," if it needed to be heard.

"I love you," Luke repeated and leaned down to capture a kiss.

It was simple and brief with only the barest flick of their tongues in earnest apology.

"You are a good Councilor," Preston said. "And a good dad."

"You are too. You are nothing like your father. Like either of your parents." Luke smiled with a little humor returning as he pressed his forehead to Preston's and even nuzzled their noses. "You know how Ethan is half Seer?"

"Yeah…."

"I think he knew better than he realized why you and me were the best choices for Jess. Because we have something very important in common—neither of us had the parents or upbringing we want to give her. And because of that, we're both scared of screwing up, and acting out in the exact opposite ways we want. Self-fulfilling prophecy." He snickered.

"When did you get so smart?"

"I've always been smart! I just hid behind a dopy smile when we met to get you into bed."

Preston laughed louder and had to clamp his free hand over his mouth to stifle it. His other hand squeezed Luke's again. "It worked. It still does."

"Yeah?" Luke beamed, and then let his smile settle seriously one last time. "We need to cut each other some slack. And I mean *we* when I say that—it's not only you who's been thinking of things one-sided. We need to remember we're a team. I promise I'm going to stop forgetting that."

"Me too," Preston said.

"So…." Luke sat up again but didn't lose his hold on Preston's hand. "Who's the little guy?"

Preston turned to take in the slumbering mouse beside his head. "No name yet. Just keeping me company."

"Gonna bring him home with us?"

"I'm not sure Basil and Dr. Dawson will approve, but I might be able to convince them."

"Give them an adopted baby too? Then if I may…." Luke reached over Preston to pick the mouse up, who wasn't disturbed in the slightest, but snuggled just as happily into Luke's palms. "I dub you… Gus-Gus! He was always my favorite in *Cinderella*."

"And I had a soft spot for Lucifer." Preston smiled. There was something equally enticing about Luke being domestic and doting as anything overtly sexual he ever did. "Maybe Gus-Gus can finish sleeping *away* from the bed?" Grabbing the other pillow, Preston held it out to Luke, who seemed to understand and grew a much slyer smile.

Even as he settled the pillow on a nearby chair and Gus-Gus atop it, he questioned, "Not worried about making too much noise?"

"I had a thought about that." Preston drew a rune in the air that pulsed with light and floated to the door, causing it to softly push closed before the symbol faded into it. "I am a talented witch after all. We'll hear anything that happens out there, without any of our sounds leaving this room." He kicked off his underwear, pulled them free of the covers, and tossed them at Luke.

With a louder laugh, now that they didn't need to stifle them, Luke chucked the underwear over his shoulder and descended on the bed with a fervent grope for every part of Preston's body as he got under the covers with him.

"Oh, I missed you." Luke nuzzled Preston's neck, letting his fangs out with a teasing graze and flashing his bright blue cat eyes.

"No more going anywhere," Preston said, taking hold of Luke's cheeks, which were softer with the first sprouts of ginger fur. "Just us, here," he finished and drew Luke into a kiss.

Chapter 17

EVEN THE click of their fangs was something not to be missed, as Preston allowed his to grow too, giving in to the need in his body and soul to keep claim on his mate—forever.

It was like the first time they'd ever locked lips, reminiscent of the tender but eager passion of their past, which had been just as much on Preston's mind as Luke's. Their actual first encounter had only been a brief make-out session, their second a nearly public blowjob, followed by glorious destruction preceding the third, which otherwise mostly revolved around lustful exploration and grinding.

The fourth....

Oh, the *fourth*.

"Remember that night after I officially moved into the den?" Luke husked Preston's own thoughts against his lips.

And why not? They'd had ten years to learn each other's bodies and desires. The old reservations and stirs of wrongness imprinted on Preston from his parents had long since faded. It was easy now, especially with the sharpness of their fight behind them.

"You mean, the night you—"

"Claimed your final virginity?"

Preston laughed. "I was going to say were graciously offered it, but fine."

"Gracious? I don't know, you can be kind of a power bottom."

"You're welcome."

Luke laughed with Preston, and their gentle teasing of each other faded from shared humor to softness and building seduction with the writhing of their still coiled bodies.

Preston pushed the covers down to give them more freedom, groaning at the first squeeze of Luke's hands on his waist that then dragged up his stomach. His cat claws were sharp but scratched with tantalizing lightness.

The roll of Luke's hips wasn't nearly as restrained, bucking hard against Preston while he wrapped arms around Preston's back to hold him in place. Luke often led, and Preston let him, with only the occasional though admittedly bossy order of what to do next. It worked, their balance, the way they fit each other better than anyone would think a rat and cat could, just like that first night in their shared bed.

"I remember," Preston whined, the slickness between their bodies making their cocks slide oh so deliciously. "That night, I wanted to get my mouth on you, to show you… I'd never back down or deny you again."

"Yeah… it was super-hot." Luke dug into the crook of Preston's neck to lick and nip up his throat.

Preston hated to cease one of his favorite ways of being claimed by his mate, but reviving their first time would be like renewing their vows—not that they'd ever spoken any in the human sense, though they'd talked about doing that someday.

This was their vows, their renewal, reliving that night as a promise to relive it every night, content in each other's arms until they were dust.

"I want my mouth on you *now*." Preston pulled from Luke's grasping arms and pushed him onto his back.

That night, so long ago, Preston hadn't been this confident—in wanting Luke, yes, but not in his skills—so he'd feigned it until he felt it. He'd slinked down between Luke's legs, grinning the entire way.

He did the same now, not bothering to retract his fangs or claws but keeping a close eye on the press of their tips into Luke's skin. He caught Luke's eyes staring hungrily down at him, aware and anticipating what came next long before Preston's head was between his thighs.

Preston's spirit chains sprang forth, wrapping around Luke's wrists and ankles to hold him spread-eagle to the bed as Preston licked Luke's slit with a slow, lapping twirl.

A thrill shot up Preston's spine at the sound of Luke's gasp.

He sucked Luke's head into his mouth, recalling as best he could how he'd done this back then, constantly moving his tongue and descending farther, one slow inch at a time, toward Luke's base. Luke was big enough that Preston's eyes watered the more he swallowed him down. He pulled back to focus on the head, thinking of how he most enjoyed having this done to him—which ten years ago had only been the experience of Luke blowing him in a shared Shelter bedroom.

Remembered laughter made Preston hum, and he bobbed back down, his throat more relaxed and able to take Luke deeper.

The room filled with a louder moan. "I-I… I love the chains, baby, but I want to *touch* you."

"Compromise, then?" Preston said.

The chains unwrapped from Luke's wrists, but the ones on his ankles spread him wider.

Strong fingers dug into Preston's hair. The strands were loose from their bun, long and kinked down between his shoulders with some fanning across his forehead from the tousle of sleep. His glasses were who knew where, but his eyesight wasn't so poor that he couldn't see what he was doing and enjoy the view.

Luke's hands didn't hold him in place or guide his rhythm, merely hung on and carded through the tangles of Preston's hair with a gentle scratch of his claws, as if needing something tactile to do with his fingers or he'd go feral.

Preston bobbed down again.

"*Pres*…."

His own cock jumped at the rasping way Luke said his name, tinged with the edge of cat's howl—and purr and *roar*.

"That's right… say my name." Preston lapped up Luke's cock from base to tip.

"*Preston*." Luke's hips arched off the bed, straining against the remaining chains, and his fingers tightened around Preston's scalp.

Once more, Preston wrapped his mouth around Luke and bobbed, letting the edge of his sharpened teeth graze down and up again along the heated member just enough to leave drag lines.

"Fuck!" Luke growled. "I want inside you. Right now. I want to fuck you so hard the walls shake."

Preston *had* been evoking their first time, when that was exactly how this culminated, but—

"I brought lube!" Luke blurted, eyes flickering down at Preston in the half light, like a playful cat caught in the dark. "In my bag. Wishful thinking?"

Preston muffled a laugh against Luke's thigh and then turned with another lick at his head, making Luke yelp. "How about resourceful?"

Drawing up to his knees, Preston stretched out an arm toward Luke's bag on the floor.

The bottle flew into his hand.

"I really love that Jedi stuff…." Luke squirmed beneath him.

It was only a tiny bit of TK. Summoning small things was easy.

And very handy.

Preston stared down at Luke, his ginger cat, with whiskers having sprouted now too, and such lovely dreamsicle hues in the patterns of his fur outlining the curves of his body. Laid out on the bed like that, flushed and naked, legs spread by the spirit chains, made it impossible to imagine ever finding fault with this man.

Preston's love.

His mate.

Luke wasn't perfect, no more than Preston, but being with him was perfect in all the ways that mattered.

"Like this, yeah?" Luke purred as he squeezed Preston's hips. "But flipped? Like our first time with you folded in half flailing for the headboard and me buried deep right up to the hilt."

Fuck yes. Preston rumbled a whine, voice high and low together with overlapping tones, and gave himself a few quick strokes through his precum. "Done."

A press of the bottle into Luke's hand and the will of Preston's now very trained portal magic were all it took to swap positions. Luke grinned when he registered the change and loss of restraints, marveling at Preston beneath him like he truly thought he was the most magical being in the world.

Preston rolled his hips, causing his length to bob against his stomach.

Luke popped open the cap on the lube in answer and poured it onto Preston's cock to slide from his tip down the length of him to his entrance. Once Luke set the bottle aside, he palmed Preston's balls, gathering some of the silky liquid, and twisted his fingers up the shaft all the way to Preston's head. Coating his fingers with what he'd poured, he passed his thumb over Preston's slit, stroked down and up, down and up, then finally, finally drifted lower.

Preston's eyes remained glued to Luke the entire time, egging him on with sharp rises and falls of his chest. Luke petted one slender digit along Preston's entrance and slid in smoothly, so easily with the coating of lube, as his eyes darted to Preston's face.

Seeking that sweet spot inside, Luke stroked inward and twisted harder, making Preston gasp. He tilted his head back, fanged mouth falling open, but kept his eyes on Luke.

Luke curled and twisted again, reaching just slightly *left*, and a far more satisfied moan left Preston.

There. Just like the first time.

Like always.

He found Luke's free hand and knitted their fingers together, hips rocking upward to pull him in deeper, proving how tight Preston was. They'd gone too long without this, but Preston was no stranger to being opened, not like that night in the den when it had taken ages, and Luke had reveled in every moment of going slow for Preston, until he'd quaked and begged to be filled.

Luke brought their linked hands between them, guiding Preston to take hold of him and add a few strokes through the wetness left by Preston's mouth. Then he led Preston to his own cock, silky from lube.

Most people thought Luke dopey and adorable, and he was, even with ten years added since an eighteen-year-old became Councilor and a wayward rat's mate, but he looked positively sinful like this, leading them through the motions of giving and seeking pleasure. Sinful in a way that could never be sin, just wickedly wonderful and so damned sexy.

Preston read how much Luke felt the same about him, gaze raking over the sight of Preston's legs bent, hips arched, as Luke's finger—*fingers* now—disappeared inside him and curled toward that same spot again and again that made Preston's voice rumble with cacophony.

Now. He needed it now. "Now," Preston commanded, rocking more steadily against Luke. "Take me now. Fuck me *now*."

"*Fuck*, Pres…. Fuck yeah, I will."

Luke reclaimed the bottle of lube and added a liberal amount to himself, more than needed. The urgency between them was an echo, making everything fumbly and hot and almost brand-new.

Grabbing himself beneath the thighs, Preston rocked backward to give Luke a better angle. One hand at Preston's hip, the other on his cock, Luke felt briefly for Preston's entrance and then pushed, hot and pulsing, inside him.

Damn, Preston had missed this.

Luke went slow, so attuned to Preston's needs and reactions that over the past decade Preston had never once felt the burn too deeply. It always blazed into ecstasy, and tonight was no exception.

"More! I can take it, more!"

Luke's hand gliding over Preston's cock made him tighten in contrast to the words, and Luke gasped at the squeeze. The soft, lazy stroking he began was the final push Preston needed to relax again, and Luke slid in halfway and back with ease. Then further on the next buck forward, and further still, until he slammed home, fully engulfed within Preston, and Preston cried out his name with a wrecked moan.

It was easier to set the pace by holding Preston's hips, but Luke kept his hand on Preston's cock for as long as he could. He went harder, harder, *faster*, eyes forever on Preston's face to be certain it wasn't too much.

He hardly needed Preston's expression to know that, since Preston keened a stream of obscenities, "*Fuck*, yes! Harder! Fuck me! Come on! More, *more!*"

Luke hissed, and a catlike yowl sounded, his eyes sharpening, with even more fur sprouting over his skin as he gave over to an almost full Stage Three. The largeness of him like that made his cock larger too, bringing Preston's cries to a choked halt.

At that heavenly fullness, he fought to keep his eyes from rolling back into his head and shifted in kind to match Luke, sleek black fur spreading and his tail growing that was usually an afterthought, not prehensile or at all useful aside from balance. He flopped it forward anyway, where it found Luke's softer, fluff-covered tail and coiled around it as best he could.

Luke pounded him hard and deep like Preston wanted, and the noises it wrought from his throat —*fuck*—it was a good thing Preston had warded the room from sounds leaving.

Too tortured without attention where he needed, Preston reached for his cock, his other hand braced on the headboard as he stroked himself swiftly, watching Luke fuck him with a glorious intensity.

"Shit, Pres... you look so hot like that...."

"You... are amazing. I love the way you fuck me. Harder... harder!"

"Told you you were a power bottom."

Laughter spurted through Preston's moans, just as come spurted hot and fast over his hand. Luke moaned in echo with his eyes on Preston's release, clenching them shut a moment later and neck arching as his own climax peaked.

If Preston could have licked Luke's Adam's apple while he finished, he would have.

Luke came, balls deep just like he'd promised, and hearing the aftereffects of his purring "mmm" noises like he was blissed beyond reason could have sent Preston right back over the edge again too.

Almost instantly, their fur receded, bodies shrinking and tails fading as they came down from the high of their orgasms. Luke kept some of his shift, so Preston did too, admiring his *kitten* and how adorable he was, how beautiful, even with his fur dampened from sweat.

Luke stayed atop Preston, slowly softening, and allowed some of the cum he'd spilled inside Preston to leak out in a wonderfully warm dribble. "I love you."

"I love you," Preston said back, hoping his face conveyed even a fraction of the love Luke could bare open so easily, because oh, Preston felt it. He loved this cat, this *man*, more than any hang-ups or arguments could ever overshadow.

They kissed, long and lazy, not wanting to disconnect, even when it became a necessity with the cum cooling on Preston's skin. His hair was fanned over the pillow now, and Luke dug his hands into it with relish. His love of it falling into Preston's eyes when it was still only shaggy had been why Preston grew it out so long.

Still kissing, Luke ran the back of his clawed fingers through the scruff on Preston's cheek. Luke liked that too, he'd often said, just as Preston liked the freckles along Luke's shoulders, and a couple new sunspots that had been added to his face over the years, one beneath his left eye and another at the corner of his lip.

Preston kissed each of them before plunging his tongue between Luke's lips once more. As they panted, needing to rest, Luke finally rolled to the side.

"Wow, I missed that," Luke said.

"Me too."

"You know… it was kinda nice being reminded of when we met. I mean, the good parts, not the arguing."

"I was thinking that myself."

"Like first learning you were a nerd."

"And that your vocabulary's shit."

"Hey! It's not so bad anymore."

"Because I got you that word-a-day calendar."

"Dick move, by the way. But it was pretty useful. So, um…." Luke glanced at Preston, mostly human now save a glow in his eyes, and gestured at their stained bodies. "Prestidigitation?"

Preston laughed. He loved how Luke could always get him to do that, even when he'd tried so hard in the beginning not to.

Prestidigitation did its job, and they pulled the covers back over them. They were missing a pillow, since it now belonged to Gus-Gus, but they snuggled close enough that one king-sized pillow was plenty.

"I don't suppose your immense intellect and improved vocabulary means you have any ideas for solving our actual problem while being here?" Preston asked.

"We just need to do some old-fashioned digging. And show Jess a good time around her childhood stomping grounds."

"Ethan said we could talk to his uncle, right?"

"Leo, sure!"

The older vampire lived in Glenwood, warded in a way that the average shifter couldn't sense him, since generally vampires were seen as pests to be killed on sight. Leo had a pact with Kate, carried over from an original pact with her father, Ken, when he was Alpha, keeping Leo under protection so long as he never killed anyone and didn't allow shifters not already in the know to discover what he was.

He wasn't really Ethan's uncle but had raised him after accidentally turning Ethan's father, Gordon, into a vampire years ago, which had resulted in Gordan killing Ethan's mother. Gordon was currently in the basement of their Centrus City den, where Ethan was trying to get through to him after he used his sire thrall on Ethan to nearly take over the pack—and ultimately, the city.

Gordon had turned Ethan into a vampire Halloween night, finally bringing to conclusion one of Bash's oldest prophecies and starting them down this path that had led them to Glenwood after the Brookdale pack survived a takeover of their own.

"What's he do?" Luke asked. "What's Leo's expertise in, ya know, cover job, that sort of thing?"

"I don't remember. We could shoot Ethan a text in the morning."

"Or now. He is our *vampire* friend. He'll probably respond."

"Fair point." Preston didn't have to bother with TK this time, since his phone was within reach on the nightstand. He fired off the message to Ethan and kept his phone in hand.

"Kate's gonna get us that list too," Luke said.

"Anyone who might have leads or has the potential to be involved."

"Someone who's part of our world, and to have donated so many shifter artifacts over the years, has vast knowledge of anthropology and some serious resources. Can't be too many who fit that bill."

"Not likely, no."

"*Leo* has a lot of resources. Big house where Ethan grew up?"

"Sure."

"And he's definitely part of our world...."

"Yeah...." Preston did not like the knot forming in his gut from the leading way Luke was saying that, especially with how it prompted the gears in his head to spin too.

His phone blinked with Ethan's response, and he flew up into a sitting position.

"Shit."

"What is it?" Luke sat up beside him.

"I really hate your intuition sometimes." He met Luke's stare with a hinting frown. "Leo is an anthropology professor."

"THIS CAN'T be happening. This can't be happening," Luke chanted.

They were in an old part of Glenwood, approaching a very old and, yes, large house that proved the expansive resources at Leo's disposal. He was a vampire, after all, and was likely quite ancient.

They'd left Jesse in the care of the Glenwood Warden and a few agents. Jesse hadn't been pleased about being left behind, but she'd seemed to notice the tension between Luke and Preston had dissipated and held her tongue against further protests. She was a good kid, and like most, didn't enjoy seeing her parents fighting.

"Leo helped us in Centrus," Luke continued. "Why would he do that if he was the bad guy all along?"

"I don't know, but there is no way this is a coincidence." Preston stopped at the gate to the grounds. His scowl made Luke wonder if the look of this place reminded him of his own family home. Large, gated manor houses didn't have many good memories for him.

"And we're not going to tell Ethan we're confronting the man who raised him?"

"Not until we're sure."

"But Pres… this is a vampire," Luke hissed. "An older-than-Ethan vampire, way older than Ethan's dad too, since he made him. Do you really think we can take this guy? We're just a cat and a rat."

"Rat *King*, and a Magister."

"Okay, but I'm still just a cat."

Preston faced him head-on, and his serious expression softened just enough to look sweet and pretty the way Luke loved—even more than the smell of pie. "You're not *just* anything. Besides, we're not doing this alone." He nodded over Luke's shoulder.

Coming up behind them was Kate, Jude, and Jordana, along with a few recruits who were very well-versed in difficult fights.

Isabella hadn't done too shabby for herself after being banished from Centrus City. Here, she helped manage some of the Warden's top agents.

"Hi, Lui!" Luke waved, picking out the large lion amongst the others in Isabella's crew. "How ya been?"

"Hey, kid," Luisa answered gruffly. "Good enough."

"I'm twenty-eight now, Lui. You can't call me a kid anymore."

"Pretty sure I can." She smirked.

"What's the play?" Kate asked, leading the others with the unmistakable air of Alpha.

Luke looked to Preston, because he sure as hell didn't have an answer.

"We knock," Preston said simply, "and have a nice conversation with a previous acquaintance."

"Forgive me," Isabella huffed, "but the amount of backup you requested makes me a bit skeptical it'll be that easy."

Luke was right there with her. They'd had about this many facing Gordon, but one of the people on their side that time had been Ethan, another vampire. He couldn't help feeling outgunned, even if they weren't outnumbered.

Isabella didn't look much older than the last time they'd seen her, but then aging for shifters eventually slowed, and she could just as easily be eighty as forty-five.

Jude had a lit cigarette he puffed on.

"I thought you quit." Preston frowned at him.

"Listen, Fievel." Jude took a long drag. "If we're dealing with the same mess as ten years ago, I can have a smoke like I did back then."

A glint sparkled in Preston's eyes.

"Don't—"

And the cigarette went up in flames.

"Have another when this is over." Preston smirked and hit the gate's buzzer.

A friendly and not at all surprised sounding Leo let them right in.

"Ethan warned me you might be coming," Leo said, smiling pleasantly as he set out refreshments for them on his coffee table.

It seemed no one wanted to pose the question of why a vampire had refreshments, but it was just tea and store-bought cookies, so it was probably for moments like this and to keep up appearances.

Leo didn't smell like a vampire. He didn't smell like anything, which was mildly unsettling but wouldn't be noticed in a crowd. The important part of keeping him hidden was to not waft too obvious a smell toward any nearby shifters of *fanger*.

"I don't remember the last time, if any, I entertained so many." Leo sat in the one vacant armchair, while Isabella and her crew had opted to stand—and farther from Leo with upturned noses regardless of his lack of scent.

He was a trim man of average height with neat blond hair and blue eyes. He looked no older than thirty, but that meant nothing for a vampire. His attire was definitely professor-like, and the house was practically a library, smelling somewhat musty of books with shelving in almost every room they had passed to reach this one.

"Good to see you again, Kate," Leo said. She sat nearest him on the end of the sofa with Jude and Jordana. Luke and Preston were the others nearest him in an opposing loveseat. "You as well, boys. And nice to meet the rest of you, but… how can I help?"

"Is this your handwriting?" Preston wasted no time handing Leo the recent donation slip for the creation tablets.

"I, um…." Leo blinked at it, seeming about to deny any knowledge of the slip, but a pinch of confusion settled between his brows. "Yes… it is."

"And this one?" Preston offered the other slip, aged ten years, from the stolen artifacts with *item number eleven*, the totem, distinctly called out.

"I… I don't understand." Leo cringed, holding one slip in each hand with a sudden tightness that creased the paper.

Everyone tensed, and a rumble was heard from Lui, but when the slips dropped from Leo's hands, all that happened was him lurching to the edge of his seat and grasping Preston's hands.

"I remember! *She* had me donate it! All of it! I remember now!" he said in excited recollection. "Eleven… the totem, it was an old vampire artifact to control shifter slaves. All she needed was for it to end up in any city center and she could control whoever held it to control others. It was only one attempt of many to upset the balance. Like with Gordon. Oh *God*…." Leo released Preston's hands and clutched his chest.

"*What* with Gordon?" Luke scooted closer. "This mystery vampire set all that in motion too? But you forgot to feed, I thought, got all frenzied, and attacked Gordon at random."

"No… no, I thought that too, but I hadn't neglected to feed. She starved me, put me in Gordon's path, planned everything."

"Who is this woman?" Preston demanded.

It was the same person who Bari encountered—more or less—in Brookdale, but who—

"My sire," Leo said breathlessly, staring unfocused forward. "My maker. That's why I couldn't resist. I'm not like Ethan, empowered as a Focus and Seer to shake off his father's control. I succumb completely when she calls to me. She's been setting different wheels in motion for decades.

"Sometimes, when she isn't near, I remember things she's made me do. Like… before I left for Centrus City to find Ethan." He turned with further recognition to Preston and Luke. "I had the creation tablets donated and sent to Brookdale to get them away from her, to try and warn someone. I knew once I was in Centrus, if she was nearby watching it all play out, I'd forget again, under her thrall.

"I'm sure Gordon empowered her too, being a Focus, but she herself doesn't have that power. She's sought for centuries, millennia to regain the control lost when vampires were overthrown by the shifters they enslaved. She can only glamour one person at a time normally, but in addition to controlling me and any others of her children."

"Others?" Kate asked warily.

"There's at least one more," Leo confirmed. "He probably doesn't remember anything either, a sleeper agent, waiting for her to need him. I can't even picture him or remember his name…."

"Reggie?" Luke remembered everything Bari had experienced in Brookdale.

"How do you know that?"

"There are a lot of things starting to come together," Preston answered.

"She gave us the job," Jordana said.

"What?" Jude turned to her, on the far end of the sofa with Jordana between him and Kate. "We never met the contact."

"I did. I just didn't remember." Horror filled her face like when she'd confessed the totem controlling her. Slowly, she lifted her head to meet eyes with Leo. "Ale—"

The word choked off and Jordana vanished.

So had Leo!

They were across the room, as if having phased right through the sofa, with Leo holding Jordana in the air with a crushing grip on her throat, eyes wild and fangs bared like an entirely different person.

"Enough out of you," he spat—only it wasn't Leo. His voice came out two-toned, with a higher female one overlapping his as if speaking through him.

Everyone readied to attack and started to shift.

"Anyone moves one step closer and darling *Jordy* will lose her head," Not-Leo threatened.

Luke knew that voice….

"Although…," it continued, and there wasn't time to let that thought finish.

"*McDonough*," Luke hissed, and Preston clearly knew what he meant since his eyes went wide. "Do it!"

That roller coaster dip sunk through Luke's stomach, and he was behind Not-Leo before their grip could squeeze any tighter around Jordana's throat.

Luke struck, claws sinking into Not-Leo's shoulders, which made them howl and release Jordana in reflex. She dropped, and Luke leapt backward, allowing Isabella and her crew to tackle the controlled vampire to the floor.

He was strong, clearly heightened by his mystery sire, but they managed to keep him down. Kate and Jude raced to Jordana to be certain she was okay, and after a pained nod proved she was, Kate left her in Jude's hands and hovered over Not-Leo with an ominous aura.

He blinked, and it seemed to be just Leo again, not bothering to struggle.

"Don't let him up," Isabella warned. "Could be a trick."

"Don't let me up," Leo agreed, looking desperate and pained and miserable beneath them. "You need to kill me. She'll only use me again.

I'm so sorry." His eyes met Luke's, and if Preston hadn't come up behind him with an anchoring grip on his arm, it might have been as good as a blow to knock Luke prone. "Tell Ethan I'm sorry."

"What? Wait...." Luke shook his head, pleading with Isabella, with Kate, with everyone. "We'll just lock him up, like Gordon."

"Gordon is my child," Leo said before anyone else could answer. "She can't control him with that gap in connection, but she could empower me to control him for her. If I'm gone, he can be saved. I hope he can be saved. But I'm a liability."

"Then you're a liability," Kate said, and Luke was so fearful she'd slash Leo's throat and kill him right there, but she merely knelt. "Even so, I'd rather that than break the pact my father made with you, all because someone else is pulling the strings. We'll keep you locked up, covered in more wards than she could ever dream of breaking, and take her out to spare you, Reggie from Brookdale, and anyone else she has under her thumb. I will not be undermined in my own city, and I know the other Alphas will agree.

"This is going to take all three of our packs together," she said as she stood, addressing the room, "or we all might be at risk to the cities around us if they see us as a threat. So far, she's had her hands in Centrus, Brookdale, and now, here in Glenwood."

"Alexa," Jordana said in a croaking voice. She was standing now too, with Jude holding her at his side. "Her name is Alexa. It's always been Centrus she wanted first. She'll return there."

"To do what?" Kate asked. "What's her next move?"

"I don't know." Jordana shook her head.

Leo shook his too.

Isabella's people started to get up, but Lui and two other especially large and strong-looking cat shifters maintained their hold.

Preston stepped around Luke to address Kate. "I don't suppose Jesse could stick around here for a while?"

This was happening fast. They'd only come here for intel, and now everything was escalating in a way they couldn't possibly slow down.

"My people can keep her safe," Kate said, "but I'm coming with you."

"Me too," said Jude.

"I…." Jordana looked uncertain, no doubt brought back to memories of that voice in her head, just like Luke remembered the sound of it too when he'd briefly held the totem.

"You'll help watch over Jess, right?" Luke offered.

"But… I…."

"*You* are going to keep our pack and young Jesse safe," Kate said, moving back to Jordana and taking her from Jude to gather her close. "The rest of us will be okay."

"Okay," Jordana said, "but if almost everyone is gathering in Centrus, say hi to Bari for me." She glanced at Luke and Preston. "Heard he bagged himself an Alpha. They can be difficult to tame." She grinned at Kate, and the pair shared a kiss.

"Me and mine will take care of Leo," Kate said after they parted. "Say your goodbyes to Jesse and go on ahead of us to Centrus. We'll be there."

Luke and Preston had to warn the others. They had to prepare for… who knew what. All they could be certain of was that Alexa was coming, and her plans so far had nearly cost them all everything at least four times.

Leo asked them to tell Ethan not to worry about him, which Luke figured would fall on deaf ears. Stepping outside Leo's large home afforded them a lovely view of downtown gothic Glenwood, but it was difficult to enjoy it.

"Not exactly how I wanted our vacation to end," Luke said.

"Yeah."

"So, we say what we can to Jess, and then…." He turned to Preston. "Home?

"Home." Preston met Luke's stare, reached for his hand, squeezing too tightly, and looked back at the view. "Our mystery villain isn't a mystery anymore. And *Alexa* is heading to Centrus."

Keep reading for an excerpt from
The Bard and the Fairy Prince
by Amanda Meuwissen!

Chapter 1

"Behold the lure of passions met in contrast to the lore,
For kings and countries join as one when curses are no more.
As when a prince in dark of night did trade his life for one,
'Twas not his friend he was to save but a kingdom thought long gone.

"For the prince found love
Where hearts had frozen cold,
And the lands rejoice
In the thaw.

"Those meaning harm were soon to find that love does conquer all.
No force of magic, might, or steel could hope to see it fall.
The prince did sacrifice once more to prove his love was true,
And oh the Ice King melted then and gave the rest their due.

"For the prince found love
Where hearts had frozen cold,
And the king found love
In return.

"So, remember well to heed a story's end,
For two kings will sing the final tune."

JANSKOLLER PAUSED in his choral recitation, reminded of the original ending to the Ice King's tale, which caused him to grin at the ladies watching him compose and perform in the market square.

He couldn't resist finishing, *"But the Ice King still comes again too soon.*

"Ha! Too crude for a wedding?" he asked. He set aside his lute, leaning against the platform that housed the great Amethyst at the center of the Dark Kingdom—once the Shadow Lands and now, Janskoller supposed, the Amethyst Kingdom once more, even if it was still a strange place. "For the Emerald Prince turned King, I certainly hope that line isn't true." He winked, and the ladies tittered.

He did so find his best inspiration when writing for a captive audience.

The sun was shining upon the strangely angled buildings and gnarled black trees interspersed with the occasional more colorful abode or ripe apple tree budding with the pink flowers of early spring. Janskoller had been told that anything angled, twisted, or glittering black was left over from the curse, though the people here didn't see it as misfortune so much as what had made them their true selves.

And what selves they were! In his travels, Janskoller had known plenty of humans and even more dwarves, and despite supposedly lacking elvish presence in the Emerald Kingdom until not less than three curses had been broken, he'd met many elves as well, and nowhere near their ancestral home in the Mystic Valley. Once he'd even stumbled upon a village of centaurs—at least as far as one of his tales told. But here the people were every myth or bedtime cautionary tale made real.

Janskoller couldn't hope to name them all—harpies, nagas, wraiths, satyrs, and any number of combinations of all the above and more. The specific nature of ending their curse had been about lowering the barrier that would have afflicted anyone new who entered these lands and killed any inhabitant who tried to leave.

Now, within these borders, a simple touch from a citizen was all it took to transform their homes, lands, and even themselves into more recognizable fare. Anyone entering remained themselves unless they chose otherwise. Anyone who left could do so safely. And if someone had been changed, they would return to human, elf, or dwarf upon leaving.

It was said that if anyone new did choose to accept the curse and stay in Amethyst, they would become unageing like everyone else who lived here. A promising prospect for many, Janskoller supposed, for little else held the grand appeal of immortality.

Most "normal" people in view were like him, visitors eager to see one of the fabled and recently rediscovered lost kingdoms, while the citizens were so comfortable in their own skin, few had altered themselves or their surroundings.

What a magical place—and an even more magical few months.

"I think I could use a break from the arduous task of bardic composition," Janskoller announced with a clap. "What say you fine lasses? Any requests for classics?"

There were three women, a naiad local and two humans, along with other passersby starting to take interest in him.

"Tell us your story, Sir Janskoller," the naiad said.

"Oh, no, no, no, my beauty. No sirs about me. Well, occasionally there are sirs about me," he added in mock-whisper, "for I am not one to turn away any pretty face. I am but Janskoller the bard, humbly at your service." He bowed low. "Though I have seen my fair share of adventures. Shall I regale you of when I first crossed over from beyond the Ruby Mountains?"

Several passersby did indeed stop, and soon, Janskoller had a true crowd about him. The Amethyst gemstone made a lovely backdrop and seemed to hum with untold power that spurred him further into his next song.

Janskoller had been here a few days already. The Shadow King's caravan, which included the enigmatic leader's fetching redheaded consort, had already departed for Sapphire to enjoy several days abroad before attending the upcoming royal wedding between Sapphire and Emerald. 'Twas certain to be a spectacle, and Janskoller intended to be gone from here in time to attend it himself and perhaps even sing the kings his song—if paid handsomely enough.

For now, he was content with the coins being tossed into his cap, set upon the cobblestones beneath his feet.

He had traveled for many years outside the Gemstone Kingdoms, but whispers of curses broken and changes in the wind had lured him back. He never thought he'd see the day, for his lot was to be on the wind itself, ever passing through and never settled. If this was what the future held, however, lands opening, magic and elves and love between all welcomed even in the Emerald Kingdom, perhaps he would travel here a bit longer and see where those winds blew.

After all, most important for any good bard was to let their stories weave whichever way was needed.

Even if most were lies.

NEMIRAC KEPT a keen eye on his surroundings as he exited the wood's path and continued into the Amethyst Kingdom. It was late now, the land cloaked in darkness like it had been for a thousand years, with stars and a bright full moon above. Come dawn, however, the sun would shine again.

No longer was this the Shadow Lands or the Dark Kingdom, but even so, already Nemirac could tell how different Amethyst was from the Mystic Valley. Also known as the Diamond Kingdom, the Mystic Valley was Nemirac's home, where he had lived his entire life, secluded with the rest of his people until *their* curse had been broken, almost overlapping with the curse broken here and in nearby Sapphire.

Nemirac hadn't initially planned to travel, but after word spread of Amethyst's curse also coming to an end, Nemirac's mother had received a letter from the Shadow King. Finally, upon reading the letter, she told Nemirac the truth. He wasn't simply the Diamond Prince. All his life he had been the Fairy Prince anyway, after his mother, the Fairy Queen. But they were no fairies. That was merely a fanciful title bestowed upon his mother for her power. And they were certainly not elves, as Nemirac had been raised to believe.

They were demons.

Nemirac reached a set of steps at the edge of where homes began to line the streets, leading to the spire-topped castle in the distance. What appeared to be a recently crafted sign was planted into the ground beside the steps, mentioning a market below and an inn "Newly Added" that wouldn't have had any use until recently.

The inn would be Nemirac's first stop, though he had no intention of spending the night.

"Hail!" someone shouted the moment Nemirac entered. "Another new face, eh? Have a seat, anywhere you like. We welcome all kinds here."

The construction of the building was nice enough. Every plank of wood was black, the inn made from the same black trees as almost everything else. Nemirac had seen a few people on the streets, but here he could truly appreciate the myriad of beings that inhabited this place.

He couldn't say he had ever seen the likes of such... monsters, other than in storybooks. There were also humans, elves, and dwarves, some visiting like him, no doubt, and some who may have once been creatures themselves but had chosen to change their forms with the breaking of the curse.

The bartender who had called to Nemirac was something like a fish-man, with puckering lips and finlike fingers. Nemirac tried not to let how strange this all was to him show, for though he had seen many wonders in his homeland, filled as it was with magic, he knew very little of the outside world, and Amethyst was hardly an ordinary example.

"Are you also the innkeeper?" Nemirac asked the fish-man, approaching the bar where a few patrons were seated, enjoying drinks.

"Not one for pleasantries, are you? I'm Gordoc," the man said. "And yes, sir, this is my establishment. Just opened. You're one of the snazzier elves we've had come through. You some sort of noble?"

"I'm looking for other travelers, not conversation," Nemirac said shortly.

He'd also thought he'd chosen a more neutral outfit when he set out from home, but looking around at everyone here, he supposed his trousers and black-and-silver tunic would have been better on their own, with a more basic cloak, instead of what he had selected. He just felt incomplete without his red mantle buttoned into the tunic like a high collar and covering his shoulders, along with the accompanying half robe that attached at his hips and billowed low nearly to his ankles.

He was a prince, after all, but at least he had foregone his coronet for simpler adornments like his yellow leather belt. His staff was ostentatious as well, he supposed, with its large diamond at the top. The staff was crucial for channeling his magic. He was only half-elf—half-*demon*—so innate magic wasn't a luxury for him like it was for his mother.

For now.

"Excuuuuse me," Gordoc said with an exaggerated raise of his finned hands. "If you're only interested in other travelers, everyone tonight who doesn't look like a local isn't one. Take that as you will. Now, are you in need of a room and drink—"

"That's all, thank you." Nemirac turned from him without further comment and ignored the irritated huff the man released at Nemirac's back.

There were many in attendance who were not monsters, but after a longer scan of the room, no one looked like someone who had seen battle or even a bar fight. There was a young human couple laughing at a table, an older dwarf who could have been a grandfather drowning in ale, and several half-elves playing a game of cards, none of whom wore weapons belts. Everyone else was just as unexceptional.

Since there were half-elves and at least one full elf in attendance, some of whom might be from the Mystic Valley, just to be certain no one might recognize him, Nemirac drew up the hood from the back of his mantle, forced to pull his long braid forward to drape over one shoulder. Even while intricately plaited, his hair was long enough to nearly reach his waist, silver-colored, practically white, as if it were made from diamond dust itself—or so his mother used to lie.

The last of the people Nemirac noticed was a cluster of young women of various races in the corner, none of whom looked formidable enough to protect Nemirac should his plans go awry.

Safe within his hood, but having come up empty, Nemirac started to turn back to the bar, though he doubted it would be fruitful to ask Gordoc if there were other inns or places travelers frequented.

A boisterous laugh from the corner drew Nemirac's attention—a male laugh, deep and resonant, amidst the gaggle of women. Nemirac headed in that direction, finally seeing that the women, five in total, weren't clustered for their own sakes but clustered *around* a man, who seemed quite pleased by the attention.

As Nemirac continued to approach, he saw more of the man revealed—human, with tanned skin, brown hair to his shoulders, a neatly trimmed but full beard, and lively green eyes. He looked large, thick with muscle beneath his teal-and-purple surcoat. He also wore an overcoat with fur along the collar and a floppy cap that tilted to one side in the same teal-and-purple colors, but with a green feather.

His laugh was infectious, though Nemirac assumed his admirers were there more for the strikingly handsome figure he cut—and because he appeared to be the one supplying the booze.

"Another round? Don't you lovelies go anywhere now," he said, sliding around several of the women to get out from behind the table.

One of them must be a local, judging by her blue amphibian-like skin, and two of them, Nemirac realized, were actually slight and very pretty young men.

Nemirac changed direction to head the man off at the bar. He was indeed large, well over six feet tall, whereas Nemirac was barely five foot ten and willowy, with minimal muscle. Nemirac wasn't built for combat outside throwing spells, but this man clearly was. He had an axe on one side of his weapons belt and a short sword on the other. He wore bracers, his surcoat was actually cleverly disguised leather armor, and his well-worn boots were those of a wanderer.

Perfect.

"Another round for my table, Gordy!" The man pounded a rowdy fist on the bar top and dropped a small pouch of gems upon it, spilling out a few that he passed to Gordoc, whose eyes sparkled at the sight almost as brightly as the stones themselves.

"Right away!" Gordoc gathered the gems greedily.

At Nemirac's approach, the man turned with a grin and raised a questioning eyebrow, one with a scar clean through it that added to his rugged attractiveness.

Not that Nemirac *cared*. What he was after was a bodyguard.

"Are you for hire?" Nemirac asked.

"Forward, aren't you?" The man's deep, boisterous voice made Nemirac's stomach grow hot. "That's far too fair a face to be hiding in a hood. I wouldn't be opposed to being paid, pretty thing, but I'd take you to bed for free."

"I-I meant as a sellsword!" Nemirac barked, feeling his cheeks grow as hot as his gut.

He was often called pretty back home, but he'd only recently come of age at twenty-two and usually avoided anyone trying to court him. Books and magical study were easier to lose himself in than people.

Nemirac recognized his own attractiveness, combining the beauty of his dark-skinned elf-looking mother and his fair human father. He'd always wondered why his hair was silver instead of blond, however, just as he'd questioned the gold color of his eyes, when his mother's were dark and his father's blue.

At least he'd wondered before discovering his true lineage.

"I'm interested in hiring a combatant, not… *dallying*," Nemirac spat.

"Pity," the man said, eyeing Nemirac openly from head to toe.

"Are you for hire or not?" Nemirac wanted this man because he looked the strongest and was honestly the only option right now. It had nothing to do with the appeal of his broad shoulders, the twinkle in his eyes, or the single dimple on his cheek beneath the scruff of his beard.

Gordoc began placing flagons upon the bar, and the man claimed one and took a long drink before he answered, "I can be. What are you offering in exchange?"

The man's gems were impressive, but Nemirac had something better.

He dropped his own pouch on the bar and opened it to reveal diamonds, causing Gordoc's eyes to saucer. "I need you to do as you're told and not ask questions. This will be a long-term arrangement, likely lasting several weeks, and I won't be staying in Amethyst, so if you intended to remain here tonight, that will change. Do we understand each other?"

The man opened the bag of diamonds farther, that same scarred eyebrow rising, though he otherwise remained impressively neutral. "The world has suddenly opened, offering many new lands for adventure. Frankly, I'm up for anything."

"*Do we* understand each other?" Nemirac asked again.

"Yes. I can follow orders just fine." He winked.

Nemirac ignored the gesture. "Where do you hail from?"

"Originally? Ruby."

"Ruby? You're not a dwarf."

"Not only dwarves live in the Ruby Kingdom, pretty, but I suppose people from other lands have forgotten that. Where do you hail from?"

"Not your concern." Nemirac lowered his voice, since Gordoc had finished with the flagons but was hovering a little too closely. "Meet me in the square in three hours, after all is still and everyone has cleared out, not a moment later. We will be making a hasty retreat, and I need to know you'll be timely." He sneered over the man's shoulder at the group of admirers watching with obvious annoyance that someone new had the man's attention.

"I'm always timely—even when dallying," he added in a whisper. "You have a deal, pretty. I'm intrigued."

"My name is Nemirac." This man hadn't come from the Mystic Valley, and since those lands had been cordoned off for two hundred years and Nemirac was still young, no one outside his home should know his name.

"Pleasure to meet you, *pretty*. I'm Janskoller," he said with a tip of his cap. "Janskoller Thah."

"Janskoller the what?"

He chuckled, more like giggled, which should have seemed disjointed coming from such a masculine specimen, yet it suited him perfectly. "T-H-A-H. But if you're asking—Janskoller the mighty? The handsome? The virile? Take your pick. Most people know me as Janskoller the bard." He bowed.

"Bard?" Nemirac hadn't noticed before, but leaning against the wall beside the table Janskoller had come from was a lute. "I need you to fight, not serenade me."

"Why not both? I can fight, don't you worry about that. The serenading I'll throw in for free." He winked yet again. "Would you like a demonstration—?"

"Three hours," Nemirac interrupted, even if the lute had him curious. He had a feeling he had just made a terrible mistake, but at least the view would be pleasant.

Nemirac reclaimed the not-yet-earned diamonds and headed away before Janskoller could say more. There was planning to be done before they met again and made their escape. It was time for Nemirac to claim his birthright—starting with the Amethyst gemstone.

Amanda Meuwissen is a bisexual author with a primary focus on M/M romance. She has a Bachelor of Arts in a personally designed Creative Writing major from St. Olaf College and is an avid consumer of fiction through film, prose, and video games. As the author of LGBT Fantasy #1 Best Seller, *Coming Up for Air*, paranormal romance trilogy, The Incubus Saga, and several other titles through various publishers, Amanda regularly attends local comic conventions for fun and to meet with fans, where she will often be seen in costume as one of her favorite fictional characters. She lives in Minneapolis, Minnesota, with her husband, John, and their cat, Helga, and can be found at www. amandameuwissen.com.

Follow me on BookBub

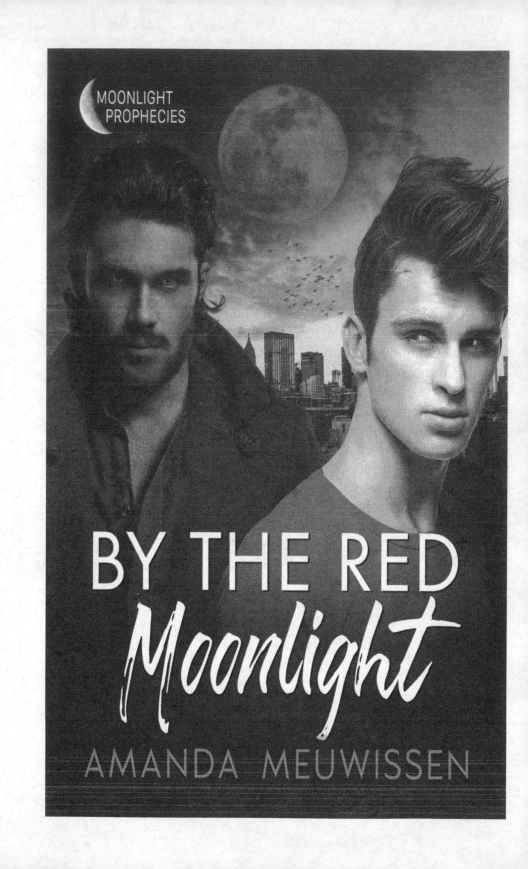

MOONLIGHT
PROPHECIES

BY THE RED
Moonlight

AMANDA MEUWISSEN

Moonlight Prophecies: Book One

Alpha werewolf, crime boss, and secret Seer Bashir Bain is neck-deep in negotiating a marriage of convenience with a neighboring alpha when a tense situation goes from bad to worse. A job applicant at one of Bash's businesses—a guy who was supposed to be a simple ex-cop, ex-con tattoo artist—suddenly turns up undead.

A rogue newborn vampire would have been a big wrench in Bash's plans even without his attraction to the man. After all, new vampires are under their sire's control, and Ethan Lambert doesn't even know who turned him. When Bash spares his life, he opens himself up for mutiny, a broken engagement, and an unexpected—and risky—relationship.

Ethan just wants a fresh start after being released from prison. Before he can get it, he'll need to turn private investigator to find out who sired him and what he wants. And he'd better do it quick, because the moon is full, and according to Bash's prophecy, life and death hang in the balance.

www.dreamspinnerpress.com

Moonlight Prophecies: Book Two

Alpha Jay Russell's broken engagement may just be the best thing that ever happened to him. His ex-fiancé's twin, Bari, is much more his type and straightforward about his flirting and desire to unite their packs.

Jay returns home after his misadventures in Centrus City to a new prophecy, an unknown enemy, and tribal unrest over a series of racially-driven murders. Furious, Jay is determined to bring whoever's responsible to justice… but the unrest upsets the fragile peace he's been working to achieve, threatens his new lover's life, and undermines his position as Alpha, which makes investigating a challenge.

Can Jay and Bari work together to fight their inner demons—and a strange adversary dead set on returning to the past—or will mistrust and political machinations tear them apart?

Blue Moon Rising is the second book in the Moonlight Prophecies series. Fans of shifters, soothsayers, and shadowy villains will fall under Amanda Meuwissen's spell in this suspenseful, sexy urban fantasy romance.

www.dreamspinnerpress.com

THE PRINCE
AND THE
ICE KING

A Tale from the Gemstone Kingdoms

AMANDA MEUWISSEN

Tales from the Gemstone Kingdoms: Book One

Every Winter Solstice, the Emerald Kingdom sends the dreaded Ice King a sacrifice—a corrupt soul, a criminal, a deviant, or someone touched by magic. Prince Reardon has always loathed this tradition, partly because he dreams of love with another man instead of a future queen.

Then Reardon's best friend is discovered as a witch and sent to the Frozen Kingdom as tribute.

Reardon sets out to rescue him, willing to battle and kill the Ice King if that's what it takes. But nothing could prepare him for what he finds in the Frozen Kingdom—a cursed land filled with magic… and a camaraderie Reardon has never known. Over this strange, warm community presides the enigmatic Ice King himself, a man his subjects call Jack. A man with skin made of ice, whose very touch can stop a beating heart.

A man Reardon finds himself inexplicably drawn to.

Jack doesn't trust Reardon. But when Reardon begins spending long days with him, vowing to prove himself and break the curse, Jack begins to hope. Can love and forgiveness melt the ice around Jack's heart?

www.dreamspinnerpress.com

STITCHES

A Tale from the Gemstone Kingdoms

AMANDA MEUWISSEN

Tales from the Gemstone Kingdoms: Book Two

Created by the alchemist Braxton, Levi was "born" fully grown and spends his early days learning about the monster-filled kingdom he calls home.

Even though he is just a construct pieced together from cloned parts, Levi longs to fit in with his mythical neighbors, but more than that, he wishes he could say two words to the Shadow King without stuttering.

Ashmedai has been king of what was once the Amethyst Kingdom since it was cursed a thousand years ago. Only he and Braxton know what truly happened the night of the curse, and Ash's secret makes walking among his beloved people painful, so he rarely leaves his castle. However, with Festival Day approaching, Ash wouldn't mind going out more often… if it means seeing more of Levi.

Ash wishes he deserved the longing looks from those strangely familiar violet eyes. He knows no one could love him after learning the truth of the curse. But if anyone can change his mind, it is the sweetly stitched young man who looks at him like he hung the moon.

www.dreamspinnerpress.com

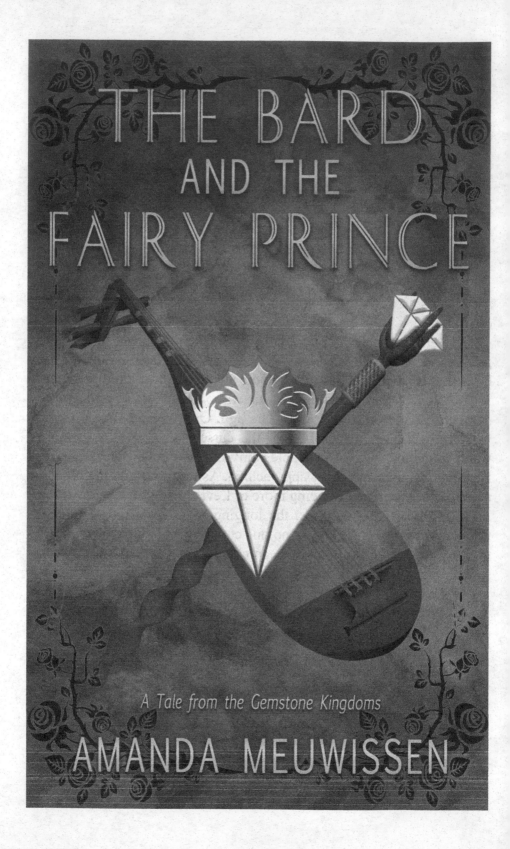

Tales from the Gemstone Kingdoms: Book Three

When Prince Nemirac learns of his heritage, he vows to become the most powerful demon in history. But he can't do it alone.

Feeling betrayed by his parents' lies about his true lineage, Nemirac embarks on a quest to visit all five Gemstone Kingdoms and drain the stones of their power to ascend as a new being. But until he obtains that magic, he's vulnerable.

Enter Janskoller the warrior bard.

Janskoller has just returned to the Gemstone Kingdoms, drawn by stories of broken curses and lands open for travel. He doesn't expect a pretty young mage to hire him as a bodyguard, but it's a good gig for a bard lots of adventure to fuel his stories, and plenty of travel to spread his fame. Besides, Nemirac's passion and obvious secrets intrigue him. But soon Janskoller realizes the peril of Nemirac's goal—an end that puts the five kingdoms at risk and corrupts Nemirac into a darker, twisted version of the man Janskoller has come to care about. As the two grow closer, can Janskoller convince Nemirac to abandon his pursuit of power in favor of the deeper, more lasting magic of love?

www.dreamspinnerpress.com